Paper Treasures

Paper Treasures

Lilly Horigan

Lilly Books
Bolivar, Ohio

Dedicated to the
Homeless Navy Veterans
in Clark County, Nevada

Inspired by true events.

Chapter 1

Paige McKinnon reached into the McDonald's bag one more time, hoping to find another french fry at the bottom—anything to distract her from her grandmother's last text urging her to reconsider leaving home. She had been on the road for hours since waving goodbye and was incredibly nervous already. The texts only made it worse, but she knew her grandmother was only trying to look out for her.

Paige tried to keep her eyes on the road in between eating, drinking, and setting up her phone to play the next chapter of the audiobook she was listening to. Sometimes she wondered how she got where she was without hitting someone or something. She never seemed to be paying any attention to the road in front of her, not with all the thoughts demanding attention in her head.

She had left early in the morning; early for her anyway. She hoped the eight-hour drive would go quickly—she was thrilled to finally be moving to Vegas! Living in Washington since birth meant there would be major adjustments to the Las Vegas climate, but she was eager to get started on her new life, a life on her own to answer questions she had waited years to ask.

She tried to concentrate on the audiobook and follow along, but her mind was going over every possibility she could think of concerning what could happen when she arrived in Vegas. She paused the book and forced herself to focus on the road a few seconds, and began lifting her anxieties up for the hundredth time that day. *God, please make a way for me to see her. Help me find a place to stay and lead me where you want me.*

Paige felt the anxiety diminish but the anticipation kept it lingering in her soul. She was taking a big risk, and it was a risk that no one was happy about back home. She was leaving her family to seek answers of her own.

She was 18 and finally able to make the decision to go. They understood her desire. They saw how her beautiful blond hair, blue eyes, and strong chin looked like no one else's in the family. They knew she wanted to see the person who gave her those unique features. She wanted to see her mother.

She knew her nose and ears were passed on from her father. She never saw it herself, however. He had died in a car accident when she was two. She didn't know all the details of the accident. Her grandmother had a hard time talking about the death of her son. She raised Paige the best she could and her childhood had been fun and healthy.

Now out of high school, she could finally see her mom and try to make a connection with her. Paige knew her mother was sick and knew that even if her mother had wanted to see her over the years, she couldn't have. There were court orders put in place to make sure there was no contact.

Did her mom even know about the orders?

Did her mom even know about her anymore?

~

After hours of staring at a computer screen, Seth Redding finally left his mom's quilt shop. Her dream would soon open and the merchant software he had chosen for her was almost ready for the big day. He had just finished setting up the system to accept credit cards and sell yards of fabric in any measurement.

It seemed there were a million small things that needed to be done, and a thousand little problems that came up that he had not foreseen. He was happy to help her fulfill this dream, but he would have preferred something a little less technical and financial. Trudy Redding had a gift for putting together fabrics and threads in amazing ways but computers seemed to malfunction with only a few keyboard strokes when she was on them.

Seth made his way to his car, contemplating if he should stop at the grocery store next door. He thought his mother had made a wise decision on where to locate the shop. The small shopping center was on one of the busiest roads in their part of town and not far from the highway. Although the shop was small, it was all his mom desired. It was cozy and inviting. It was a perfect addition to the shopping center, which looked more like a quaint downtown village. The parking lot had what patrons would want—practicality and close proximity. It seemed, to Seth anyway, as if she had taken longer to name the shop than any other decision. She had settled with *Quilts On*.

Seth would never forget how thrilled and giddy his mom was the night she had come up with that name. She thought herself so clever putting two of her favorite things into one name—quilt and son. She even had her sign made up so that the text color was different for the last three letters. He suggested maybe the name was a way of hinting that he should start quilting. She laughed at the idea of ever trying to get him to quilt. Sitting at the dinner table watching her squeal with delight when he gave his approval to the name made Seth chuckle again as he walked to his car. She was easily pleased, and he loved that about her.

Seth's interests didn't include fabric or computers. When he wasn't helping his mom, he played his guitar. He had taught himself with the help of online videos, and was amazed that he had been able to get right into the band at church. They attended a big church in Vegas, and they welcomed new people who were willing to be part of worship. There was a growing Christian population in Vegas, although the world would probably never know it. The news only focused on "Sin City" when events lined up with its sinful reputation. Seth was looking forward to being a positive part of the city.

After mentally going over the to-do list to get his mom up and running for the big opening day in less than a week, he decided to stop at the store and pick up food. His little apartment a few blocks away was just the right size for him, but he ate out most of the time. Sitting in an empty house and having dinner alone was less than exciting.

At just over 22 years old, Seth knew he was not like other guys his age. He had returned from serving 4 years in the Navy, and he wasn't interested in bars, gambling, or meeting a different girl every night. Seth was ready to start the next stage of his life—ready to meet the right girl and, in time, start a family. But first, he needed to figure out what he was going to do to support that future family.

Heading for the beer aisle, he picked up a case from a local brewing company. He only drank occasionally, and when he did, he wanted quality beer. After hours of computer work, and repeating the same instructions over and over again to his mom for what seemed like the simplest of tasks, a beer or two would taste great. He picked up a couple ready-to-eat foods at the deli and headed home.

His apartment was on the third floor of a decent complex only five minutes from his mom's new shop. He'd been there less than two months and the refrigerator was not the only thing that looked empty. He had not brought, nor bought, much furniture. There was no point in going into debt or depleting his savings for a couch or table.

Getting out of the Navy in less than four years without any debt was a miracle. Many service members made a lot of dumb financial decisions that took years to fix. Seth's mom, however, had taught him to make use of everything he had and not to go in debt unless necessary. Sometimes they disagreed on what was necessary.

~

Paige finally made it to Vegas late in the afternoon. She had picked a neighborhood that her aunt had visited once. She recalled the letter in her bag that her Aunt Marie had sent her:

Dearest Paige,

I will, of course, share any details I can with you about your mother. As you already know, the last time I saw my sister was a few years ago. Unfortunately, she was in one of the areas that I would not recommend you frequent without someone with you. Also, after visiting Vegas year after year and looking for her, I have come across a few wonderful neighborhoods that I think would be a great place for you to live, work, and begin your search for her. I have included important maps, a bus schedule, and a little money for you. My email and number are on the back of the map. Call me with any questions I can answer for you.

Love,
Aunt Marie

Paige got off the highway and made her way to the area her Aunt recommended. She passed the bus station and an amazing park. Paige knew it was the park her Aunt had written about in one of the many letters and emails she'd sent over the years. Aunt Marie had once run a Veteran's Day 11K race there when she and her father, Paige's grandfather, had come to visit her mom.

Paige continued on, all while praying for God's hand to show her where to stop and what to do. The shopping centers were small and unique. It was hard to imagine that the Strip, with all its lights and craziness, was only ten minutes away from this seemingly quiet area.

She drove down the road she had seen on her map numerous times before, but now she looked at the places in light of needing to find a job and a place to live. Paige had only enough money to stay in a hotel for a few days.

Her family couldn't believe she had left without knowing where she was going to stay. Equipped with her phone, a car, and some money, she felt she had all that was needed to handle the journey. Paige trusted that God would lead her where she needed to go. However, the weight of the unknown and realization of what she was doing suddenly pressed down on her.

Ready for a break, she entered the parking lot of a shopping center with a large grocery store. Without a place to live, she couldn't shop for groceries yet, but she could buy some water and a sandwich. She was tired of eating fries and cheeseburgers.

The shopping center, along with the grocery store, had a dry cleaner, a quilt shop, and a pizza place. She noted the walkway that connected the house-like shops and was impressed with the cleanliness and the flower pots hanging along the entire property. Someone cared about this area—not many places have this much attention to detail. Even the parking lot was clean and had numerous lantern-type lights along the rows.

Paige instantly liked the area. She could see why her Aunt had recommended it. After getting out of the car and stretching her legs, Paige scanned the area across the street. Although not as cozy as the side she was on, with its pansies and lanterns, it did have a bank, a flower shop, and a café. Purse in hand, she headed to the grocery store but made sure she passed the quilt shop first.

Paige adored any type of craft store. She was drawn to the colors, ideas, and creative possibilities. She always collected beautiful fabrics and threads for future projects. Although Paige didn't do any traditional quilting, many of the women in her family did. In fact, Aunt Marie had recently made her a quilt for her high school graduation. It was in the back of the car, with the rest of her "life," awaiting a new home.

The quilt shop was directly next to store but didn't seem open. Strange, since it was the middle of a weekday. Deciding to take a quick look, she tried the door. Locked. She moved on toward the grocery store and heard the quilt store door unlock and open. A sweet-looking lady, probably in her fifties and about Paige's 5' 4" height, stepped out.

"Can I help you?"

"I'm sorry. I was just checking to see if you were open."

"We're opening next week. I haven't put a sign out yet. Oh, I should get to that. I'll have my son do that this week. And I should put something in the paper. Oh, why didn't I think of that sooner? And some balloons..." The lady seemed to forget all about Paige standing there and was looking in the window, counting on her fingers, and seemed to be mentally adding items to a list.

Paige didn't feel comfortable just walking away. "I'm sure it will all work out. This looks like a great location. Will you have quilt classes for beginners?"

"Oh, I'm sorry. Yes, yes. We'll have classes for all levels. Have you ever quilted before?"

"No, but I have done some embroidery and cross-stitching in the past."

"Then you'll have to stop by for the beginner's class when it starts, probably in a month or so. Oh, I'll need to get a schedule up and the instructors in place." Again, seeming to forget Paige was there, she opened the door to head back inside. "Would you like to see the store, dear?"

Seeing that the lady was overwhelmed, Paige decided to leave her to her mental checklists. "Um, thank you, but I can see you are busy. I'll stop by some other time. Right now, I need to get some food and find a place to stay for the night."

The woman's head snapped over to Paige. "You don't have a place to stay? Are you new to the area?"

"I am. I just drove in from Washington state. I'm moving here and don't have an apartment lined up. Is there a hotel near-by that has reasonable rates?"

"Well, yes, but if you're in need of a place to stay, I have a room right here above the shop you can use. In fact, I was going to rent it out to offset the cost of the suite and employees. It's small, in a shopping center, and connected to a quilt shop; but it's also right next to a grocery store!" The lady smiled, her concern and kindness shining brightly across her face. She had a sweet spirit, and Paige liked her instantly.

"I don't know what to say. This is a surprise and, if I can be honest, it's an answer to prayer if you mean it."

"Oh, I do, and I love hearing that I'm a part of God's handiwork. Here, let me show you the room. There's a separate door to the apartment right next to the shop entrance. Let me go get the keys and you can decide after you see it." The woman disappeared back into her quilt shop and came out faster than Paige had thought possible after seeing her completely overwhelmed a couple of minutes ago. "Here it is. The door has a separate lock so you can be safe and confident. It doesn't have a buzzer or speaker system; you'll need to coordinate leaving this outer door open for folks coming over."

The door was wrought iron and well cared for. It was another sign that this property was loved a great deal by someone. The door led to a staircase that was a little steeper than Paige expected, but easy to manage. The interior was painted in neutrals and led to a small landing where a brown door with a tall, plastic plant with red flowers next to it awaited the two women. Thrilled there was no graffiti or smell, Paige's heart was already galloping with excitement. God had provided way more than she could have ever dreamed.

"This lock has a different key than the first door. Again, it doesn't go to anything else. Only you, the landlord, and I will have one. There's also the ability to lock it from the inside to be sure no one can get in." The shop-keeper opened the door and Paige walked into her second answered prayer: the apartment. The first answer had been the sweet shop-keeper herself.

Chapter 2

The next morning, Paige opened her eyes to an unknown room and suddenly her heart raced and her muscles tensed. Once her heart caught up with her memories of the night before, her adrenaline dissolved. She recalled how smoothly the evening had gone. After getting some necessities at the store and taking a quick shower, she had fallen asleep with deep gratitude. The apartment was fully furnished and there were sheets on the bed. Even more impressive: they smelled fresh.

During the apartment tour the previous evening, she got to know the sweet lady. Trudy was a single mom and had lived in Las Vegas for about two years. She had a son who lived locally, and he was helping her pursue her dream of opening a quilt shop. Due to time, not much more was discussed. Trudy had handed over the keys and a few phone numbers for contacting her—all with a complete confidence that shocked Paige.

After bringing in the essentials from her car, Paige had called her grandmother to let her know she had arrived safely. Gram had obviously been fretting all day and endlessly wondering how Paige was doing. Although Gram, as Paige always called her, didn't know exactly how the journey was going, she did know where Paige was at all times. One of the conditions of her grandmother paying for her cell phone bill was that she got to see where Paige was via the Find Friends app. Paige was glad she had agreed to it; it was the lifeline her gram used to be sure that her only granddaughter was alive. Her grandmother only pictured the bad of Vegas; never the good surrounding it.

After a quick shower and some unpacking, Paige had been eager to go to bed. Yet being in a new state and a new place hit her like a ton of bricks. She was tired but wound up from the day's events. She was also more than a tad nervous about the situation she so quickly had found herself in. She had assumed she would spend the first night in a hotel. Lifting up prayers of thanksgiving and peace, she pulled out her favorite way of relaxing: a book. One chapter was all she needed though.

Once the confusion of waking up in a new place passed, she was ready to start the day with coffee and some quiet time across the street. She dressed, texted her gram that she was still alive, collected her favorite books, and looked back over the cute apartment.

Father, thank you for making all this possible. Lead me today in the next steps of this this journey. You've provided a place for me to live, and I'm excited to see how you'll help me earn money to stay here. May I be mindful of your guidance throughout the day. Please continue to keep Mom safe. Help me find her.

~

Almost every day, Seth entered the café across the street from his mother's new store. Sarah's Café had opened sometime earlier in the year and it looked like it was going to be a success. Ironically, it was a non-profit coffee shop; the first Seth had ever seen. The owners, a young local couple from the same church Seth attended, didn't post or give suggested prices for its products. Instead, everything was donation only and a portion of the profit went to mission projects. He wasn't sure how they paid for all the expenses, but he loved buying coffee knowing a portion was sent to missions.

One of the owners was usually behind the counter and today it was Sarah herself. Sarah wiped down the blue and green marble looking tile and straightened the home-made donation box. It was obvious she loved what she was doing and that her coffee shop was a dream come true.

"Hi, Sarah."

"Seth! How's your morning going?"

"Great. Mom's shop is only a week away from opening. I'm not sure if I'll get everything done, but it should be close."

"You can do it. I know your mom is thrilled with the progress and is so excited to have you helping her. She knows she couldn't do it without you."

"Thanks, Sarah. I needed the boost of confidence. She has wanted to do this for so long. It's nice to see God's timing working out. It would've been hard to do while I was in the Navy and she was on her own."

"She always lit up when she talked about you at church. But she giggles and hops around like a little schoolgirl when she talks about her shop. It's so cute to watch."

"It is. I think she's going to ask you to put up a couple of signs in here for the opening. I wanted to give you a heads up."

"That's no problem at all, Seth. Thanks for letting me know. Want your usual today?"

"Yep. Thanks, Sarah." Seth put his money in the box and went to his usual seat.

~

Paige had watched the guy walk in and listened to his conversation with the café employee. He was obviously comfortable here, which made Paige feel even more out of place. She was glad he had not been there when she walked in earlier. Trying to pay for her latté had been an awkward experience after the lady had informed her that the business only took donations in a cute box on the counter.

With just a $20 bill on her, it left Paige wondering if she could get change or if she would have to order more food. Twenty dollars for a latté was way too steep for Paige's wallet. Thankfully, the kind lady saw the confusion pass over Paige's face and opened the lid of the box to get change. The young woman, who Paige now knew was Sarah, gave all the details of the shop and how it worked. Unfortunately, Paige was unable to learn any more information about the shop or the woman because they were interrupted by the loud grumbling sound coming from Paige's stomach. She had been so embarrassed but Sarah had smiled and then recommended a muffin as well to appease her stomach.

The kindness and the purpose of the shop was another breath of fresh air for Paige. She had never seen anything like it where she grew up. She couldn't imagine how the shop survived, but it seemed to have a steady flow of people coming in every few minutes. Some stayed and others took their coffee to go. The tables were cute and the decor was calm and inviting.

Paige tried not to look up at the guy as he turned away from the counter in search of a seat. It appeared he was going to stay and Sarah knew it. Since Paige had, without permission, listened to his conversation, she knew this was Trudy's son. Waving him over and saying, "Hi! I overheard you talking and know who you are. I'm new in town, and I'm living above your mom's quilt shop. I met her yesterday and she gave me the apartment on the spot," seemed something only his mom should tell him. Not her. Yet it also felt uncomfortable not saying anything. Paige felt unsure of what to do, so she ignored him and tried to look as busy as possible with her books.

But ignoring him proved impossible, once a pair of brown leather shoes and blue jeans appeared next to her table. Paige looked up to find a pair of deep blue eyes looking at her. He had light brown, short hair and a green button-down Polo shirt. He was slightly older than her and his brown eyebrows were drawn down in an intrigued "who are you" kind of way—along with a slight smirk. "Hi. First time at the café?" he asked.

"Um, yes. I like it." She didn't understand why he had come straight to her. The café was small but the place had at least ten open tables. She was still debating whether she should mention the apartment or not.

"Yeah, it's unique and benefits amazing causes through mission projects. I didn't mean to bother you while you were studying. I just wanted to say hello. I usually sit in this spot and didn't want to not welcome you to the place knowing it was probably your first time here." He grimaced, regretting something he had said. "That was a double negative. Sorry." He chuckled a little at what seemed to be not only the act of catching himself with his bad grammar but then apologizing about it. "My mom always tells me not to use double negatives." He suddenly looked really embarrassed with his comments which Paige immediately found hilarious. "Anyway... Welcome!"

"Thanks." Paige laughed softly and smiled. "I appreciate that."

"Enjoy," he said, and turned to go to the other side of the café with a small, but sincere, apologetic smile.

"You too." She watched him go over to a round table in the opposite corner of the shop. She knew she probably should have apologized for being in his seat and then offered to move, but she never got the chance once he went into his criticism of his double negative sentence. Paige looked down and laughed silently at the encounter. The thought of going over and telling him who she was and where she lived entered her mind. When she looked over; however, he already had a book out and seemed to be concentrating. She sat back and looked out the window, enjoying the sun in her face and the view of the street.

~

After Seth had taken his seat at the other corner of the restaurant, he tried to concentrate on what he always did when he came to the café: quality time with God. This time usually lasted about 15 to 30 minutes, but it energized him for the day. A consistent God time was a new habit his mentor, Patrick, had urged him to start.

Some days he spent the time reading a particular book of the Bible. Other days, he went back over the notes from the previous sermon at church. Today, he planned to read a book.

After Sarah brought his coffee over, he held it and stared at the page he was reading in his new book about being a Godly man in the 21st century. Unfortunately, the words were floating in front of him. He could not concentrate sitting in a different corner with a new girl in his usual spot. Seth knew he was, at times, a creature of habit. He enjoyed doing things the same way and it could get him into trouble sometimes. He had learned over the years to adjust to change; it was very necessary in the military. He didn't get angry or agitated, but it did require him to alter his expectations.

The new girl had probably thought him strange and awkward. He had tried to come off as welcoming and not as the token creepy guy at the coffee shop. Unfortunately, that boat had sailed.

After some time, his thoughts had finally settled down and he was able to get into his reading. He put the situation behind him and accepted the fact that he would probably never see her again. He underlined and made marginal notes as he finished his coffee. He would go over them with Patrick on Thursday night when they met here for their weekly meeting. Patrick was older, married, and went to the same church. They would sit in their usual spot, now occupied by the beautiful stranger across the room. It was the best seat in the café from a security perspective.

Chapter 3

Trudy was so thankful she had enlisted the help of her friend, Julie, to get all the fabrics priced and sorted. All the shipments had finally arrived, and the walls were arranged by color and then categorized by season. She knew there was a small community of quilters in the Vegas suburbs. She hoped she could get the locals to frequent her shop, not only for tools and fabric, but also with some classes and quilt meetup groups. Trudy realized that most quilters purchased a lot of their fabrics and tools online these days—creativity would be key for the store to be successful.

As she was finishing up the Christmas section, Seth came in. He had his coffee and was ready to start working on the electronic side of the business. She didn't know what she would do without him. He had learned so many skills in the Navy, and he handled all of the website configuration and the computer software that was needed for the shop.

Thankfully, Trudy wasn't completely lost when it came to computers. She did go to all the required sites to learn what she needed to officially start the shop. Seth had been impressed with her work, and it tickled her heart to see him proud of her. Oh, how the tables had turned. It used to be Seth who sought approval from his mom. Now she thoroughly enjoyed seeing him pleased with her 21st century assimilation.

"Hi honey. How was breakfast?"

"Great. Sarah's on board to help you out in any way she can. I told her you'd be talking with her."

"Wonderful. I'll go over at lunch and discuss the plans with her." Trudy was ready to get the word out about the shop. Sarah's Café had been a great addition to the area and its popularity had been a wonderful blessing. "I'd like to print off some simple flyers. I'll just use this computer if it has the right software on it." She logged on to the shop's main computer and looked over to Seth.

"That's fine. The printer is hooked up."

Trudy smiled. "Wonderful. I'll take some over to the church and library bulletin boards."

Seth pulled out his laptop and placed it on the cutting table. He brought up his mother's website. It was simple, plain, and had the info needed for her shop. There were no plans to do online sales yet, so adding pictures of the shop for the homepage was all that was left to be done. "I took the pictures of the front of the shop yesterday, and I'll load them onto the website today."

Trudy looked over at him. "Oh, I added a few things to the windows last night. Could you re-take them today? I'm sorry, hon. I realized it was a little bland last night when I was talking to Paige."

"Paige?"

"Yes, she's renting the apartment upstairs."

"Oh, I didn't realize you'd rented it out."

"It just happened. Last night, in fact. I can re-take the pictures if you want."

"No, Mom. I can take them again. It'll only take a second."

"Great. Thanks, hon."

Trudy had originally rented the suite and the apartment thinking Seth would want to live there. Yet, when he had returned home from the military, he chose another apartment. He didn't know she hoped he would occupy the space. He was used to being on his own and Trudy understood his desire to not be attached financially to his mother. He didn't want to be a burden or a leech, but the apartment needed to be rented if she was going to make her own rent payments on time.

Seth didn't ask who Paige was; he probably assumed it was an older woman. It was tempting to fill Seth in on all the details from the night before. Although Trudy was excited to have the two meet, it was not her job to be a matchmaker for her son. God knew what each of the kids needed.

~

After breakfast, Paige went back to the apartment to drop off her books and grab the information she had on her mom's past whereabouts. As she got in her car to start her first day of searching, she was still wondering if she had done the right thing in the coffeehouse by not introducing herself to Trudy's son. She came to Vegas to find her mother and didn't want to waste time thinking about a guy. Finding her mom was what this trip was all about.

Aunt Marie had told her that mom's last apartment was near the Fremont Street Experience. Unfortunately, that was eleven years ago. No one had seen or heard from her mom since then. The only way the family knew she was alive was by following the arrests and court cases against her.

Paige took the long way to get to Summerlin Parkway so she could see the park and soccer complex in the daylight. It was a lot bigger than she thought and had twelve soccer fields, a tennis complex, and trails that went around it all. The park was only a block away from the shopping center. Now she knew where to go to run. It was strange to think that her aunt had been there about 15 years before. *If she hadn't done that race, would I even be here right now?*

Making her way around the park, she got on Summerlin Parkway East. She had the MapQuest directions for getting to Fremont Street. With no traffic, it would take about 20 minutes. It was almost 10am, so she assumed traffic would be minimal and was right. Highway 95 South was busy, but not backed up. Aunt Marie had told her that looking before noon would be most likely fruitless. Unless Mom was going to a shelter for a bed and breakfast, she would be sleeping off whatever she had been doing the night before. However, Paige was too excited and decided to start earlier.

The arrest records Aunt Marie had obtained through the years had many things in common. One of them was the very late, or early, depending on how you look at it, hour Mom had been out at the casinos. She seemed to get kicked out of them pretty regularly. Unfortunately, one of the things they did not have in common was where they were located. She was arrested at the Strip and in Old Vegas. It would take a miracle to find her, especially since going out late at night was the one thing Aunt Marie had asked Paige not to do.

Her aunt had also warned her about Fremont Street.

The area is very inappropriate. There are half dressed, to practically naked, people all over. Many are drunk even in the afternoon and the mentally ill and homeless are walking up and down the streets begging for your money. Be very careful and only go during the day. Take the last photo we have of your mom and show it to the cops that are on patrol there.

Once she arrived, Paige felt ready to ignore whatever was going on around her and keep her focus on looking for her mother. Being under 21, the only place Paige couldn't go was to any game tables or slot machines in the casinos. She was grateful her age didn't keep her out of the casinos all together. Aunt Marie had told her that finding her mom in them would be nearly impossible. She planned to look around for her mom in the casinos she entered, but she would go in them primarily to use the bathrooms, get out of the heat, and take advantage of the free Wi-Fi.

~

Seth had finally gotten his mom's merchant account squared away so she could charge credit cards. He was quickly learning the ins and outs of starting a small business. His mom had shown him how she acquired all of the licenses and paperwork needed to start the shop. He was so proud of her. Together they made a great team.

He was thankful he had not taken her up on her offer to use the upstairs apartment. She could make more money by renting it to a stranger. He also felt led to start civilian life on his own. Renting from his mom was too similar to being under her roof again.

Thankfully, he had saved up 60 days of military leave and was able to leave his duty station two months early. He hadn't found a job yet, but he'd put a number of resumes out in Vegas and around the country for the last few months. Seth's job in the military was working with weapon systems. Unfortunately, it is a program that doesn't exist in the civilian world, and so it did him little good in finding a job. He had acquired a security clearance, but he was not interested in continuing as a government contractor or working with military systems. He wasn't sure what he was going to do, but he knew his future didn't include the military, at least not directly. He had a heart to be near his only family: his mom. A military job in his area of expertise would have landed him in DC or Virginia.

The apartment he had rented was down the street from the quilt shop and only five minutes from his mother. His mom had helped him find the apartment when he told her he would not be living with her or renting the upstairs unit. Apparently, the same man who owned the shopping center also had multiple town homes in the Summer Springs area of Vegas. He gave Seth a great monthly rate on a two-bedroom apartment. As a Veteran himself, John Wilkins understood the difficulty of transitioning from military life to civilian life. He had waived the security deposit and didn't require a one-year lease. Except for finding a job, Seth was very happy with how God had worked things out. He kept praying that the right job opening would make itself known.

"Mom, your credit card system is up. Come and take a look."

Trudy had spent the day arranging fat quarters of fabrics according to color on the mini wire shelves in front of the quilt bolts. The shop was arranged so that when the customers came in, they had bolts of fabric sorted by type and color on the right wall. The cutting area and register were on the left. The center of the room had small tables where special bolts of fabric for holidays, babies, and novelty prints were arranged. It also had rotating racks of quilting supplies, patterns, and books. Directly across from the customer entrance was the door to the two back rooms. One was for storage and the other for training and classes.

"Oh, I'm so excited to see it. Can we test it?"

"Sure."

Trudy picked up a package of needles and handed them to Seth. "No, no. You're going to do it. I'll be here for the opening days, but you need to know how to work the entire system without me. I've got to find a job, remember?" Seth handed the package back to his mom with a smile.

"You're right. Such a smart boy!" She lovingly tapped his face with her hand. "OK, so first I scan the item?"

"First make sure you are on this screen and then click here," Seth said pointing to the screen, "so that what you scan will fill this spot with the product code."

"This is so exciting, sweetie!" She did what could only be described as a giddy happy dance. Seth laughed and drew her attention back to the screen.

"Now you can scan it." Trudy did as he said and watched the numbers populate the field. "Good. See how it filled in the information? Now enter the quantity."

Trudy soaked in everything Seth was telling her. With a little guidance, his mom was able to work quite well with the system. Leaving her to her own devices; however, proved that she was very impatient and too clicky with the mouse. "So now I just hit save?"

"Not yet. You have to ask the customer how they want to pay and then select it here," Seth said as he pointed over her shoulder again.

"Go ahead and select credit card." He reached into his pocket and got his wallet out. "Here. Use mine."

Fifteen more minutes of training and Trudy felt ready to handle transactions. They had five days left, so Seth decided to wait to teach returns and exchanges. He thought writing up an operating procedure would be best so that anyone helping his mom, be it Julie or whomever she eventually hired, would be able to do any task on the system. He had a feeling; however, he would be getting many trouble-calls in the future.

~

Paige arrived at the shopping center, her new temporary home, around 4:00 later that day. She had spent 6 hours in and around Fremont Street, and it had been nothing like she expected. She thought it was going to be a street with crowded sidewalks; when, in fact, it was completely blocked off from cars, had a clear, cage-like roof, and spanned multiple blocks As soon as she walked into the area, a couple of tourists zip-lined over her, getting their Fremont Street Experience from above. Vendors were everywhere, but evenly spread out. The place was not as packed as she thought it would be and multiple security guards walked up and down the area.

The homeless were easy to spot, as were those aiming to bring folks into their establishment. Aunt Marie's warnings were helpful when it came to seeing how casinos and restaurants sought new customers. It seemed their advertisement approach was that "less is more." Literally. The women, and even some men, were half-naked with the frilliest of outfits to encourage folks to come in and eat or gamble. Nothing was left to the imagination.

Paige had wandered the tourist destination for hours. She approached every cop and asked about the homeless, the local jail, and how the mentally ill homeless were handled by the authorities.

Although she had come away without seeing her mother, she had received tons of information on where the homeless go to eat and sleep. Paige also got the numbers and locations for all the shelters. The police officers carried a business card with all the local shelter information for those who needed help. One officer had given Paige the card after she explained why she was there. She was thankful it was passed out to those who needed help in the Vegas areas, and it was another example of Vegas' efforts to keep folks off the street.

The difference between the locals, homeless, and tourists was amazing. One could see all three in less than twenty steps. At times it was beyond heartbreaking. She didn't have enough money to give to all those holding cups and make-shift signs. She also knew that giving cash was not a good idea. At one point, Paige stopped to talk to a homeless couple a block away from Fremont.

The homeless were always cautious of people coming up to them. Apparently, they were often spit on, so Paige had quickly shared upon approaching that she was looking for her mom who was last known to be homeless in Vegas. The woman had welcomed Paige to sit down. Twenty minutes later, Paige was walking away from the woman and wiping away a stream of tears. The woman, who now held all the cash Paige had brought, had told her heartbreaking story with a numb acceptance that nothing would ever change.

Mothers, wives, fathers, husbands, toddlers, and babies begged and roamed the streets. Each homeless person had a tragic story. Only God knew the beginning and ending of each; including her mother's.

Only God knew if her mother was even alive.

Chapter 4

Seth was ready to go home. He had spent hours fine-tuning the system and needed to do a final practice his guitar part before the evening's worship service.

"Mom, I'm heading home. Are you coming tonight?"

"Yep, I'll be there. It is tempting to stay and get more work done, but I know God can do more through me in less time when I take time to worship Him."

"True. I'll see you after." Seth left the shop and brought up the app with the music for the service as he walked to his car. He wanted to have the song memorized, so he didn't have to stare at a music stand the whole time. He wasn't looking where he was going and brushed up against someone. He apologized, looked up, and saw a girl look up from her own phone with an apologetic smile.

Seth recognized the girl from the coffee shop immediately. But as soon as he met her eyes, he could tell she had been crying. She was red and puffy. "Are you OK?"

"Yeah," she said with a smile that did not reach her red eyes, "I'm fine." She smiled her fake smile again, looked down, and continued walking. It was obvious she didn't want to talk, and he wasn't sure if she remembered him from the café. He watched her go and unlock the door to the upstairs apartment.

Seth's mouth dropped open. *The girl from the coffee shop is Mom's new tenant?*

~

Paige tried to get the lock open as quickly as possible. This was the first time she had used it, since it locked automatically when she left. She could tell Trudy's son was still watching her and prayed he would not come over to talk or question why she was there.

Thankfully, she saw him take a couple of awkward steps backward in her peripheral vision, turn around, and leave. Finally, she got the door open and went upstairs. She opened the second door much faster and laid the keys on the kitchen table. She flopped onto the couch as the exhaustion of all the walking in the heat and emotional stress caught up with her.

An hour and half later, she awoke and was ready to get cleaned up and get something to eat. But before she could consider dinner, she felt the need to talk to someone about what she saw on the streets. She showered and dressed quickly, noting she had yet to take her clothes out of her suitcase. She opened up her laptop, connected to her phone's hotspot, and prepared herself for the onslaught of questions she would get from her grandmother.

It took two seconds for the other end to pick up.

"Oh, honey! I've been waiting. How did it go today? What did you do? Did you find her? Were you safe? Do you have enough money?" Gram's questions were non-stop. Paige laughed and thought how the last time she had laughed was earlier that morning in the coffee shop.

"Gram, I'm fine. I am taking all of your wisdom and Aunt Marie's advice very seriously."

"I'm glad to hear it." Gram's eyes narrowed and she tried to look into her screen harder. "Have you been crying?"

"A little."

"Oh, honey. I knew this was going to be hard on you."

"I know."

"So, tell me what happened." Gram settled into her chair waiting to hear what had brought her one and only grand-daughter to tears.

~

Paige took a deep breath and let it out slowly.

"I walked up, down, and around Fremont street for hours. It was hot and the homeless were shielding themselves from the sun with their cardboard signs. They switched locations over and over again as the day went to avoid the police. A couple of people came up to me that looked to have some obvious mental problems. I kept my distance and usually walked in another direction. Only when it was men though, and when I was farther from public than I would like.

"I talked to a few police officers. None of them recognized Mom's name, but I did get a card with all the numbers of the local shelters. I'll start visiting them this week."

"Don't forget what your aunt said. They won't give you any information on whether she is there or not."

"I know, but maybe God will make a way."

"I hope so. Then what happened?"

"On the outskirts of Fremont, I decided to stop and talk to a lady. She was in her 40's. She was surrounded by dirt and bent cardboard signs. One said 'Just had a baby. Anything will help.' Gram, she had just got out of the hospital less than 2 days before!"

"Where was her baby?"

"Her husband, who is also homeless, walks the baby and their one-year old son around the streets of Vegas all day long until she has begged for enough money to get a room."

"Unbelievable."

"I know. It was heartbreaking, and I had just passed a guy with a baby slung to his chest and pushing a stroller only five minutes before. That was her family."

"Did you come home after that?"

"Yes. I gave her all the cash in my pocket and it was getting late."

Gram's mouth opened. "Honey, you can't give all your money away every time you hear a sad story."

"I know, but it was heartbreaking. I wanted to be able to pay for a room for them all for at least one night." An understanding smile crossed Gram's lips. She understood Paige's desire to help the homeless. It was an outlet for her when she was unable to help the one homeless person she wanted to help.

"Why doesn't she go to the shelter for mothers?" Gram asked.

"Because then the family would be separated. It's very rare to have an entire homeless family."

"Most homeless are single, divorced, or widowed, I imagine."

"Many of the women are trying to hide from a guy and an abusive relationship. That's why the privacy is so strict," Paige said.

"What are you going to do tonight, hon?" Paige hadn't really thought about what she was going to do for dinner. She had only bought a few things at the store the night before and didn't have anything to make a meal. "I don't think you should stay in being so sad, but you don't know anyone yet so you can't go out either."

"Well, I can go out and get food without someone else," Paige said with a grin. "But I know you're just worried about me. I promise I'll be careful."

"Ok, sweetie. Please send me a text before you go to bed tonight and let me know you're doing alright," begged Gram.

"I will. Love you."

"Love you, too." Paige hit the end button and closed her laptop. She felt depressed and it was tempting to go back to bed. She was all alone and overwhelmed to the point where skipping dinner was also a temptation. She could tell she was going to second guess coming to Vegas if she didn't get out of this rut quickly. She grabbed her journal, purse, and keys and headed to the one place that she knew.

~

The café had only a few people in the booths. It was six o'clock and most people would be at home or out to dinner. The menu for the café was on a blackboard on the wall neatly decorated with different colored chalk and drawings. They had over 50 drinks and 10 food items. Simple food that didn't require much work or space.

"Hi. Can I help you?" asked the girl behind the counter. She was younger than the owner she had met that morning, but about the same age as Paige.

"Yes. Can I get a bagel with ham, egg, and cheese? Or is that just for breakfast?"

"No, you can get that. Would you like a drink?"

"I'll have a white chocolate latté, please."

"No problem. Go ahead and sit down, and I'll bring it right out," said the girl.

"Thanks." Paige placed eight dollars in the box and went to the table by the window. Thankfully she had left money in her room before leaving for Fremont, so she had not given it all away. She was empathetic, but not completely stupid. She knew she would have to tighten up her budget and that her four-dollar latté and four-dollar sandwich were the last extravagant things she would purchase for a while. She needed a job.

"Here you go," said the employee, bringing Paige out of her thoughts.

"Thank you." Suddenly Paige realized what she needed and couldn't believe she had not researched it yet. "May I ask you a question?"

"Sure," said the girl.

"Do you know of a good church close by?" Paige realized that she should have asked Trudy that question last night.

"Yeah, my church," said the girl with a big smile. "It's right down the road. It's pretty big, so you can't miss it. It's called Creek Community Church."

"Great. What time is service on Sunday?" Paige was suddenly disappointed that it was only Wednesday. Sunday felt forever far away.

"Services are at 9:00 and 11:00. But we also have a Wednesday service. It's tonight at 7:00. The Wednesday service is more like a Bible study service. It has fewer people and is more in depth than the Sunday sermon." Paige couldn't believe it. A church down the street with a service that was going to start in 45 minutes. "If you want, you can come with me. We close up at 6:30 on Wednesday's, so I can take you."

Paige looked at her watch again. It was 6:15. "You close in 15 minutes? I'm sorry. I didn't realize that." She stood and picked up her sandwich which she would have to eat a lot faster than she had anticipated.

"It's no problem. Please, sit. There's still time to eat. We always take orders up until closing."

"Are you sure? I can take it to my apartment."

"Very sure. It's not even closing time yet and I still have to cleanup. I'll be on time for service though, so you can come with me if you want.

"Thank you so much for offering, but I have a car. I can drive over." Paige didn't want to inconvenience the girl, or be at the mercy of someone else's schedule if she wanted to leave early.

"Ok. When you get there, go in the front door and the sanctuary is straight ahead. There is an info desk at that entrance and they'll give you a coupon for the café that you can use on Sunday since you are a first-time visitor."

"Sounds wonderful. Maybe I'll see you there," Paige said.

"Yep. Enjoy your food." Paige was able to journal for a few minutes in between eating, but she found herself to be too rushed to concentrate on putting her thoughts in any coherent order. She placed her empty plate on the counter and her trash in the bin. The customers had thinned out and the girl was finishing up cleaning the coffee machine when Paige approached.

"I am so sorry, but I forgot to ask your name."

"Oh, no big deal. It's Kelly."

"Thanks again for the info on your church, Kelly."

"Sure. Hope to see you there."

"You too," said Paige. She needed to get back to the apartment and clean up before she went anywhere in public. She wasn't use to the heat, and she suddenly realized it had put a layer of sweat on her. Vegas in the middle of June was probably not the best time to go searching for her mom. But there was no turning back now.

~

Seth had been at church since 6:00. He was playing rhythm guitar for three songs for the evening service. He was still amazed that a month into his attendance at the church he was on the worship team. They were welcoming and willing to give new folks a chance to serve. The church was huge and one of the largest in Vegas.

Prior to joining the military, he had attended a much smaller church in Ohio. Almost every Sunday since birth had begun with a church service. But that is where it started and ended. Seth knew God existed, knew Jesus died for the world, knew God loved him; but he had not fully accepted it—had not lived it. His worldview was not all-in for Christ, but more all-in for himself. Growing up he was confident that all the boxes had been checked in heaven for him. He was good to go.

But then he got the call that changed everything.

While on watch in the Navy, his Master Chief had pulled him off the floor to talk to him in his office. When he entered, the Chief handed Seth the phone.

"Hello?"

"Seth? It's Aunt Pam."

"What's wrong?" He knew nothing about that moment was normal. He rarely talked to his dad's sister.

"I am so sorry to have to tell you this, but your father has had a heart attack. We're at the hospital now, and he's on life support. The doctors don't think he's going to recover."

Seth's world stopped. He took a breath when he realized he was aching for air. "When did it happen? How long has he been on life support?"

"It happened a couple of days ago. We've been trying to reach you. The attack was severe and it has left your dad comatose. The doctors do not expect him to recover. I am here with your mom. She is holding my hand and wants to speak to you but knows she will just breakdown.

"Your dad has no brain activity, and he has a living will on file here at the hospital. Two doctors have signed off that he is not expected to recover, and so it moves to the next step which is notification. They must notify you and, of course, your mother. Since you are not here, they need you to confirm over the phone with two witnesses. You will need to let two people know that you have heard and understood the information. They are here with me. Honey, I am so sorry. As a nurse, I can tell you they have done everything in their power. Your dad is gone."

Seth breathed in and felt outside his own body. The shock and suddenness of it all left him speechless. His dad wasn't unhealthy, but he wasn't super athletic either.

"Seth? I know this is a lot to take in. Do you have any questions?"

"You are his sister. I trust you. Do I have to do it right at this moment, though?"

"Yes, honey. They are following the orders in his living will. Then you can stay on the line with us as they proceed."

After speaking to two nurses, Seth acknowledged that he had received the information. He listened as they proceeded to end his father's time on earth. Only the sobs of his aunt, his mother, and the slowing, electronic beat of his dad's heart filled the other end of the line.

He flew home a few days later, wondering what he was going to say at the funeral. His father had been a great dad and a wonderful husband. The accolades would be plentiful.

Yet, it was during that time that Seth learned that his father most likely was not spending eternity in heaven. The unexpected realization that Bruce Redding had probably never trusted Jesus as his Savior was devastating.

His father had been a great guy who paid his taxes on time and didn't break the law. Mom and Dad attended church, tried to be good people, and even gave money consistently in the offering plates. They taught Seth to do the same and always gave off a confidence that they were living the right way; heaven was the assumed place they would all end up.

The pastor leading his father's funeral service was new to the family and filling in for their own pastor who was out of town. This pastor didn't really know the man in the coffin. He only knew the bullet points: Bruce Redding was a hard worker for a local company, attended the small church down the road, and would be greatly missed by his family. The pastor then proceeded to share a dangerous and truth-filled message that revealed a scary fact for his entire family: knowing about Jesus was not enough. Being a good guy was not enough. Believing Jesus lived, died, and even rose again was not enough. Going *all-in* for Jesus was the only way to be in the Army of God and enter the eternity of heaven.

The pastor had unknowingly put the message in terms Seth understood. He needed to make Jesus his Commander and Chief. It was no coincidence their own pastor had been unavailable.

And so, Seth enlisted. He kneeled and went all-in for Jesus just days after his father's funeral. That decision led him to learn, grow, and walk in a new life in Christ. His mother had also let the message into her heart and was changed as well. Seth remembered her pouring her thoughts out at the kitchen table just days later.

"I loved your father with all my heart, Seth. But despite our church attendance and our small offerings each week, going to

church was just part of our culture. Your dad and I never thought of Jesus as the Leader and Lord of our lives. Only God knows the faith that was in your father's heart, but I am very certain that if you lost me a week ago, I would not have been spending forever with God in heaven. I've been the leader of my life. I've never given it over to Jesus."

His mom quit her job and moved to Vegas months later to work at a local charity with her long-time friend, Julie. As her only son, Seth felt not only led to live near her when he was done with his four years in the Navy, but also to share God's love to a city that needed to see it.

Here he was, 22 years old and part of a worship team in a large church in Vegas. How quickly things had changed. Spending 20 years in the Navy was no longer his desire. In fact, he wasn't quite sure what the next step in his journey was going to be at this point. He had enough money for a few more months without a job. Time off was what he needed to rest, focus, and take the right steps toward the rest of his life. He planned to enjoy it.

~

Paige pulled up to Creek Community Church, also known as CCC by the signs, only a few miles down from her apartment. She found it amazing that something so welcoming and wonderful was so close, yet had remained hidden to her. She hadn't traveled north of her apartment yet. The highway and everything she needed to live and search for her mom had been in every other direction.

The church had a large parking lot, a few parks for kids, and some type of school associated within it. Outside were folks directing traffic and saying hello to the people as they came in. There was a special parking area for guests, but Paige decided to follow the crowd and go to regular parking. She knew that parking in guest parking drew everyone's attention to you. That was affirmed by the signs which stated that guests were VIP's. She did not want to stand out and receive special treatment. That was better suited to those who were looking into what the church was all about. It made those who did not know Christ or the church feel welcome and loved. She was glad to see they put a lot of effort into greeting new folks, but she liked to stay low key.

She said hello to those walking into the building around her. With such a large church, it was easy to be a guest and not be singled out with "*Are you new?*" questions. Paige's home church was not nearly this big, but she had visited other churches in high school and understood that a person could be as active or as invisible as they wanted to be in any church of a good size.

Each entrance was inviting with music over the speakers and greeters at every door. Not one person looked unhappy. It was just the lift Paige needed to end her day.

"Hello. Welcome," said a kind middle-aged woman at the door. She was dressed in jeans and a T-Shirt that had the church's name and logo on it.

"Hello," replied Paige and returned the kind smile.

"Are you new here?" Paige had tried to be all natural and own the place while she walked in, but it had not worked. Paige's smile widened. She laughed a little at being found out so easily.

"I am. Is it that obvious?"

"Just a bit," the lady responded. She softened up her smile and tilted her head in a way that reminded Paige of a teacher directing a new kindergarten student in school. "I can see it in your eyes and the way you are looking around. The sanctuary is actually our gym and it is straight ahead. Feel free to sit anywhere. There are also ushers if you want to sit up front and can't find a seat. Don't forget to stop by the VIP desk and get a gift and some info about the church. Let me know if I can help with anything."

"Thanks so much. I appreciate it."

Skipping the VIP desk, Paige slipped into the gym now converted into a sanctuary. It was impressive. The place was not full, which was probably normal for a Wednesday night, but it had more people than her church did on a normal Sunday. She took a seat in the middle aisle and read through the bulletin she was given at the door.

Paige was in awe of the number of activities and opportunities at CCC. She closed the bulletin, took a deep breath, and thanked God for the peace, safety, and comfort she felt at that moment.

Chapter 5

"Paige? Oh, I'm so pleased to see you. How are you getting along in the apartment? I didn't see you today. Do you have everything you need?"

Paige couldn't believe it. In a city as huge as Vegas, she had ended up at the same church as her landlady.

"Trudy! It's great to see you too. I'm doing great and, yep, I have everything I need so far. Thank you again for letting me stay. When do you need me to leave? I don't have another place lined up yet. To be honest, I haven't started looking or thought about it, but I'll start tomorrow."

"Oh, no, dear. I'd love for you to stay and rent the apartment if you want. We can sit down and discuss rent this week sometime." Paige wanted to rent the apartment, but she wasn't sure she could afford it.

"Sounds good. I haven't found a job yet, but when I do, I'll know for sure how much I can afford. Everything is still up in the air for me right now. I hope to find a job within the week."

"Take your time, sweetie. I had no plans to even try and rent it out until everything was done with the store. You just concentrate on getting settled and finding a job. Would you like to sit with me up front?"

Paige knew that sitting up front would just draw more attention to herself. The thought that she might not care for this service or church, and knowing it would be hard to not show it on her face, made the decision easy. She knew she had a tendency to wear her feelings on her sleeve.

"Oh, thank you for asking. If you don't mind though, I'd like to stay back here."

"That's fine, hon. You enjoy the service. My son is playing guitar tonight. I'll try and introduce you after." And with that, Trudy moved to her seat. Another woman about the same age was up front waiting for her.

Paige was still standing and thinking of how Seth was in the building. That wouldn't have been so bad had he not seen her with red, wet eyes earlier in the afternoon. And now he knew she was the new renter above his mother's store.

The service began and the music, lights, and sound were amazing. Seth played an acoustic guitar and stood on the far side of the stage from where she sat. He wore the same jeans, but now had on a simple T-Shirt. She didn't recognize the logo on his shirt, but found it interesting that he'd had on a button-down shirt during the day and switched to a T-shirt for service.

She forced herself to look away and concentrate on the music. Her home church didn't have the money for any fancy sound or light equipment. Here, worship was more like a concert where God was the one on stage and the audience gave themselves to worshiping Him. With the lights down, the lyrics on the screen, and the flow of music and praise from one song to another, Paige was able to lose herself in worship. It was an amazing ending to a very hectic day.

She lifted up her cares and her desire to find her mom. She thanked God for Trudy, her gram, and her aunt. She could have gone on for hours. But after four songs, someone came up to give the announcements. Once the lights went up, everyone sat down to hear the message of the evening.

Completely at peace, and ready to hear what God wanted to teach her, she looked up to find the stage empty. A middle-aged man in jeans and a plaid, untucked button-down shirt walked up and led the congregation through a message on trusting God in all circumstances. It was exactly what Paige needed to hear.

God put her where she was at that moment, and she would trust Him to get her where she needed to go.

~

Seth was in the back row listening to the sermon. He was praising the fact that he hadn't messed up any of the songs. He was still very new to guitar and wanted to do his best. The music director was just a little older than Seth and, thankfully, was a great encourager. Seth knew any mistakes would not push him out of the band, but he didn't want to make it difficult for the team.

Looking around he noticed his Mom's new renter near the wall. Seth chuckled to himself. How many times was he going to see this girl today? He tried to remember her name. His mom had said it, but he hadn't really listened well enough to remember. Was it Peyton? Pam? He knew it began with a P. And then he remembered. It was Page. Or, more likely, Paige with an i.

He looked over to her again, now that he remembered her name, and wondered where she had come from. What had made her so sad earlier? He could tell she was not sad now. She looked as if she was on cloud nine. She had an air of peace and joy. Seth wanted to talk to her, but felt they had seen quite enough of each other over the course of the day. With her living above his mom's shop, he knew it would be only a matter of time until they bumped into each other again.

Pastor Eric's message had come to an end and he closed the service in prayer. Seth watched as Paige got up, grabbed her stuff, and almost ran out the door. She seemed super eager to get out and not talk to anyone. This didn't surprise Seth at all. She probably knew the folks would want to know all about their visitor--and she did look tired. Seth watched her leave and then made his way to see his mother.

"There you are, dear," his mother said with a big smile. "You did a great job up there tonight." She kissed his cheek and smiled proudly.

"Thanks, Mom. It went well. I liked the songs we did. I saw your renter here. She was sitting toward the back."

"Yes, Paige. I didn't know you had met her. I was going to introduce you. I told her she could sit with us, but she chose to stay by herself." Trudy looked around and saw no sign of Paige.

"She left. I saw her leave right after service was done."

"She's a smart girl. Many people would have tried to stop her and say hello. That is not bad on a Sunday morning, but on a Wednesday night that can make for a late evening." Trudy watched Seth as he stared out the back door, nodding and agreeing with her words. "When did you meet Paige, hon?"

"Well, we haven't officially met yet. I saw her in the coffee shop this morning, but I didn't know she was your renter. Then I saw her this evening going up to the apartment when I left the shop. You told me her name earlier today.

"Oh, that's right. She is so sweet. I'm not sure how she came to be in this area yet. But she came blindly and without so much as an apartment or a job lined up. I think God's doing something in her life, but I have no idea what it is."

Seth considered this and was amazed that someone that young would take such an unusual risk. Of course, he didn't have a job lined up either, but he still had income coming in from the military. Most high school graduates don't choose to go to a rural part of Vegas to find themselves. It was definitely strange, and only made Seth's curiosity increase.

~

It was almost 8:30 when Paige reached the apartment, but it felt like 11. She was emotionally and physically exhausted. She took another shower and then climbed into bed. She had brought up one more bag from the car when she returned. This one held every memory she had of her mother; second-hand memories that fit into a box. She had no memories of her own of either her mother or her father.

By age two, her mom had lost all custody of her and her dad had passed away. She was an orphan, but it would take years for that to sink in. Her paternal-grandmother shared all about Paige's father, but left the details of her mom's past to the other side of Paige's family. It was never a secret that Mom was mentally ill; Paige always worried she would up the same way.

A little shoe box decorated with stickers and drawings from when she was little held her most prized possessions. Rare pictures of Paige with her father and mother were the most prized of all. She didn't know a lot about how her father and mother met. It seemed no one wanted to talk about it, or didn't know much of those details themselves.

Over the years, Aunt Marie had sent a bunch of pictures of her sister from before she had lost touch with reality. They showed a happy, beautiful blonde at various events like weddings, graduations, and parties. She changed her hairstyle often, and sometimes even the color, but always loved to cheese it up for the camera. The pictures didn't show the hurt and problems going on in her mom's life. Aunt Marie had shared, and only after Paige had asked for details late in her teens, that it wasn't always fun and lighthearted. Her mom struggled with problems. Problems with anger, acceptance, and commitment. Problems that led to bad decisions that often included drugs.

From the box, Paige pulled out a picture of her mom from her high school years. The 80's were her mother's generation. With big bangs and tons of bracelets, her mother was the poster child for what was in-style for those graduating in the late 1980's. Her mother had been gorgeous.

The next picture was of her mom here in Vegas 10 years ago with Aunt Marie and Paige's grandfather. But there was no similarity. The woman in the picture had strange clothes, dark glasses, black hair, and was just skin and bones. She looked like a drama queen who did too many drugs and, standing next to her sister and father, was in a completely different universe. They all smiled in the picture, but it seemed that her mother's smile was beyond normal and held an air of pride and fantasy. Aunt Marie and grandpa smiled with sadness and a touch of fear.

Mom was unstable. She was unpredictable. She was on drugs, and she was mentally absent from all reality, yet still survived on the streets. Aunt Marie had warned Paige about how her mom had acted all those years ago. She had written Paige multiple letters that included history and ideas about searching for her. Those letters sat in a stack in the back of the box with the treasured maps her aunt had also sent. Some were old and cherished. Some were new. She wondered if she should go over the new maps now that she was here. Tired, and ready to crash, Paige decided she would look at them when she had the time.

She closed the box and thanked God that she had at least some pictures of her mom. She could have had far less. She knew she had been born in the midst of her mother going in and out of mental institutions. Paige was thankful she was alive at all. She knew that many in her family still believed abortion was the best option for women in difficult circumstance, or for those who just weren't ready for a baby. Thankfully, God had put it on her mom's heart to keep her.

Paige was determined to not waste the life God had provided her. Despite all the pain, heartache, and unknown; God was fully in control of her past, present, and future.

Only He knew if that future included getting to know her mother without letters and pictures.

~

John Wilkins sat in his favorite chair and could barely keep his eyes open. He was ready to call it a night. When his phone suddenly vibrated, he hoped that nothing major was broken in one of his rental units. One downside of renting was sometimes the renters themselves. They wanted everything fixed immediately. They rarely realized that if they owned the place, they wouldn't be able to immediately fix it either. He was a businessman, and, unfortunately, not a plumber, electrician, or carpenter. Being knowledgeable in those things would have helped so much and could have saved him a ton of money. But he was never good at that kind of stuff, and he didn't really like it anyway.

He picked up the phone reminding himself to be patient no matter what the person on the other line said. "Hello?"

"Hi, John. It's Mike." John released an inaudible *phew* and smiled. Mike was one of the least high-maintenance renters he had. However, a late-night phone call from him was unusual so John didn't relax too much.

"Evening, Mike. Not like you to call this late. Something going on?"

"Yeah, sorry about the hour. But I wanted to make you aware that there's a car in the parking lot that's been here now for two nights, and that's pretty unusual. I wasn't sure if you wanted to tow it or something. It has out of state plates, and it's far enough from the pizza place that it doesn't seem to be connected. It doesn't look broke down, but maybe it has a bad battery and they haven't been able to get back. Just thought you should know."

Mike was the General Manager for the grocery store and knew that John tried to keep the plaza clean and safe for customers.

"I appreciate the phone call, Mike. I don't know any reason why it would be there. I don't think I'll tow it until I talk to all the other folks in the plaza. Maybe they know why it's there. Thanks for letting me know. I really appreciate it."

"No problem, John. You have a nice evening."

"You too, Mike. Night." John clicked *end* and thought about what he would do. He was so thankful nothing was broken. A rogue car was easy enough to take care of with the tow company. John knew the signs in the parking lot said no overnight parking, but people rarely read signs.

John smiled to himself as he got out of his chair. This would give him the reason he needed to go talk to Trudy. He would call all the other renters, but he was not going to pass up an opportunity to talk to her. Just thinking of her brought color to his face. That hadn't happened in years. Only one other woman made him get all mushy thinking, and she'd decided years ago that they were better apart than together. He thought he was done with women, but obviously his heart had other ideas.

Chapter 6

With the store opening in only a couple of days, Trudy realized she had made a big mistake by not hiring another person. Including Julie, there were only two people to run the store and one helper in case it got bad: her son. Seth didn't mind helping, but Trudy doubted he wanted to get stuck in a quilt shop for the remainder of his final, paid time off from the Navy.

It was early, but she thought maybe Paige would be awake. Hoping the young girl would need a job, she decided to make her way up and see how she was fairing with the apartment--and her finances. Grabbing her keys, she left the shop.

As she unlocked the lower door, she realized what a pain it would be not knowing if someone was knocking at your front door. Trudy could get in because she had a key, but how would Paige know if there was someone at the door? She decided she would talk to John, the owner, about getting some type of buzzer and speaker system installed.

Once at the top of the stairs, she knocked softly.

Paige, Trudy was happy to hear, asked who it was first and then opened the door. It seemed Trudy was just a little too early. Paige was just out of bed and in a cute plaid pajama set. "Oh, sweetie. Did I wake you up? I'm so sorry," Trudy said.

"Oh, no. I got up about 15 minutes ago. I was just sitting on the couch and watching some T.V. Please come in." Paige led Trudy to the living room. A clean living room. Trudy was glad to see that she had, so far, been wise in letting the girl stay here. She didn't want to admit it, but she didn't know this girl at all and the younger millennials had a bad stereotype of being lazy. The only evidence Trudy had that Paige would be perfect for the place was the peaceful feeling that had led her to offer it to her just days before. "I don't have any coffee, unfortunately. I am hoping to buy a coffee maker as soon as I can."

"Thanks, sweetie, but I am fine. Did you see the coffee shop across the street?" Trudy watched Paige grin.

"Yes, I did. It's a really cute place. But I can't afford it every day. Please, have a seat." And with that, Paige took her own seat on the other side of the couch, put her feet up, and wrapped her arms around her legs. Trudy had another rush of realization of how young Paige really was. What had brought such a young girl to Vegas?

"The café is a cute place, and it's donation only. I'm sure they would not mind a lower donation amount from a young college student.

"I'm actually not a college student." Paige said rather cryptically, lowering her eyes. Trudy could tell that she didn't want to go into details. Understanding the need for privacy, Trudy decided not to press.

"I think I have an extra coffee maker, if you would like it. Also, if you're interested in earning some extra cash, I could use some help in the quilt shop when it opens." Trudy hoped that whatever had brought Paige to their neck of the woods was not something that would end up hurting the sweet, young girl huddled at the end of the couch. She seemed confident, yet uncertain. Trudy had to force herself not to pry into the young girl's life. She wasn't Paige's mother.

Paige shifted on the couch and tucked her feet under herself. She was biting her lower lip and had a very intense expression.

"Everything alright, dear?" Trudy asked, hoping to break the girl's thoughts.

"Yes, sorry. I was just thinking. The job offer sounds wonderful. I think I'd fit in really well considering I did so much quilt work with my gram growing up. And I could use the money. But I am also here for another reason that may take up some of my time during the day. Were you looking for someone part-time?"

In truth, Trudy wasn't sure she could afford anyone. There was no certainty of how successful the shop would be in the area. Although the life insurance money was enough to start the shop, it wouldn't last forever. If the shop was to survive, it had to be successful and make a profit. She didn't want to deplete all of her accounts and end up living with her son, penniless. She wanted to be wise with what her husband left her. He had gone to great effort to be sure she was taken care of if anything happened to him. She would do her best to make sure that she would never be a burden to her son.

"Yes, I think part-time would be best. In fact, we could exchange hours for rent payment to keep it simple. Unless you are going to need cash, then we can go a different way."

"No. I don't need cash. I have been saving my money since I was 8. I have enough cash right now to live, but not enough to pay rent for very long. Do you know what hours you were wanting someone at the shop? Unfortunately, I would need to be gone most afternoons."

"Well, I think we could arrange something. The shop will be open from 10-6 every day except Sunday. Most women like to shop earlier or later. After lunch is usually the quietest time in quilt shops based on my own shopping patterns and what I've seen in other stores. Would 9:30-12:30 work for you? That would give you 18 hours a week. It would be nice to have help opening and preparing for each day. My friend Julie may be able to help for closing."

Trudy could see Paige was thinking again. She looked like she wanted to be excited but then her smile would fade into some painful memory, or a heavy burden would intrude. Trudy hoped to put the girl at ease.

"Now, you won't offend me if you say no. I'm sure working at a quilt shop was not your plan when you came to Vegas." Paige looked up suddenly, realizing she had been in her own little world during most of the conversation.

"Oh, I would love to work with you. I'm sorry. I was just thinking and being amazed all at the same time. I really can't believe how God's led me to you. It's all been so...wonderful." Trudy thought that this girl was just the beam of sunshine her family needed in their life. It was obvious she had some issues she was working through, but what 18-year-old didn't have issues?

"Wonderful," Trudy said, clapping her hands together. "I wasn't sure. You looked quite lost in thought." Trudy smiled and hoped to encourage the young girl to share her thoughts. How lonely it must be to come to a strange city and not know anyone. Or did she? Maybe it was family she visited in the afternoons.

"I know. Sorry about that. I was just trying to figure out how I would handle everything if I had a job close to the apartment. I guess I expected to get a job more toward the Strip."

"The Strip?" Trudy asked. "May I ask what you were going to do?" Trudy hoped Paige was not planning to use her body to get money. Once in that business, Trudy could only imagine how hard it would be to get out.

"I'm not sure. Maybe selling tickets to shows or working at a coffee shop."

"You chose this area for an apartment though. You could have rented a closer apartment if you wanted to work at the strip. What made you come here?" Trudy knew she was getting into some personal questions, but it was dangerous at the strip. The young girl seemed to be winging it all--maybe just letting God work it out. If that was it, what a faith the girl had. It amazed Trudy. She was still learning to live by faith herself.

"My aunt recommended this area. She visited once many years ago and loved it. She's guided me a lot in my moving here. She used to come to Vegas all the time for work. But she definitely didn't want me working at the Strip, so she'll be very happy to hear that I have a job in this area." Paige was smiling now, remembering the words of her aunt. "I've been praying for any job. My aunt has been praying for a great job that would keep me safe. Seems like we both have had our prayers answered."

"It sounds like you have a wonderful aunt."

"You guys would get along so well," said Paige. "She loves to quilt."

"Really? Maybe I'll meet her someday."

~

When Paige closed the door after Trudy left, she leaned against the door with a sudden realization of what she had just done. She accepted a job where she would be seeing Trudy's son all the time. Paige didn't have time to get distracted by boys right now. She had waited years to go searching for her mother. A boyfriend would just get in the way.

Paige pushed herself away from the door and rolled her eyes at her presumption. Who said he'd want to date her anyway? Maybe a mysterious, hopeful, and emotional blond wasn't his type. Paige pushed the thoughts away. She was too excited about the job to worry. She immediately texted Aunt Marie and Gram to let them know the good news. The money she'd saved all those years from cards and gifts would last a lot longer with no rent to pay.

After showering, Paige made her way to the coffee shop. She was determined to find a way to celebrate her new job. They had decided she would start the next day. It was only four days until opening, and Paige would need to learn how to run things right away.

It was about 10:00 in the morning, and the small café was pretty quiet. The morning rush had come and gone. The owner greeted Paige with a smile. What a wonderful feeling to have someone recognize her as a local so soon after coming to town. The warm colors of the café and the inviting feel of the place was so welcoming. Paige hoped the place would be permanent.

"Good morning. Back again, I see," said Sarah from behind the counter.

Smiling with the joy of getting a job and someone recognizing her, Paige was almost giddy as she approached the owner. "I am celebrating, so I will have a large white chocolate mocha and a bagel with cream cheese, please."

"Sounds good. What're you celebrating?"

"I just got a job."

Sarah beamed. "Congratulations! Where will you be working and what kind of bagel would you like?"

"Everything bagel, please," replied Paige. "I'll be working across the street at the quilt shop. Trudy asked me this morning. She's also my landlady. I'm renting the apartment above the shop as well."

"Wow! That's awesome. I'm sure Trudy could use the help. I'm sorry. I haven't asked you your name."

"Paige."

"I'm so excited for you, Paige. And for Trudy. Seth will be pleased she has more help. Do you know Seth?"

"I know who he is, but we've not officially met yet."

"Oh, he was here yesterday at the same time. Now I remember. He's a really nice guy. Treats his mom so well. I assume you want your bagel toasted, correct?"

"Yes, please. Could you put the cream cheese on the side?"

"Yep. It's in the pre-packaged containers already," said Sarah, as she grabbed the cream cheese from a small refrigerator under the counter. Finishing the mocha, she added whipped cream, a stirrer, and hung a lid from it on the side. The attention to detail in the small café was such a nice change from the fancy coffee shops that treated you like a number. "What brought you to this area?"

Paige silently groaned. She would have to start telling people why she was there, but she really didn't want to. It was a depressing story and folks always got down themselves after she told them about her mother. It was so much a part of Paige's life, that it didn't affect her to tell the story anymore. It was what it was.

"My aunt recommended this area to me. It's so pretty and the community is great. What a change from the Strip."

"Ah, the Strip. I'm glad you're not staying or working there. A lot of good folks work in that area, but it's dangerous and enticing for those who don't have self-control."

"I was initially planning to work there. But you're right; it's dangerous. Living here will also save me money on gas and parking fees."

"If for some reason you need to go down there, or anywhere for that matter, the bus stop is only 3 blocks down the road. You can get a day pass, three-day pass, or even a month pass. The buses are pretty safe. They always have security and monitors on them, and it keeps those who are not able to pay off. Just stay back away from the doors and keep your belongings close to you."

Paige wasn't planning to use the bus system at all. She had the routes listed on a map, but she hadn't spent any time looking at it. Her aunt had sent it to her a few months back. She placed it in the box with her other information on the homeless shelters, library, and other maps that she'd collected over the years from her aunt.

Aunt Marie had continued to come to Vegas every year to look for her sister and had kept Paige up to date on what the homeless were doing and where they were hanging out. The details of her trips had increased as Paige had gotten older, but it always seemed like her aunt was hiding something about her mom.

"Here you go," said Sarah, drawing Paige out of her thoughts. "I put your coffee in a to-go cup. Most people prefer the cup over the mug because it keeps it warmer longer. Just let me know if you prefer a mug next time."

"That works, thanks. I usually never finish my coffee. I only started drinking coffee a few months ago, and I get caught up in my books and forget it's there."

Sarah laughed. "Most people do. I can also warm it up for you before you leave. Let me know if you need anything else, Paige."

Paige placed seven dollars into the box and thanked her. She made her way to the same seat she had sat in the previous day and began to get her books out of her bag. She was reading a Chuck Swindoll book that she picked up at her local Christian bookstore back in Washington. It was his book *Embraced by the Spirit*.

Paige grew up in a loving home, but she'd still been an orphan from the age of two. It seemed, because of that, she was more drawn to books about the Holy Spirit. He was her Comforter. Her Encourager. One of her best friends.

In high school, her friends joked that she was young on the outside and old on the inside. She enjoyed the things older folks enjoyed: cross stitch and reading. But Paige was young at heart, too. She made mistakes like most kids and also dreamed like them. The majority of her friends were from broken homes; when their parents divorced, they always dreamed they would reconcile. Paige couldn't remember anyone ever saying that it actually happened. She dreamed of her mom getting better and having a cute house where it would be just the two of them. That dream, she knew, was just like her friends wanting their parents to get back together. A dream that was unrealistic, but hopeful.

Why is it that the older I get the less hopeful I feel?

God was still the God of miracles and of the impossible being possible.

Paige took a deep breath, pushed the past and her dreams back down where they would not distract, and read her book. She took notes in her journal and tried to eat and drink her food before it got cold.

~

Seth saw Paige in the window at the café. He was tempted to go in and talk to her. However, after watching for a few minutes, it was clear she was really into whatever she was studying. She looked young. Was she even eighteen? Where did she come from? Why was she alone all the time? How did she meet his mother?

The questions came like a tidal wave, and he was drowning in them and her. Her long hair was blond and her eyes a blue that seemed to go on forever like the ocean horizon.

Seth shook himself out of his trance. He was in a car staring at a girl he didn't know. What was wrong with him? He was acting creepy.

He turned off the car, grabbed his pack, and headed into his mom's shop. There were only a few days to get the shop ready for the opening. He wasn't sure how she was going to handle the big day, and he wasn't certain everything would be done by then. He needed to prioritize the things that were incomplete and decide which to tackle first.

The little bell above the door rang when he came in. "Mom?"

"I'm back here, Seth," called his mom from the back-storage area. Seth locked the door behind him and made his way to the little room behind the front of the shop. The store also had an emergency exit in the back that he hoped his mother had remembered to lock; unlike the front door he had just came through.

"Mom, you have to lock that front door when you are here alone."

"Oh, I forgot again."

"Do you have your gun with you."

"No."

Seth groaned. He had helped his mother get signed up and trained to use and carry her gun with her at all times. She was living alone and would be working on her own a lot. She needed to protect herself. They were in the suburbs of Vegas, but crime didn't stop at the Strip.

"I know, I know. I'll work on it. I'm just not used to grabbing my purse, keys, and gun when I leave the house."

"Yes, but we talked about all this," Seth said, grabbing the bucket of water his mother was hauling in from the back door.

"You're right," She patted his cheek after he took the bucket from her. "Can you take that to the front? I want to wash the windows."

"Did you get that last shipment of fabrics you were waiting on?" The shelves of the shop were full except one. Seth made his way to the windows and set the bucket down. "Did you want this inside or outside?"

"Outside. I think the windows in here are alright. What do you think?"

Seth looked at the windows and put every effort he could muster to not look across the street at Paige. "Um, these look fine. The front, too."

"Oh, no. We need to do the outside at least." Seth smiled inwardly. This was not prioritizing. The windows were about the least important task to be done. But he was not surprised. His mom had always been a neat freak. He walked outside and set the bucket down.

He took a moment and glanced across the street. Paige was still reading. Still writing. Still looking pretty in the sunlight.

Seth shook himself again. What was he doing? He didn't want to be in a relationship, or even date right now. He was just out of the Navy and needed to think about the future. He had dated a few girls since high school. One he had even proposed to and lived with while in the Navy, but it didn't work out. When he had accepted Christ, and put God first in his life, she left him. She told him that he was putting his new, fancy "God" ahead of her.

"You spend all this time reading and going to church now. We hardly ever go to the bars or parties anymore," she said.

"I know. I don't want to. I have been lukewarm, or at least fooling myself, for so long. I'm on fire for God now, and I want to spend more time with Him. Going to those places are too much of a temptation for me right now."

She threw up her hands in frustration. "Who talks like that? You are one of those religious nut jobs now." Seth cringed. He was hoping that his love for Jesus would excite and maybe entice her to want the same thing. It didn't. "Do you love this God more than you love me now?"

He knew she was not going to like his answer. "Yes," he said quietly. Her mouth dropped in shock. He was waiting for her to yell, but decided to take advantage of the moment. "How can the created not love the Creator more than any other?"

She stood and grabbed her purse from the chair. She was in his apartment in Virginia; an apartment they now shared. She'd arrived only a couple days before from her own deployment. They had been dating for over almost two years and most of that time had been long distance. Now that they were finally able to spend time together, his faith was separating them.

"No one thought we could make a long-distance relationship work. We told them they'd be wrong, and they were. But now that you're here, we're not any closer. You're in love with someone else, and I can't compete with God." She made her way to the door and Seth stood.

"It's not a competition. Loving God doesn't mean I don't love you. Please don't go. Let's talk about it."

"No. I'm done. I don't want to be a third wheel. I'll come back and get my stuff later."

And with that, she left. He never saw her again. He had felt like such a failure for so long. She did not want to come to know God as he had: as a Father and a Friend. It took him months to learn that it was not his job to convince her she needed Jesus. No one can do that but God himself. Looking back, he knew that it was all for the best. He'd been living as if he was already married. But Seth also knew that God could do amazing things with past mistakes. If she would have stayed, and accepted him as the new person he was, they could have worked through it.

Seth glanced again at the café. Could this be the girl that would accept him and his relationship with Jesus?

"I did get that shipment of flannels. I'm going to put them out after I am done here," his mom said, drawing him back from his past.

"Oh, great. I'm going to do some mock sales and see what problems need to be fixed." Reluctantly, Seth moved toward the register and away from the window.

"Wonderful, I'd like to do some as well. I'm going to need to start showing Paige how to do it tomorrow morning."

"What?" Seth asked, whipping his head back to his mother.

"I hired Paige."

Chapter 7

Paige couldn't believe the number of homeless people in the library. Of course, there was no way to prove they were homeless. In fact, many may have just been poor and jobless. The Las Vegas Public Library had a room full of computers where folks huddled behind black boxes and stared at their screens. Paige didn't want to think about what inappropriate things some might be looking at.

She knew her mother used to come to this library. Her aunt had told her that her mom once sent emails and had a P.O. Box in the area. As long as no one made a scene or was violent, anyone could use the library; but it was not a safe place. Security walked the floor at all times.

Paige had driven to the library after leaving the café. She saw Trudy and Seth hard at work in the quilt shop, but decided not to go in. Since she would not start working tomorrow until tomorrow, Paige wanted as many hours to search as she could get in. This would be the only time she could get to the library by noon for a while.

The chances that her mom was even up and around before noon were slim, but going different places at different times was part of the strategy Paige decided to try. Her mom's last arrest had been at 2am at a local casino years ago. Since going to casinos at 2am would be crazy, Paige had to trust that God would make a way.

She was at a small table that had a view to the front door and the computer area. If her mom came in, Paige would see her. She had already walked around the entire library and also verified her mom wasn't one of the many people hunched into those black tunnel boxes that held the monitors.

The men in the room all stared at her. Every person had a phone. No one had a book. It seemed libraries were rarely used for books anymore. Paige had her own books out in front of her, but she was too anxious to do any reading. It was hard to imagine that any time she could turn or look up and see her mother. Ironically, the thought of it brought so much anxiety that Paige's heartbeat quickly elevated and she could feel herself sweating in the air conditioning. All the men staring at her was not helping.

Paige had a picture of her mom on her phone. The picture was about 10 years old and she knew it was a long shot that anyone would recognize her. Her hair color in the picture was black and not the dirty blonde that it was supposed to be. It was short and self-cut. If her mom was still on the street, and not in an apartment like she was when the picture was taken, her hair would be her original color now. Her teeth would be stained, her face scarred from acne she always battled, and she would undoubtedly be so skinny that she'd probably be blown over by the wind if it wasn't for all the clothes she had on.

Aunt Marie had said that if Paige actually saw her mother, it would be a shock. All those physical features were present years ago and would only be more prominent now. Of course, there was no way to know if she was even alive. There'd been no arrest records for years. One of the best things for her mom, Paige knew, would be to get arrested again. Maybe another arrest would be the help she needed to get moved to a psych ward where she could get medication to clear her head and time to detox her body of whatever was in it.

Paige's anxiety continued and she found herself jittery and antsy. She had waited years to be here. Years to come and search. Yet 10 minutes at a table in the library felt like a lifetime. Besides her God-time in the morning, it was 10-15 minutes with her favorite fiction books that helped her relax the most. Yet even losing herself in 19th century England wouldn't keep her mind from racing this morning.

It was the first time since arriving in Vegas that she wanted to get on social media. But her gram had asked to her to stay off. Letting all her friends know that she was in Vegas alone was not wise. Since Paige never told many of her friends about her mom, it would only invite tons of questions anyway.

At the table next to her, there was an older man with a Veteran's hat on. He was holding a small flip phone and putting great effort into hitting the right buttons with his large and dirty hands. Paige couldn't tell if he was homeless himself.

"Excuse me, sir." He didn't seem to hear her so she reached over to touch his shoulder. She stopped short when he turned to her with a confused and defensive look. "I'm sorry to disturb you. I'm looking for my mother. She's homeless here in Vegas. Do you know anything about the homeless in this area?"

The man looked around to see if anyone else noticed her talking to him. Not sure what he was thinking, Paige went on. "I don't mean to interrupt you, but she's very sick, and I'm hoping to help her or at least find out if she is alive. I don't know all the places I should look." Paige shared a soft smile with the man, and he seemed to relax.

"It's too dangerous for you to be out there on the street looking for someone." He dropped his hands down to his lap; temporarily giving up the work he was doing with his phone. His defensive look was quickly changing to one of sympathy and concern.

"I know. But the shelters don't give any information, so I'm forced to take her picture around and see if anyone recognizes her or know where she hangs out." Paige grabbed her phone and pulled up the last picture she had, anyone had, of her mother. With all the years that had passed, Paige knew it was a long shot. She lifted it up to the man's eyes and he grabbed the phone from her fingers. He held the picture up close to his eyes. His fingers were shaking. Paige tried to remain calm; she didn't expect the man to grab her phone from her.

"No, sorry, I don't recognize her. Did you go to the women's shelter?" He asked, handing the phone back to her.

Paige sighed. "They're not allowed to give out any information on the people who stay there." The privacy laws had always been the most difficult problem when it came to looking for a loved one. But the privacy of those who came to the shelter was always the first priority, and no amount of proving good intentions or relationship would help get any information. Paige thought it ironic that the shelters let the homeless eat and sleep there at night, but then made the people leave all day to roam the streets. Yet, for those people who have family looking for them, there was no assistance from the shelters. The first priority was not getting the people help, it seemed. In fact, to Paige, their policies seemed to keep many of the homeless stuck in homelessness unless there were programs being offered that Paige had not heard about. Most women were escaping abusive relationships, and Paige understood the need for secrecy. But there was no abusive husband or stalker looking for her mother. Her privacy for that reason was non-existent. But it didn't matter.

"Have you checked the park?"

Paige looked up.

"What park?" she asked with excitement.

"There's a park just down the street. A lot of homeless go there during the day. Just go down two blocks and take a left after the McDonald's. But you should have someone go with you."

Paige ignored the man's warning. "Thank you. I'll check there. Would you like a bottle of water?"

"Sure," said the man, looking up to see if someone was watching. Suspicion was normal. Most folks didn't talk to the homeless or poor.

Paige reached into her backpack and took out one of the bottles of water she had picked up at the store near her apartment. Her aunt had told her not to give money, but food and water instead. Paige had already ignored that piece of advice the first day she had come out to Fremont.

She handed the bottle over. "God loves you, you know."

"Does he now?" asked the man. He grabbed the water and put it on the table. He looked like he was concerned that Paige was going to either ask him for money or preach to him. "Thanks."

"You're welcome. And thank you for the advice." Paige packed up and decided to go right over to the park. "Have a good day." She swung the backpack over her shoulder and looked at the old man. "And thank you for your service."

Momentarily confused as to how she knew he was a Veteran, he lifted his hand to his hat. "Oh, um, yes." He smiled and Paige saw some color come into his cheeks.

"Bye."

"Bye." He watched her head to the lobby. Paige looked back as she was about to leave the building and saw the man pick up the bottle of water.

~

Seth had spent the morning on the small details that seemed to take too much time, yet they needed to be done. He fixed the sales receipts so they printed correctly, verified the accounts in the software, and confirmed the merchant account was accessible and linked. Seth had decided to trickle information down to his mother on a need to know basis, so it didn't overwhelm her.

"Mom?" Seth called from the register. "Are you ready to go through this one more time?"

"Coming!" His mom was stacking fat quarters along the wall of the best-looking fabrics. He knew that the opening was going to be a very hectic day. But having the fabrics looking perfect was going to be the last thing to worry about when items needed to be rung up and credit cards started flying.

Seth had learned a lot about the problems that came with opening a retail business from one of his buddies who separated from the Navy a year before. Jim had been his chief, and the two had got along well. Soon after separating from the military, Jim had opened his own gun shop in Virginia. Keeping in touch on Facebook, Jim had even offered Seth a job at his shop. But Seth felt like he needed time with his mom and wanted to help her dream come true. Nevertheless, it was nice to know that if he had to work, there was a place he could go. He just wished it wasn't on the other side of the country.

"O.K. I'm ready," his mom said. She was bouncing up and down again on her toes in excitement. Although she was very nervous about the money side of things, she loved the idea of having a cash register.

"Alright. Let's say someone picks a fabric and wants 2 1/4 yards." He switched places with his mom, and watched her take a hesitant step to the computer. "I would like 2 1/4 yards of this fabric, please," said Seth with a high old lady voice. His mom laughed and rolled her eyes.

An hour later, both mom and son needed a break. They locked up the shop and made their way to the café. Sitting near the window, Seth had a thought. "Mom, I think you need to have a soft opening."

"What's a soft opening?"

"You just open your doors earlier than expected without publicly announcing it. You only tell a few folks and, hopefully, they come in and you practice on them with their purchases. It's a way to work out the potential kinks."

"But I told everyone we will open this Saturday! The flyers are already up in the area," she said with growing concern.

"We don't need to change the grand opening. We just open our doors tomorrow so that we can see what you need to learn, or I need to fix."

"Wow. This is happening so fast now," she said. Seth noticed a hint of panic in her eyes. "But I like the idea. What should we do?"

"I picked up the OPEN sign from the office store yesterday. It's in my car. I say we hang it up and turn it on tomorrow and see what happens. If no one comes in by noon, you can let a couple of your friends know so that they will stop by." Doing his best to hide his thoughts that had been trying to distract him all day, Seth grabbed his coffee and quickly added, "That will also give Paige some time to learn the system with actual customers."

"What would I do without you, Seth?" his mom asked.

"Oh, you'd be bored and miserable," he said smiling. They both laughed and finished their coffee. They had a lot of work to do if their doors would have customers walking through them tomorrow.

~

John drove into the parking lot of the shopping center at four o'clock. This was the only shopping center he owned and he hadn't been to it in days. Commercial properties were so much easier to manage than the residential ones. Business owners were more likely to take care of their units and only call in an emergency.

His call from Mike gave him reason to come back earlier than he normally would. He was happy being single and only had to concern himself with his business. Yet when he sat and read the paper while listening to the news each evening, with nothing more than his plans for tomorrow going through his mind, he now sat wondering what she was doing. He felt like a foolish old man. He was a divorced 58-year-old who had an extra 15 pounds and a head full of gray hair. Thankfully, those 15 pounds were easily hidden since he was taller than most guys. Still, he knew he was not a catch in the visual sense.

He parked his car between the grocery store and the quilt shop. He had one more unit in this shopping center to rent, and he hoped it would go soon. The rent from all the other units easily paid the mortgage and expenses, so he wasn't working too hard on getting a renter.

When Trudy had called his number three months earlier and asked if she could rent the unit for a quilt shop, John had been pleased. The shopping center was beautiful and well-rounded. He wanted it to be an asset to the community. He didn't rent to just anyone who had the money. He wanted to see shopping centers come up a bit on the impression scale. Too many were old, falling apart, and even dangerous because of a lack of security or oversight.

John had hired a man to keep the place looking nice and went to great effort to make it a shopping center people would want to frequent. By the look of the renters in the complex across the street, it seemed his vision of a nicer community was catching on to the other business owners in the area.

As the bell on the door rang, John saw Trudy look up from her computer. She was a little younger than he was, but single as well. Unlike his ex-wife, who hated him, Trudy missed her husband. He had learned about him when they had met to walk through the building. Trudy held her late husband with high regard. It had pained John to think he would never have someone who would miss him like that.

"Afternoon, Trudy," he said. "How is the preparation going for the grand opening?"

"Hello, John. I can see I forgot to lock the door again. Would you mind locking the door behind you? Seth has been bugging me to keep it locked for safety."

"Smart kid." John locked the door and made his way to the counter.

"Yes, and ever since his father died, he's paid much more attention to my safety. Sometimes too much, I think."

"Better to be safe than sorry," he said as he made his way toward her and leaned his hip against the sales counter. He crossed his arms and tried to seem calm, but inside it was like he was a teenager again. After the first phone call to ask about the rent, he had seen Trudy only a handful of times. Some visits were necessary: walk through, signing documents, and handing over keys. Other times, it was for any reason he could think of including making sure her utilities worked and that she knew which container to use for trash at the back of the building. "What time will you open on Saturday?"

"We will open at ten on Saturday, but we're also going to have a soft opening tomorrow. I need more practice with this computer."

"I can only imagine the difficulty, especially with inventory. I still do most of my books by hand, but my accountant is always telling me I need to convert over to some financial software. "

Trudy laughed and smiled at him. "I would stick with the paper for as long as possible."

He nodded. "I plan to." He looked out the window, not seeing the reason he was visiting in the first place. "I don't want to keep you from your work, but I got a call from the grocery store manager letting me know that there was a strange car in the parking lot the last couple of nights. Do you know anything about it?"

"Oh, yes. I should've called you. I'm so glad you stopped by. I rented the apartment upstairs. The goal was to have my son use it, but he decided to stay elsewhere." Trudy slammed her hand down, startling him for a moment, and stared at him. "And do you know what happened? A girl from out of town came to the grocery store a couple of days ago and peeked into my store. We got to talking about the opening, and, long story short, she needed a place to stay, so I am letting her rent it." Trudy beamed with amazement. "She is the sweetest dear, and I felt a tug on my heart strings when I saw her and spoke to her. I can't explain it, but offering her the apartment, as well as a job, was the right thing to do."

"Then it is her car? That would explain the out of state plates." John smiled inside. He knew what it felt like to have those heart strings pulled. They had pulled for Trudy almost immediately.

"Yes. Another reason I am glad you stopped by is that I'm concerned for her safety. There's no way for her to hear if anyone is at the bottom door. If she invites visitors, she would have to leave the door unlocked and then they would come up and knock on the second door. That has a lot of potential for trouble. Have you ever considered putting in a button or intercom below so that the person upstairs could buzz someone in?"

"I'm not sure what the original owners of the center were thinking when they put an apartment above the unit. The setup is unique. In truth, I never thought about it either from a resident's perspective. I will have my handyman stop by and see if we can get something worked out."

Trudy started laughing.

John smiled. "What's so funny?"

"My son must be rubbing off on me. Here I am worried about security on a door, yet I keep forgetting to lock my own!" As her laugh died down, he decided it was time to ask her out for dinner. He loved the sound of her laugh. He watched her take a deep breath and look at him. "Thank you, John. The girl is so young. I would hate to see her get hurt."

John heard a noise from the back.

"Mom? Oh, hi, John," Seth said, as he made his way from the back room. John shook the young man's hand.

"Seth, how's civilian life going? Are you missing the Navy?"

"Definitely not. Four years was enough for me. How about you? You missing the Air Force?" John had got to know Seth well on his last visit to see Trudy, and the boy was very pleased that his mother's new landlord was a retired Colonel.

"No, not at all. Twenty-six years was enough for me."

John began walking toward the front door. He quickly decided that asking Trudy out in front of her son would be an awkwardness he wasn't ready to endure.

"I'm going to get out of your guys' hair. Thanks, Trudy, for letting me know about the girl. I will have Tom come over and see what we can do for a buzzer system. Maybe we can get one of those new high-tech Wi-Fi doorbells or something."

Seth shot a confused look over to his mom, but didn't question what was going on. The kid was so well-mannered. Had John had children, he would have liked a boy like Seth.

"Sounds good, John. Drive safe and thanks."

John made his way to his car. As he opened the door, a blue Honda Civic with Washington plates made its way to the front of the quilt shop. After a moment, a young girl climbed out. With long blond hair and a determined look, she grabbed her things and went to the apartment door.

He could see what Trudy was talking about. That girl could probably pull on many a heart strings.

Chapter 8

After Paige had dropped her stuff in the apartment, she grabbed her laptop and made her way to the café. She was eager to call her aunt and talk about all that had happened during the day.

The café had only a few people in it and Kelly was working. Paige dropped her stuff off at the window seat first and then made her way to the counter. "Hi, Paige. Did you make it to church last night?" Kelly asked.

Enjoying the feeling of being treated like a local, Paige smiled. "Yes, I did. Thank you so much. It was wonderful."

"Great. There's a singles group, which has now turned into the 'everyone under 30' group, if you're interested in meeting some more folks. It's social, but we also do Bible study and discussion on the sermons. It's every other Sunday night. So not this Sunday, but the next."

"That sounds great. Can you give me your number, or can you take mine, to send me the details?"

"Sure," Kelly said, reaching for her phone in her pocket. "What's your number?" Paige gave her number, ordered her latté and a bagel, and sat down at her now 'usual' spot.

Opening her laptop, she glanced out the window across the street. She was so set on telling Aunt Marie about her day that she hadn't thought about stopping at the quilt shop and going over details about tomorrow with Trudy. A black truck was one row over from her car and Paige figured it was Seth's. She was going to have to get over trying to avoid the guy. He was her new boss's son, and their being around each other was inevitable.

"Here you go," said Kelly.

"Oh, I forgot to put money in the box," Paige said, pulling her thoughts back in.

"No problem. You can do that whenever you want. Even the next day. We are really relaxed here." Kelly made her way back to the counter and Paige looked out the window again. What was she doing getting distracted by a guy? She had waited years to come to Vegas and search for her mom. Of course, that didn't mean she had to ignore the world either. She needed to be balanced, that's all. She had to put her priorities in order.

Determined to do just that, she looked over to the counter. "Kelly, do you have a password for the Wi-Fi?"

"Yep. It's john316. No spaces or colon and all lowercase."

Paige smiled. "Thanks." She got online and opened Skype. Aunt Marie was three hours ahead and usually home in the evenings. She noticed that her aunt and her grandmother were online. Paige put on her headphones and clicked the video chat button for her aunt.

"Paige!" Her aunt almost screamed when she answered. "Oh, I have been waiting to hear from you. Your gram has been keeping me updated on your progress. I'm so glad you arrived and are safe."

"Hi, Aunt Marie. I'm sorry I haven't texted or called you."

"No, no. Don't you worry about that. I'm sure your plate is full. I'm praying for your trip all the time. Your gram says you found an apartment already."

"The whole thing has been amazing. As soon as I came into the city, I met a wonderful woman who has given me an apartment and also a job." Paige shared all the details of her trip, leaving out her boss's son—who was a small detail no one needed to know about.

"Well, I'm just thrilled how God has been working in all of this, Paige. It truly is awesome to watch. Do you have enough money then? Are you using the bus system? Have you gone through the brochures I sent you?"

"I have them all, thank you. But no, I've not gone through them yet. I'm still driving down to the strip and back. If money gets tight, I'll use the buses."

Her aunt bit her lip and hesitated. "It wouldn't hurt to know the routes though, just in case."

"True," agreed Paige. "I will take a look at them. Today I made my way to the main library and talked to a guy there who led me to a park about five blocks away. He said a bunch of homeless people go there. On my way, I spoke to a group of older homeless men for directions to the park. I shared the details of why I was there and showed them mom's picture. They recognized her."

"Really?" Marie said, breaking into a huge grin. "That is wonderful."

"They kept referring to her as that really skinny one."

"That doesn't surprise me. She was super skinny when I last saw her. Did you find the park then?"

"Yes. But there weren't many homeless there at that time of day. On the way there I passed a McDonald's. There was a married couple outside that I stopped and talked to. They asked me for change, and I offered food for information. After getting them two value meals, they told me their story, which of course was heartbreaking, and mentioned some other areas where the homeless hang out. The couple said they've been homeless in Vegas for twelve years after being stranded there by a friend. The wife then got cancer which left them broke. I'm amazed that these people don't have one family member to contact for help. It seems like they have just accepted that they're going to be homeless for the rest of their lives. It's so depressing."

"I know, sweetie," Aunt Marie said, in a semi-passionate tone. Paige wondered if Marie thought the couple had told Paige the truth. It was hard to tell which stories were just refined lies.

"But at least someone recognized mom's picture. That's awesome."

"Absolutely. But I worry about you going to all these places by yourself. Do you want me to come out and search with you at all?"

"I only look for a few hours every day, and I'm paying a lot of attention to my surroundings. I also have my job starting tomorrow at the quilt shop below my apartment, so that will take up a chunk of my time. I'll only have a couple hours every day to search once I drive downtown."

"It's astonishing that you have a job in a quilt store after being there for what, three days?" her aunt asked excitedly.

Paige smiled at Aunt Marie's astonishment. "Yes, it's opening this weekend. You would love it."

"Wow, sweetie. What an awesome trip God's giving you."

"I couldn't have done it without you," Paige said. "You led me here and you've given me funds to make this trip happen. Oh, and there is a great church just down the road that I visited last night. It's wonderful."

"Unbelievable. And where are you now? Are you in your apartment?"

"No, I'm at a coffee shop across the street. It's an adorable little place." Paige was about to swing the laptop around to show her Aunt when another video call came in. "Aunt Marie, Gram's calling. I'm going to let you go. I'll talk to you soon, OK?"

"Alright, hon. Thanks for calling. Love you."

"Love you, too." Paige took a deep breath, ready to tell the day's events all over again.

~

With the soft opening the next day, Seth knew that they would be at the store late into the evening. At 5:30, he looked out and saw Paige's car in the parking lot.

"Mom, do you need a break? Are you hungry?" She was placing patterns on the rack and was getting ready to hang her quilts on the wall for display.

"No, honey. I'm fine."

"OK. I'm going across the street then to get a sandwich. Text me if you change your mind."

"Alright, I'll lock the door behind you." Seth made his way from the store and it wasn't long before he saw Paige in the window at the café. He slowed his walk, wondering if he should still go over. He decided it was time to talk to her. Starting tomorrow, they would be working together—at least for a while.

After entering, Seth saw that Kelly was working instead of Sarah. They knew each other from the church singles group.

"Hey Kelly, how are you?" Kelly, her long black hair in a pony tail, looked up with a smile.

"Seth! Sarah said you were in earlier. How's the shop coming?"

"It's just about ready. In fact, we're going to have a soft opening tomorrow. Would you be interested in stopping in and buying something to give mom some practice?" He hated asking, but he was more concerned about his mother right now.

"Sure. I'll stop over before work. You want a coffee?"

"No right now. I'll take a can of Pepsi and a ham and cheese sandwich, please. Hot." Seth took out his wallet and placed the money in the box.

"No problem. Go ahead and grab the Pepsi out of the cooler, and I'll bring your sandwich over."

"Thanks, Kelly." Seth took a deep breath and turned. He had not looked over at Paige when he walked in. A stupid move, really. What person didn't look over a place when they entered. Had she even noticed his obvious avoidance of eye contact? He shook his head. Ugh. What was wrong with him?

He grabbed his drink and approached her table.

"Hi, Paige. It's probably time we officially met. I'm Seth, Trudy's son." He extended his hand when she looked up. He reminded himself to breath and not come off as a creep again.

Paige smiled and shook his hand. "Hi, Seth. I guess we should have officially met right here yesterday morning. I'm sorry I didn't say hello. I overheard your conversation with Sarah and knew you were Trudy's son before you came over and spoke to me." Her smile morphed into a guilty, apologetic cringe with a cute crinkle of her eyes as she bit her lower lip.

"Well, I really didn't give you the chance with all my babbling." He smiled, trying to make light of that first conversation that he would rather forget. She smiled again, which caused her cheeks to go up and her eyes to close even more. Seth shook himself. He was not doing a great job of being normal.

"May I sit with you a minute? I'd like to fill you in on what we're going to do tomorrow at the shop. Mom says you'll be working there."

Paige set her pen down and moved her hands to her lap as she sat up. "Sure, sit down." She placed her elbows up onto the table and then back down again to her lap. It was nice to know he wasn't the only nervous person in the room.

Seth took a seat and opened his Pepsi. "I've set up the computer for the shop, but it s new and a little complicated for my mom. So, we decided to have a soft opening tomorrow to feel out the problems and issues that may need to be fixed before the grand opening on Saturday." He took a sip and watched her over the can. She was listening and had scrunched her eyes a bit and drew her eyebrows down some when he mentioned a soft opening.

"Alright. I'm not sure what a soft opening is. Is it like a practice run?"

"Exactly like that," Seth admitted. He felt himself relax a little. "Have you ever worked in a store before?"

"No. I worked in a nursing home for about eight months serving food and such, but I've been doing crafts and quilting with my gram for years." Seth smiled, glad that his mom had found someone who understood the quilting side of things.

"I will be there tomorrow to help out with the cash register and the technical side of things. Our soft open will begin at ten, but we don't expect people to be rushing in or anything. We're only telling our friends so that'll give me time to teach you the system in the morning. I'll be over there this evening finalizing the receipt printouts and writing up a quick guide for mom."

"Would you prefer I stop by tonight? I'm right upstairs, and I don't have anything going on. That'll help make sure you have more time to fix problems as you find them tomorrow instead of training me while the store is open and customers are there," Paige said with an air of interest and hesitation. "That is if your mom is going to be there, too," she quickly added. She seemed to be rethinking her suggestion.

Seth smiled. "She's there." Someone had taught this girl to be mindful of being alone with a complete stranger. "Why don't you stop by when you're done here, and I'll show you how the system works?"

Seth saw Kelly coming over with his sandwich. "Kelly, would you mind putting it in a box for me? I'm going to eat over at the shop. Sorry, I forgot to tell you."

Kelly stopped and smiled. "No problem. Hold on." As she turned, Seth looked back at Paige who seemed deep in thought as she watched Kelly go.

"Will I see you soon?"

Paige brought her attention back over to him, as if catching herself. "Yes. I'll be right over."

"Sounds good." He grabbed the box from Kelly on his way out. "Thanks, Kel. See you tomorrow."

"Yep, I'll be over to buy something."

Seth glanced over to where Paige sat as he left and smiled. She returned his smile and then shifted to put away her things. Seth took a deep breath, amazed at how nervous he had been to meet someone. He pushed the door open and ran right into Patrick.

"Whoa, you're going the wrong way, friend." Seth stumbled back a little and then let the door close behind him.

Seth smacked his forehead. "Oh, no. I'm so sorry, Patrick. I completely forgot about our meeting tonight, and I need to go help at the store for tomorrow."

"I didn't hear from you much this week. I knew you would probably be super busy with your mom's store opening. I thought about texting you a reminder, but I didn't follow through." Seth took a quick glance back into the café and Patrick followed his gaze. He saw a young woman at the window seat, and he looked back to Seth with a smile. "Is it more than just the store opening that has your mind preoccupied?"

Seth felt his cheeks flush. "Maybe."

"Sounds like we will have lots to talk about next week. What's her name?"

"Paige, and I think I need to have a conversation about it sooner than next week." He worked hard against the urge to glance back over to her and hoped Patrick would do the same. "How about rescheduling for tomorrow night? Same time and place."

"That works. I'll be praying for you, Seth. Make sure you text me if you need anything."

"Will do. Thanks, Patrick."

Patrick smacked Seth's back. "No problem, buddy. See you tomorrow night."

~

Later that evening, Trudy sat in her kitchen journaling the day's events. She was simply amazed at how her dream was coming true beyond ways she could ever have imagined. Seth and Paige had stayed with her to clean, practice, and prepare for the next day's soft opening. Julie had even stopped by to help.

Trudy knew she could have never opened the store without her son's help. God's timing was awesome, as usual. Yet the pain of losing her husband was always just under the surface waiting to bubble over with the smallest reminder of their days together. He had always supported her crafts and hobbies, in his own way.

He never suggested she bought too much fabric or threads, which she did. He always took an interest in what she was making, and in the evenings, as he watched football, she quilted and shared her progress with him. They did their own thing, but they were in the same room and that was all that had mattered. Now he would miss the opening of her store, yet it would not have happened without him.

The term life insurance money had given her the means to take on this adventure. She didn't use all of it for the store; he would have thought that foolish. He had taught her to have an emergency fund and a budget. After that was done, the next step was to invest and then spend. One of the blessings of her marriage was that they always talked and agreed on money. They discussed every purchase over $50 and what to do if the other passed away.

Seth had learned so much about money from them over the years and had done financially well in the Navy. He saved and prepared for the future, which now meant he was there to help her open the store.

Trudy smiled thinking of Seth. It was so obvious he was interested in getting to know Paige. And she saw Paige's nervousness and looks toward him as well. Yet both had been so professional working together this evening. Paige took his instruction and Seth had been as patient with her as he had been with his technologically clueless mother. It was quickly clear, however, that Paige took to it all naturally.

As she sat at the kitchen table, which was her routine each evening, with her elbows on the table, hands clasped, and her forehead leaning on them for support, she spoke quietly to her sweet husband. "I wish you could see Seth, honey. He is such a wise young man and he is doing a great job of taking care of me."

Trudy always tried to focus on the love and beauty of God and the comfort that maybe, somehow, God would allow her husband to hear her words. But he had not known Jesus as Lord of his life, and the agony that she would not see him in heaven was, at times, beyond heartbreaking and debilitating. She had to force herself to focus on the truth: God is just. Her husband had had his time to choose Christ. She was thankful God knew her husband's heart at every moment, and she trusted that God had done only what He could do after his death on earth: what was right.

"I wish you could see the store. Oh, I am so nervous about the opening. I hope that I did the right thing with the insurance money. Thank you for taking care of us and thinking of us. If only we would have taken some of our time and spent it on things of eternal value."

Trudy squeezed her eyes shut, forcing herself not to go down a path of depression and regret. "I love you, sweetie."

Giving herself just a few minutes each day to speak to her husband was a routine that helped her during the grieving process. She had found that it was best to limit it to a few minutes, otherwise the memories and regrets would try to build up and then press her down. She then opened her prayer journal and spent the rest of the time with Jesus.

Journaling her prayers was the only way she could stay focused and not distracted by the numerous thoughts that tried to invade her time with God. She didn't know how some of her friends were able to quietly pray continually for long periods of time. Trudy found her thoughts went in eighty different directions.

Father,

Thank you for another wonderful day. I am amazed at your continued grace and mercy in my life. I hope that this store will be a way to reach others for You. Show me, each day, to walk the path of love and righteousness.

Thank you for Seth and for blessing him as he aims to make the most of this life. I am so thankful he is here and that we can work on this project together.

I lift up Paige to you. She has not told us why she is here, but it is obvious you are doing something in her life. And she knows you! Oh, to be eighteen again and know you as Lord. How blessed she is, at such a young age, to be on fire for her Savior. Give her wisdom in whatever has led her to our little part of town. May I be wise to see how I can help her.

It is tempting, Lord, to arrange and push Seth and Paige to get to know each other. But you know everything, and I have very little knowledge of what has led her here. Therefore, I am going to put my matchmaking desire aside and trust you in this.

Love you, Father.

Amen

Trudy closed her journal and set it aside. She prepared herself for her least favorite moment of the day: turning off the lights, locking the doors, setting the alarm, and going to bed. It was when she missed her husband the most and the feeling of being alone weighed heavily upon her heart. As she ascended the stairs, the faint, still small voice came up into her soul to encourage her.

I am with you.

And she breathed in deeply, closed her eyes, and whispered, "Thank you, Father."

Chapter 9

P aige turned off the alarm on her phone when it went off at eight the next morning. She laid in bed thinking about the previous evening. Working on the computer and learning the system had come easily to her. She smiled thinking of Seth's reaction to her picking it up so quickly. He had shaken his head and smiled. He quietly shared his concern about how his mother was going to do in the shop when he wasn't there, and that Paige's presence was definitely going to help him worry less.

Paige was thrilled to be an asset to the family. They were the cutest mom and son team. Off and on through the evening, the three of them had engaged in small talk to get to know each other. Thankfully, neither had asked her why she was in Vegas and she could tell they were giving her space to tell her story in her own time.

It was Seth that Paige had learned the most about. Trudy praised him often through the evening and it always connected to something in his past. *Seth learned so much about computers in the Navy. I'm so grateful he is out now and can help me. Seth is a big reason this store is opening. He has been so encouraging since his father passed away, and he's given me so much wonderful advice on how to use the money we gained from the insurance.*

When Paige heard that Seth had lost his father, she had looked over at him. He had a small, sad smile as he looked down at the counter with a tint of red cheeks. Paige couldn't tell if he was more embarrassed by the praise or sad due to the memories. Paige had compassion for him. Though she had never really known her own dad, the loss of him seemed fresh whenever she heard of someone else losing their own father. It was obvious he had had a good relationship with his dad. Paige couldn't imagine what that felt like.

She decided that it was time to get this day started and jumped up for a shower. Over breakfast in her little kitchen, she journaled and then texted her aunt and gram. Each was so thankful for her new job and wanted to know more details. Thankfully, Gram never begged her to come home anymore and Aunt Marie hinted often that she would love to come out and help her search. Paige had told her that once she was more settled in her routine, a visit, along with her help, would be appreciated.

Paige took out her memory box and counted the cash. She wasn't using the emergency credit card that her gram had helped her get except to get gas for the car. She was supposed to tell Paige the total of the credit card bill once it arrived there, but she had not said anything yet. Paige wouldn't be surprised if her gram "forgot" to tell her the total and paid it herself, so Paige had been keeping an eye on the account online. Her gram was the co-signer on all of Paige's accounts, but she wanted to be responsible for her own bill payments now. She realized she could pay it online before the statement arrived at the house, if she timed it right. Unfortunately, she hadn't had time to convert all the accounts to her own name after turning eighteen. The trip had consumed all of her thoughts.

Her maternal grandparents, along with Aunt Marie, had been sending Paige cash on holidays since she was little. Paige now had over a thousand dollars to use for this trip. She wanted to use as little as possible though. She didn't know how long it would take to find her mom. Now that she had a job, she wouldn't need to worry about rent. The money would feed her for quite a while, but she would need to find a way to earn some cash if she wanted to stay for more than a couple months.

Paige made her way to the shop, locking the doors to the apartment as she went. It was 9:30 and the store would open, softly, at 10:00. She wanted to get there early and take time to walk through store, see if anything last minute needed to be done, and maybe get some coffee across the street for her and Trudy. If Seth was there, she would buy him some coffee too. She wanted to thank him for teaching her and being so patient with her questions. He had a level of patience that she had never seen in anyone before.

Paige was surprised at how easy working with him had been and how she had unnecessarily worried about spending time with him. He had been professional and not at all flirtatious. It was refreshing to have a guy act normally around her. Over the past couple of years, it felt like most guys looked at her and assumed she was dumb because she was blond. They would hit on her and never treat her respectfully.

Unfortunately, the fearful anticipation of spending time with Seth because he was cute and a distraction from her mission had now turned into a hopeful anticipation that they could spend more time together, which effectively went against the goal of not being distracted.

Paige knocked on the quilt shop door, reminding herself again of why she was in Vegas. And it wasn't to date.

~

When Seth arrived at the café, he saw Paige at the counter talking with Sarah. Each turned when he walked in and smiled at him. Different smiles—one knowing and carefree, the other hesitant with a hint of joy.

"Hey, Seth. Paige was telling me that you guys are ready to start having customers. I'll be in later to help out. Kelly is coming over as well before her shift."

"That's great, Sarah. Thank you." He approached the counter as Paige moved over to make room for him. "Paige is going to be a huge

Lilly Horigan

help to mom. I trained her last night and she is a natural," he said while glancing over to Paige. She looked down and blushed a little.

"It really is a lot of fun and a little dream come true. I always wanted to run a cash register when I was little. This one is a computer and doesn't make the same sounds, but it gives the same feeling," she said. Seth heard the little, dreamy girl inside her. She looked up at Sarah with a sweet smile. Then she turned her head slightly and looked over to Seth with a question in her eyes. Did she think he was going to laugh at her?

"I know what you mean. I felt that same way a lot when I was in the Navy. I wasn't working directly with any artillery, but I was responsible for intelligence that could alter where we went and what we did with them. It felt a little like boyhood dreams coming true."

Paige's smile increased and Sarah joined in, getting caught up with the childhood excitement. "This shop is the same. Serving and pouring coffee checks off some little girl part of me in some way. I guess God has a way of making even little, unknown dreams come true that we don't even think about until they happen."

"Absolutely," Seth agreed and put some money in the box. "Today is mom's day to have her big dream come true." Sarah handed Paige two drinks in to-go cups and asked Seth what he would like. He looked over to Paige. "Is that extra one for mom?" he asked.

"Yes. I stopped in to talk to her already," Paige replied. "She is really nervous, so I am not sure if coffee is the right way to go, but it calms me."

"No, I think that will be perfect. Thanks," Seth said.

"Did you want any food, Seth?"

"Not right now, Sarah. Just a caramel macchiato."

"Coming right up," she said and turned to prepare them.

"I'll see you over there, Seth," Paige said as she grabbed the coffees and moved toward the door.

"Here, let me get the door for you."

"Thanks." Seth opened the door and went back to the counter. He peeked back to make sure she got across the street alright.

"I'm sure she can cross the street without problems, Seth," Sarah said with a grin on her face when he turned back to face her.

"I know. I know," Seth conceded. He decided not to waste time trying to pretend like he didn't know what she was talking about.

"She seems to be on a mission of some sort here in Vegas. Do you know what it is?" Sarah asked. She handed him his cup.

"No, but I agree. There is no other reason that I can think of to come to this town, or this part of Vegas anyway."

"Don't rush her. She will tell us when, and if, she wants too." Seth nodded and would take Sarah's advice to heart. He took a sip of his drink wondering if Sarah was going to ask anything else about how he felt about Paige. He was going to talk to Patrick about the whole thing on Thursday night when they met for their mentoring meeting. Talking to Sarah about it was tempting but inappropriate, so he decided to just go on as if everything was normal. "Thanks, Sarah. I'll see you later at the store."

"Sounds good. Have fun!"

He made his way across the street and went to open the store door and he found it locked. He smiled and knocked. Paige came over and unlocked it.

"Glad to see the door is locked, Mom. You are getting better at that."

"I told Paige you are a stickler for safety. She did it." Seth grinned and looked over at Paige. She was smiling as well. He re-locked the door and made his way to the computer. "Do you want me to make a copy of my keys for Paige, Mom?"

Paige's head came up with a surprised look.

"Sure, that would be great. Thank you, sweetie." Paige went back to her work of arranging patterns. Seth saw her suck in and bite her lower lip. What did that mean? Was she scared of the responsibility, happy with the trust they had in her, or unsure of something? Seth forced himself to not to question her and began getting the computer ready for the day.

~

At ten o'clock, Trudy unlocked the front door and turned on the open sign. She clapped her hands and looked back at her helpers. "Well, this is it," she said with an excited grin. "I can't believe how nervous I am, and it is not even the real opening day."

Seth came up to her and put his arm around her shoulders. "It's a big day, Mom. But remember, we may not have but a few people come in. Don't get down if there are hours between customers. Only a handful of people know we are open today."

"Yes, you're right," Trudy said. "Today is all about making sure I know how to run the computer and process sales correctly." She looked up at her son, now a foot taller than her. "I don't want to mess up all the work you have done on it, hon."

"Don't worry about that. If you mess up, it can be fixed. While we wait for someone to come in, let's go over what you need to do each morning to get things ready."

They both went back to the computer. With the cutting table next to it, it was a perfect fit for two people at a time. One to cut, and one to check the person out.

"You'll have to balance the register each day and get the computer up and ready. I made you a sheet with steps on it that you or Paige can use to get everything ready."

Paige came over and leaned on the table when she heard her name. "Mind if I listen in," she said.

Trudy reached over and patted Paige's hand. "You must. I'll need all the help I can get." Trudy turned back to look at the document Seth had created and printed out for her. "Seth, this is wonderful. When did you type all this up," Trudy asked as she looked over the steps entitled "Morning Routine Checklist?"

"I did this yesterday morning when I was here." Trudy could not believe how much the military had changed her son. It brought out a disciplined and organized man from the independent, yet lackadaisical, boy she had known.

"Thank you, hon. This will help so much."

"What we need for the shop are a set of Standard Operating Procedures. SOP for short. This checklist is the first part of what will become the store's SOP. It will be very helpful if you are sick or busy, Mom, so that anyone with a little knowledge of the system can run the store for you."

"Perfect," she said, as she leaned over to Paige. "Don't worry. I will try not to get sick."

Paige smiled and continued to lean her chin on her hands to watch the training.

"So, I want you to work through these steps on your own so we can see if any need to be tweaked or explained. Paige? Will you read them to her while she clicks through them? That way you can learn as well."

"Sure." Seth slipped around the counter and Paige came in next to Trudy.

"I need to make a few phone calls. Just let me know if you get stuck," Seth said, as he made his way to the window and got his cell phone out.

Trudy took a deep breath. "Alright, Paige. What's the first step?"

As they worked on their checklist, she tried not to listen to Seth's phone call. Even after he had been out of the house for four years, she still had to fight the urge to parent him. It was clear; however, he didn't need any parenting from her anymore. She was so proud of him. They had grown so close since his father passed away. She worried that her dream was putting his life on hold, but he seemed pleased with helping her. She was truly blessed to have him.

"Trudy?" Paige asked, bringing Trudy out of her trance. In trying not to hear him, she let herself start thinking, which usually put her in a mini-paralyzed state. "Everything OK?"

"Yes, dear. I just zoned out there for a sec thinking about things. Sorry."

"No problem. I do that a lot myself. My gram used to call me Space Cadet because I would go off into my own little world."

"Is your gram still alive?" Trudy asked. Not wanting to pry but she didn't know much about her new tenant and employee.

"Yep. She lives in Washington. I text or Skype her every day. She is helping a lot to make this trip possible."

"She must be so worried about you down here all alone."

"She is worried, but much less now. I told her about you, the apartment, and the shop. She's grateful I have found good people to be around. She was concerned I would be alone."

"Well, I am glad I was outside my shop when you drove in the other day then. God had it all arranged."

"Yes, He did." Paige said, and Trudy could see her smile grow wider in thinking of the moment.

"What does your mom and dad think of you coming here all alone at such a young age? They must be worried too."

As soon as she had said it, Trudy knew that she had gone too far. Paige's demeanor fell and she brought the checklist up to go over it. She bit her lower lip and seemed to consider what to say and do.

"My gram raised me." Trudy could see Paige didn't want to say anymore. She seemed conflicted.

"Oh, well I bet she is an amazing grandma. You are such a fine young woman. She did a great job, it seems."

Paige smiled and looked over to Trudy. "She definitely did the best she could with what she had. She loved me, and she has always supported me."

"That is wonderful. Please tell her I said hello the next time you talk. You said she taught you to quilt a little?"

"Yes. She loved to quilt and make projects. She was very crafty."

"Then make sure you also tell her I said thank you. I am benefiting from her teaching."

Paige blinked slowly, as if taking in the comment. "I will. She will be very happy to hear that." Trudy and Paige continued with the checklist and finished it without any problems. And then the bell over the door rang and in walked the first customer of Quilt's On.

Chapter 10

The blast of hot air as Paige left the shop was a shock. She was not used to such hot and dry conditions, and it wasn't even July yet. It was almost 3 o'clock and she had worked five hours with Trudy. Seth had left for an hour at lunch time and brought back subs for them. He had fixed all the problems that came up through the day and showed her a few of the fixes as well. Paige had managed to stay busy the entire time helping a few customers and learning more about the fabrics, threads, and patterns the store stocked.

So far, Trudy was very pleased with the folks who came in. News that they were "open" made its way through Trudy's small group and other ladies in the church. In five hours they had had twelve women come in. Many shopped and chatted, which made the day pass quickly. Trudy had introduced Paige to each woman with sincere affection and gratitude. It was wonderful knowing she was playing a part in the big event. Trudy was treating her like the daughter she never had.

Paige definitely felt like a daughter around her. But she wasn't actually the daughter of a kind, loving woman who was wise and living a life filled with friends, hope, and Jesus. She was the daughter of a crazy woman. Although her gram had left many of the negative details of her father's life out of earshot, Paige knew that he'd had problems of his own. He had all his mental faculties, but he did not always make good decisions with them.

Her father had worked at the hospital cafeteria and had met her mom there. He knew she was not well. Yet, he loved her. Soon after being cleared from the mental facility, mom was pregnant. If only carrying and having a baby could make one mentally well! But it only got worse.

Her father was forced to leave and took Paige with him. The battle for custody was short and her mother was not allowed near anyone in the family anymore, including Paige. Her mother took off and her father grieved.

A few months later, her father would be pronounced dead on the side of a state highway. The details of the accident were few and Paige never looked into them or asked about them. Sober, drunk, on drugs, off drugs, tired, or not at fault, what did it matter? Her father was gone. Whatever the case, the family was thankful she had not been in the car--which always left her with a deep-down feeling that the accident had been a result of one of his "bad decisions."

When she thought about the messed-up circumstances of her past, it often put Paige in a paralyzed state of fear and anxiety. Yet, she knew God. Neither of her parents had known Him. She had a Rock she could stand on. She knew that although she was a product of a difficult time, she was also a child of God. She recalled what Gram would say when she could see that Paige was getting down about her family.

"Paige, do you know how amazing God is? Out of all the women in the world, he chose your mom to meet my son. Of all the places your mom could have run to in her mental state, she came here. With all the hospitals in the state, she was in the same one as your dad. Do you see God's work in all that? Your mom received a lot of bad advice to end her pregnancy, and she didn't. You were born healthy and strong. Do you see God's power in that?

You are here for a reason and for a purpose. It is OK to feel sad that your mom is sick and that your dad is gone, but don't feel sad that you were a result of their time together. You are the beauty that came out of many tragedies. You are not your mother or father, and you have God on your side. Trust him when you are down and scared. OK?"

Paige could not imagine what her life would look life if she didn't have her grandmother. She had repeated those similar words to Paige for years. They were in Paige's heart, and she would pull them like threads of truth and joy when grief tried to paralyze her. God definitely knew what He was doing with all her past and, she remembered, her future.

After changing from her jeans, T-Shirt, and sneakers to a sundress with sandals, she made her way to her car. The downstairs door was open and an older gentleman, probably in his seventies, was measuring the inside door frame. He looked up when Paige locked the upstairs door and made her way down.

He had a pair of well-worn overall jeans on with a clean white shirt underneath. His hat said U.S. Army Veteran and his boots were dirty and brown. His face was kind, and his eyes shone a sweet humility when he glanced at Paige. Once she reached the bottom step, he had already backed up and propped the door with his foot. He put his hands in his front overall pockets and dipped his head to her. "Good afternoon. I'm Gerald", he said, as he touched the brim of his hat. "John told me to stop by and see if we can get a buzzer system installed so you will know when you have visitors."

Trudy had told Paige about the landlord just that morning. Paige was looking forward to meeting him. Trudy spoke of him highly and was obviously impressed with how he ran the plaza.

"That's great," Paige said, slipping past him, "I'm Paige." She turned around and extended her hand.

"Nice to meet you," he said, as he let the door close while he shaking her hand. He seemed to get a little nervous, or maybe giddy, and he put his hands quickly back into his pockets. He relaxed a little and looked at her eyes. "Everything alright in the apartment up there?

If you have any problems, I am sure John will send me over to fix it. Since I am here, I could take a look today for you."

"Oh, everything is great. Thank you." Remembering what her gram had drilled into her over the years, she naturally stated, "I see your hat." She motioned to the older man's head. "Thank you for your service."

The man naturally reached up and touched the brim of his hat again. His face turned a tad redder as her words sank in. "Um, thank you." Seeing he was stuck and didn't know what to say after that, Paige quickly went on.

"Thank you again for all of your help. I'm heading out. It was nice meeting you, Gerald," she said and turned and took a few steps toward the parking lot.

"My pleasure, young lady. Have a good day." And with that the gentleman raised his hand to wave goodbye and went back to his work on the door.

Paige smiled after waving back to him. She enjoyed seeing older Veterans' reactions when she thanked them. Yet, it was also unfortunate because it probably meant many didn't take notice and thank them at all. The maternal side of Paige's family had too much military in their past for her not to take notice of their service.

Getting into her car, which was smoldering in the afternoon heat, Paige lowered all the windows as soon as she turned the car on. Hot air blew on her as she waited for the A/C to kick in. She got out her phone and searched for the address of the Stratosphere. Paige planned to walk the casino in it and the surrounding area. Her mom, aunt, and grandfather had visited the Stratosphere before mom went missing. Aunt Marie said Mom left them at the top of the Stratosphere to go and gamble. Aunt Marie and her grandfather had a soda at the bar and enjoyed the view while discussing the obvious diminishing mental state of her mom.

Forgetting she needed water for the afternoon, she grabbed her purse and decided to leave her car on while she ran into the grocery store. The car was parked right in front of the shop, so she was confident that leaving it on and unlocked would be fine.

Once she had a twelve pack of bottled water, not cold but at least not heated by a hot car, she hit go on her map app and made her way to the Stratosphere, not realizing that a young man was watching her from a computer in the quilt shop.

~

Once her shift at the café was done, she made her way across the street. Kelly had gone over just before coming in for her shift and said it was the cutest little shop. Sarah wasn't sure what she was going to get, since she wasn't crafty at all. Kelly had said she had had the same problem, but figured she could use thread for buttons and such. She had come back into the café with black, white, and brown polyester thread.

As she opened the door, and heard the soft bell ring above her head, she immediately saw Trudy peek up from behind a counter to see who entered. "Sarah! So sweet of you to come over. How was the café today?"

"Pretty normal today. How is the soft opening going?" she asked, approaching the counter. She saw Seth working on the computer. He smiled over to her as she took in the shop.

"We got more folks than we expected," she said excitedly.

"We've found a few problems," Seth added, "but they were easily fixed."

"That's great. Where's Paige?" Sarah asked, scanning the store for the sweet blond.

Seth quickly said, "She left. She had something she needed to do. Whatever it was, it required a lot of bottled water." Seth looked down; he sounded both confused and concerned.

Trudy glanced over at her son disapprovingly. "She told me she won't be able to work the late afternoons. Her business is her business, Seth. If she wants to tell us she will."

"I know. But she is alone here and new to the area. I'm just concerned."

Sarah smiled. "I think we all have taken to Paige already, and I'll bet that as she gets to know us, she will let her guard down. She doesn't know us well enough yet." Trudy smiled over to her.

"Why don't you take a look around Sarah. We are going to start the beginner quilting class in 3 weeks, once we have time to get some people aware of us and signed up. Maybe you would like to join us?" Trudy asked with anticipation.

"I'll think about, Trudy. I've never done anything like quilting before, so I'm not sure I would be any good at it."

"Why don't you look around awhile at the fabrics and books and see if anything catches your eye. Your heart will tell you if you want to try it. But once you start, it is hard to stop." Trudy said, with a teasing tone and a smirk.

"Thanks for the warning." Sarah smiled and turned to browse the shop. The fabrics were arranged perfectly by color, feel, and pattern. Sarah had never been in a quilt shop before, so she wasn't sure where to start. She rubbed her fingers along all the fabrics stopping at a unique cream fabric with different colored plant cell looking shapes. It looked so cheery and she pictured it on her couch somehow. Maybe as a pillow or a quilt?

She moved on to the flannels and reached the baby themed fabrics. Sarah's heart sank as she caressed each fabric, picturing it covering her cute baby one day. Each month, she waited expectantly to be expecting. But each month, she and her husband, Tim, were disappointed. They had spent 7 months trying for a baby. Maybe next month. Maybe never? She could feel the all too familiar tears burning behind her eyes.

Trudy came by and stopped next to her. "Don't give up hope, Sarah. God's still in control of the good and the bad. He knows your heart's desire. Continue to trust His wisdom," she said, and placed a comforting arm around Sarah's shoulder.

Sarah leaned her head over and it met Trudy's. "Thanks, Trudy. One way or another I know God has a plan to bring children to our home. Maybe it won't be the traditional way."

"Very true. Perhaps making a baby quilt will be a good project to keep your mind focused on staying hopeful. It would also help you keep faith in God's amazing ways of answering prayers."

Sarah lifted her head. "That's a really good idea. I'll think about it."

Trudy gave her shoulder a squeeze and went back to the counter. Sarah picked out a cute teddy bear fabric and took it to the cutting table. "Can I have a little of this?"

"Sure, sweetie. If you don't know what you're going to do with it yet, then I suggest a quarter yard."

"Whatever you suggest. You are the expert," Sarah said smiling. She turned back to the shop and went to peruse the books and then the threads. After taking in all the fun colors and ideas, her desire to create was fully ignited. Knowing she had no clue how to go about it, she decided to just get the fabric for the day and think about what Trudy had said.

~

Seth felt like a fool. He should have kept his mouth shut about Paige. He was also keenly aware that Mom and Sarah were secretly smiling at each other over his reaction. He was not fooling himself or anyone else. He liked her, and it had only increased as they had worked together. She was smart and teachable. He now fully understood why mom had stepped in and offered Paige the apartment. A sweeter girl he had never met. Yet, she was mysterious as well.

Where did she go every afternoon? Why did she need so much water? He imagined she would open up to them soon. After all, she was living above his mom's shop, working in her business, going to their church, and drinking coffee at the same café every day. What was she holding back and why?

Seth couldn't believe his line of thoughts. She had only arrived a few days ago. He knew his family was kind and safe, but she didn't yet. That would take more time. More time than he wished.

The day had gone so smoothly. At lunchtime, he forced himself to leave and go run some errands. He didn't really have anything he had to do, but they needed to be able to run things without him there. He was glad to hear when he came back, about an hour later, that they had had two customers and everything had gone without any problems.

He was feeling more and more confident about not being there all the time for that reason, but he was pretty sure that he would find himself there more than he had expected to a week ago.

It was five o'clock and almost time to close up the shop. "How do you feel about your first unofficial day as a quilt shop owner, Mom?"

Trudy was looking at the reports he had shown her to see the totals for the day as well as the gross profit. "Oh, honey, it was wonderful! What a dream come true. Thank you for all of your help. It was such a good idea to have our friends stop by and help us practice. They were also quite inventive in picking out things they would end up using. I know many of them are not quilters at all.

"You have wonderful friends. I'm glad to see that. I worry about you being alone."

"I know, dear. And you have been very supportive, but you need not worry about me so much. I am fine, you know that," his mom said. He did know in his heart that she was doing well, but being the only child, and her being alone, left a concern in him he never had before his father passed away.

"Alright, Mom. I will try not to be a helicopter son," he joked. "I think Paige being here also gives me a lot more peace about you and the store. She picked up everything so fast. She is a quick learner."

"She is. I couldn't believe how quickly she picked it up. I tried very hard to not compare myself, but it was obvious that she was more gifted for it than me."

"Just a little," he teased. "What time do you want to lock the doors?"

"I was thinking six o'clock."

"It really doesn't matter, since we are not officially open. We can wing it if you want."

"That's fine." Trudy and Seth looked up when they heard the doorbell ring. It was John. Seth hadn't expected to see him today. "Hello, John. Did you hear about our soft opening?"

"Soft opening? No, I didn't. I drove into the center and saw your open sign. Thought you just decided to open early, so I came in to buy something and congratulate you as well."

"Aw, thanks, John. That's very kind of you. I'm not sure if there is anything in here you would be interested in though."

"Hmm, you might be right. But I see some tools over here. I could always use some new scissors." John made his way to the quilt tool stands and noticed the rulers. "These are the strangest rulers I have ever seen," John remarked, picking up a yellow triangular ruler.

Trudy came up beside him and chuckled. "They all have a purpose."

As John turned it over in his hands, he looked over at her. "I will have to trust you on that." He returned the ruler. He picked up a pair of scissors and made his way to the counter with Trudy at his side. She moved to the other side and Seth cleared out of the way.

"You go ahead, Mom. It might be the last sale of the day." Seth made his way to the end of the counter.

John cleared his throat. "Trudy," he began, looking down at the wallet he retrieved from his back pocket. "I was wondering, if you are free that is, if I could take you out to dinner tonight to celebrate your success today?" He looked up and met her gaze and then looked over at Seth. "That is if Seth is alright with that?"

They both looked up with shocked expressions, although his mother recovered a lot faster and began to blush as she looked back to the computer.

Seth glanced from his mother to their landlord and back again. He wasn't sure if his mom wanted to go out with the man, but she seemed very pleased to have been asked.

"My mom is a grown woman, John. You don't need to ask me, but I appreciate it. And I would be fine with it, too." He smiled at the older man, and he visually relaxed with the endorsement.

His mother looked up. "I would like that, John. We are going to close up soon, and I need to go home first."

"I could pick you up at seven, and we could head over to the Italian restaurant over on Fairview Street if that sounds good."

"That sounds wonderful. Let me give you my address."

Seth watched his mom write down her home address on a sticky note and hand it to the man. Seth had such a mix of emotions, He wasn't sure what to do with his eyes, hands, or feet, so he looked down and pretended to work. He saw John take the note and read the address. "Oh, I know this area. It's very nice over there. Do you like it?"

Seth had to hand it to the guy, he was obviously nervous but knew how to cut the tension. "Yes, I like it a lot. It is safe and the neighbors are very friendly."

John folded up the paper and placed it in the pocket of his khaki pants. "Wonderful. What do I owe you for the scissors?"

Mom at first seemed confused by what John had said. She jumped a little, suddenly remembering why she was there. "Oh, yes, $8.09."

John handed over ten dollars and Mom made change, much slower than he had seen her do it earlier that day. She seemed to be having trouble subtracting nine from a hundred. Finally figuring it out, she gave him his change and scissors.

John waved off a receipt. "I will see you at seven then. I promise I won't keep her out too late, Seth," the man joked, as he looked over at him. Everyone laughed and John turned and left the shop.

Mom went back to working on the computer with a smirk Seth had never seen on her. Seth wondered if she was going to say something. The tension in the room seemed to increase as soon as

John walked out. Although he was shocked at John's request, Seth was also happy to see mom excited and blushing.

"So...," Seth spoke softly and tried to suppress his own smirk.

"So, what?"

"Mom, stop," Seth teased. "What do you think about John?"

"I've never thought anything about him except rent stuff," his mom said and her smile gradually increased. "I was not expecting him to ask me out to dinner, that is for sure."

"That makes two of us."

"He is a very nice guy though."

"Yes, he is."

"I'm thinking we can close the shop now," she said. Seth looked up, surprised by her sudden change of topic.

"OK. I'll lock the door and turn off the sign." Fifteen minutes later, they were ready to leave. The sun was close to setting and Seth noted Paige wasn't back yet as he locked up the door. His mom waited and then turned to go to her car after he checked the lock.

"What time will you be here tomorrow, hon?"

"We open at ten and need to get ready like we did today, so I will be over here by 9:30 if not sooner. Do you want me to stop and get you coffee or anything?"

"No, I gave Paige some money today so she could get me one and one for herself in the morning. She said she goes over there every morning."

"Yes, I've seen her. She studies a lot."

"Maybe soon you can take a chance and ask Paige out like John asked me out?" she hinted with a sly smile.

Seth could feel the shock and embarrassment he had seen on his mom's face earlier now appear and flush his own. "Maybe." He quickly turned to walk towards his car. "Night, Mom. Be careful and call me if you need me."

"Yes, dear." And with that, his mom turned toward her own car with a little skip that Seth had never seen before.

Lilly Horigan

Chapter 11

Paige got back to her apartment later than she expected. It was just getting dark when she'd left the parking lot just down the block from the Stratosphere. She had found numerous homeless people to talk to in and around the casino. The bottles of water were welcomed and many seemed to recognize her mom's picture.

Paige was beyond pleased that her mother's picture was recognizable, but it wasn't clear if they were giving her fake details as a thank you for the exchange of water for information. By the end of the day, she'd received multiple "observations" by the people who spoke to her. They told her that her mom had been seen walking around with a short Mexican girl, a large black man, and a small dog. She was described as super skinny and very loud. Those latter details did not surprise Paige and seemed the most accurate. Aunt Marie had told Paige her mom had been very skinny and had always been loud, especially when angry.

Paige ignored all the details the homeless provided her unless they were directions to where other homeless frequented in the area. The details she received were so strange and without any thread of similarity. A couple of men she spoke to inside the Stratosphere Casino asked her if she wanted a ride somewhere. She declined with a smile and thanked them for their time. When she started to leave, they got up to follow her. She knew going outside the casino would make her more susceptible to trouble, if that was their intent. She changed direction and made her way to the front desk of the hotel. She waited there until the men were long gone.

It was in those moments, however, that Paige wished she wasn't alone in this search.

She had walked block after block for hours around the area and had spoken to two police officers. Unfortunately, they seemed annoyed that she was interrupting them, as they stood there not doing anything particularly difficult. It irritated Paige. Some officers had gone above and beyond to help her, especially at Fremont Street the other day. But today she had come across officers who couldn't care less about one more homeless, missing girl.

When she got out of her car, she cringed at the pain in her feet. She had stood all morning at work and then walked for miles on hard concrete. She needed to get a pair of sneakers.

She decided to grab food at the grocery store and then find a movie to watch. As she walked over, she saw that the quilt shop was closed up. Paige didn't see Trudy's car, but Seth's truck was there. He was most likely in the coffee shop. It was easier just to walk over than to drive and repark.

As she entered the grocery store, she stood and enjoyed the air conditioning wash over her. She was so sweaty from walking all day. She wondered how many more bottles of water she needed to drink each day to compensate for all the sweat she lost.

When she got to the deli in the back of the store, she saw Seth looking into a cabinet of sushi. He picked up one of the packages, inspected it, and turned in her direction. He paused mid-step, surprised to see her there. "Hey Paige, how was your afternoon?"

"Good. No problems," she said and noticed Seth wanted to ask her something but then seemed to change his mind. After a few seconds that felt like a couple of minutes, he tried again.

"You did a great job today at the shop. Thanks so much."

"It was fun. Thanks for teaching me. Are you a big sushi fan?"

He looked down. "I never used to be, but a year in Japan will change that. You?"

"I've only had a California roll. Nothing more exotic."

"Then you're missing out," he said emphatically. But if you were not turned off by the California roll, then you have potential to grow." He smiled.

"I always thought getting sushi at a grocery store was just as bad as getting sushi at a gas station."

"Well, in most cases that is probably true. But here they have a dedicated sushi chef."

"Oh. That's good to know. She walked over to the sushi cooler. Being that you are an expert, can you pick out something for me? I'm here to pick up some dinner anyway."

He watched her look down at the cooler and then laughed. "I'm not sure I can be labeled an expert, but I think I can help. Do you prefer to go with the California Roll or do you want to try something a little more 'exotic?'"

Paige looked up at him. "How about the next step up?" He pursed his lips and began searching the cooler again.

"Here. Try this one. It has cream cheese, salmon, tuna, cucumber, a mild spicy sauce, and tobiko on top. Do you like spicy foods?"

"Mild is fine. Hot will have me searching for a glass of milk." She took the package from his hands. "What is tobiko?"

He smiled a little. "Why don't you try it first and then tell me what you think it is?"

Paige gave him a suspicious frown. "It's not somethings super gross is it?"

"No," he chuckled, "nothing gross." He stepped back from the cooler. "Are you headed back to your apartment?" They turned and began to make their way to the front of the store.

"Yep. I'll probably watch some TV, or try and find a movie."

Seth got quiet as he approached the self-checkout line. "Can I buy your sushi as a thank you for all of your help today?"

She looked down at her package, not really seeing it at all, and wondered what to do. She looked up and saw kindness in his eyes. "Sure. Thanks."

He took it from her hands and checked them out. After paying, he handed her the package and they made their way, rather awkwardly, side by side to the door. Once outside, Seth turned to her. "If you are interested in some company, we can go over to the café and eat. I have a meeting there in an hour with my friend, Patrick."

"Sarah won't mind us bringing food in?"

"No, not at all. She knows her menu is limited and she encourages folks to come in for whatever reason they choose--even if they are doing a Bible study and don't order anything. But we will get drinks there, if you want one."

She loved that he had not suggested her apartment or his own for dinner. He seemed to feel her hesitation at each question. He waited patiently, with a hand in his jeans' pocket as Paige looked over at the café. "Alright. Let's go."

They crossed the parking lot and street together and entered Sarah's café. A few tables were taken, but Paige and Seth instinctively went to the table by the window. "This is where we unofficially met," Seth joked as he sported a grin at the memory of that moment.

"It's a great spot. I love the sun coming in through the windows."

"I love that you can see everything and everyone who comes through the door," he replied.

Paige hadn't thought of that, but realized he was right.

They sat down and Seth asked her what she wanted to drink. She looked up at the menu on the chalkboard. "What goes with sushi?"

"Japanese beer," he said seriously, as he opened up his plastic container. "But there is no alcohol here, so soda or water would probably be the next best thing."

"I think water then." Paige began to get up and Seth stopped her by putting his hand up.

"Nope, this is my treat. You stay right there. I'll get them." She pushed her chair back in and grinned. Was she on an impromptu date? She glanced over to the counter where Seth had grabbed two bottles of water and was paying "the box." Kelly was behind the counter and asked if there was anything else he needed. Seth said no and took a moment to ask how she was doing. She smiled and said she was good.

It was clear that Seth and Kelly knew each other from church, Paige assumed.

Two water bottles in hand, Seth made his way back to the table. He handed her the bottle and then pulled a package from his back pocket and placed it next to her container.

"What's that?"

"Your chopsticks." He had another set in his hand for himself and opened them up.

Paige laughed, "I don't know how to use chopsticks."

"Then I'll have to teach you. I've seen you in the shop. You're a quick learner. I'm sure you'll pick it up." She smiled apprehensively and opened up the package. For the next five minutes, Seth patiently showed her how to hold the chopsticks. He watched her try and pick up her sushi, dunk it in the soy sauce, and aim it for her mouth without dropping it on the table. After much laughing and pieces of sushi mangled on the container from her failed attempts, Paige finally was able to pick up a portion, dunk it, and get it into her mouth successfully.

"You're a natural," he said.

"Yeah, right. How long did it take you to learn?"

"When you get to Japan, the Navy puts you through Japanese culture school. You have to get to the point where you can pick a penny up off the table with them. I was about the same speed as you."

"Was it scary, going to Japan?"

"Definitely. You go out in town and you have no idea what you are ordering. You just point. When I first arrived at the airport, just finding my way to the base was difficult. My sponsor, the person assigned to meet me and take me to the base, was late and an idiot.

Sometimes when I think about it, I am surprised I ever made it to the base."

"That sounds so scary. I have never been outside the United States."

"Really? It can be a little scary, but once I went through all of that, I felt like I could travel anywhere."

Paige took another bite. She didn't want the questions to start coming in her direction, so she quickly swallowed and went on. "How long were you in Japan?"

"About a year. My father passed away, and I came home. The base was closing anyway, so the Navy didn't send me back. I was in Virginia after that."

"I'm sorry to hear about your dad."

"Thanks. He was only in his fifties and had a massive heart attack. It left mom heartbroken."

"I can imagine it did," Paige said.

~

Seth looked over to see Paige, playing with the pieces of sushi left on her plastic tray. She seemed suddenly lost in thoughts.

"Since I was in the Navy when it happened, I only had a couple of weeks with her after the funeral. I hated leaving her alone. She had some family in the area and good friends that helped her get through that time, but mostly it was getting right with God that started the real healing for her. Both of us came to know Jesus then. Therefore, we not only have that mother and only child bond, but we also share a newness in Christ.

"That all happened less than a couple of years ago. Mom moved here last winter to start fresh. Her friend Julie lived here and invited Mom to come out and stay awhile. With the insurance money that Dad left her, she was able to sell the house and move wherever she wanted. I think leaving the Midwest behind was a good way for her to move on."

Paige was looking at him more, meeting his eyes when she wasn't nervously fiddling with her chopsticks. She was genuinely interested in what he was saying. It was like she was taking it all in and trying to imagine...something. "I met Julie," she said finally. "She seems very sweet."

"She is. Their whole women's group is nice. There are about eight of them that get together regularly for Bible study and community activities." He chuckled, as he pushed his plastic tray forward and set his arms on the table and leaned forward. "They are a fun group of women. I dropped by mom's house a couple of weeks ago when it was their monthly card club night." Paige began smiling, too, as he recalled the group of women. "They can get pretty rowdy."

"I bet that's a sight to see."

"It is. If Mom ever invites you to her card club, make sure you go. I doubt you will stop laughing for hours."

"Are most of them widows?" Paige also pushed her tray to the center and took a sip of her water.

"I think so, but I know one is divorced. There may be a few that are married." Seth looked out the window. "Some of the ladies may even be dating, like my mother is tonight."

Paige choked on her water and covered her mouth as she almost spit all over him. "What?" she asked, after recovering from her surprise.

Seth thought she had the cutest smile, but her surprised face was adorable. He smiled and suppressed a laugh.

"Sorry. I just didn't expect that."

"That makes three of us now. Mom wasn't expecting it either," Seth said honestly. "John, the landlord of the plaza, came in and asked her out to dinner tonight. But not before he asked me if it was alright."

"Aw," Paige sighed, "that's sweet. What did you say?"

Seth leaned back and put his right foot on his knee, as he grabbed his shin. He was feeling more and more comfortable as he talked to her. The anxiety he held over the past couple of days was quickly subsiding, at least for him. Paige still seemed quite tense and nervous, but he hoped to put her at ease. "I can't tell my mother what to do or not do, so I told John it was up to her. In truth, I was so shocked someone was asking my mother out, and that he was asking for my permission. I just stared at him until I felt I could answer without making light of it, or without getting angry."

Paige took his cue and relaxed a bit in her seat, crossing her legs and putting her hands down in her lap. "How did your mom respond?"

"After a moment of shock, she turned her face down while he prompted me for my permission. It was pretty clear she was not expecting him to ask her out to dinner. She then turned back to the computer pretty quickly. She was definitely blushing, and I saw that she was smiling."

"I have not met John. Is he a nice guy? He seems to do a great job taking care of the plaza. He had his handyman, Gerald, stop by the apartment this morning to put a buzzer system in for me."

"That doesn't surprise me. He is a great guy; retired Air Force, too. I think he is divorced and spends his time taking care of his properties. I am not sure if he is a Christian though. I'd put money down that mom will find a way to ask him that tonight."

"I hope she has fun. She has been so kind to me since I arrived." Paige looked down quickly, seemingly agitated by her own comment. Seth could tell she didn't want the conversation turned to her, but not asking her anything was out of the question for him. She appeared so fragile and conflicted, yet confident and persistent, too. He decided to try and keep the conversation plain and general.

"How is the apartment?"

"Great", she said, looking up with a relieved expression. "I could never afford a place like that on my own, so your mom's offer to trade work hours for apartment rent was perfect. She mentioned having an extra coffee maker. That will be nice to have, and it will save me a little bit of money." She glanced over to the counter. Kelly was sweeping the floor and mouthing the words to the song playing on the speakers. "I love this café. The lattés here are so good—but not good for my budget. Yet I am drawn here in the morning. The sun that comes in through this window is perfect for reading and writing."

"I've seen you studying. You look pretty intense."

Paige smiled. "I do tend to enter my own little world and block out everything else."

"Nothing wrong with that, unless you are in a public place and not aware of some creep who could be stalking you." Paige leaned back in her chair and crossed her arms.

"Well, there was this really strange guy the other day talking about double negatives. He did seem a little creepy," she joked and tried to suppress a grin at his expense.

"Ah, yes. Exactly," he said, realizing his own cheeks were probably getting red. "Crazy people are everywhere."

~

"Thank you for dinner, John," Trudy said, as she put the key in her door.

"It was my pleasure, Trudy." He watched her trying to steady her key. "Congratulations again on your shop. May I stop by tomorrow on the official opening day and say hello?"

Trudy turned, relieved she finally had the door unlocked. "I would like that."

John extended his hand, as if to shake hers. She reached out and he softly grabbed it, turned it over, and leaned down to kiss it. He looked up, still holding her hand while the feel of her skin was still fresh on his lips, and smiled. "Thank you for a wonderful evening. I will see you tomorrow." He put his other hand on top of hers, gave a gentle squeeze, and let go. Turning, he made his way back to the car.

He heard her open the door. When he got to his car he looked up. She was waiting, the door half open, and waved at him as he got in. He waved back and she closed the door.

He smiled to himself as he made his way home.

He felt twenty years old again.

Chapter 12

It was early Saturday morning, and Paige sat at her kitchen table, looking out the small window toward the plaza parking lot. She felt as if she had been there weeks already, not less than a week.

Was she officially an adult now? Here she was: on her own, with a job, in another state, with no family, surviving. The thought was exhilarating. She felt alive and wanted to celebrate this little victory.

With time to spare and energy that felt like bursting out of her skin, Paige decided to get some exercise. She had slowly unpacked all her bags over the last few days and felt settled in her apartment. Her closet was small, but with a large dresser it was more than enough room for her clothes. Not needing a bunch of winter clothes definitely helped.

Her running shoes were a couple of years old and were not in great shape. If she was going to wear them during the day at the store, then she would need to go shopping and get some new ones. Of course, she had no idea where to go. She decided she would ask Kelly or Sarah the next time she saw them if her Around Me app didn't show anything.

Exercise clothes on, phone, headphones, and keys in her hands, she made her way down to the parking lot. The café was already open, but the shopping center was pretty quiet. Only a few cars were in front of the grocery store, and most of them toward the back of the lot. Probably staff.

She checked the quilt store; the lights were off and there was no sign of Trudy. It was 7:20 and already 60 degrees. She made her way to the street and turned toward the soccer fields down the road.

The sport park was massive in size. The track around the soccer fields and tennis club was perfect. Realizing she hadn't run in a while, she jogged easily for a mile and then walked for half mile. She repeated the process again and made her way back to the apartment. She felt great, but she needed water. The dry heat was going to take some getting used to. Her nose was dry and she needed Vaseline or something to help it. She would grab some at the store later, but water was in her car.

She headed toward her car and knew something was wrong when she saw it. She hadn't seen anything wrong when she left, but her car now looked crooked. As she approached, she saw a front tire was flat. Then she saw the broken window.

Her heart dropped. Everything had been going so well, and it took a good couple of minutes for reality to sink in. It didn't feel real. The door was cracked where they had opened it and she tried to remember what she had left in there. Nothing of any value; but the thieves didn't know that.

They had gone through the glove box, back seat, and console. They had taken her CD's, her phone charger, her spare phone battery, and the few dollars she had laying around. The damage they had left was going to be pricey.

She felt violated.

She felt like crying.

~

John approached the young woman slowly. "Paige?" The young girl, leaning on her car with her head in her arms, was obviously distraught. He didn't want to scare her. She looked up quickly and took a step back. She was trembling.

"My name is John. I own this plaza. Are you alright?" As soon as he said it, he knew it was a stupid question. Her car had clearly been broken into and no one handles that well, especially a young girl from out of town. She seemed to have a moment of recognition at his name, so he continued, hoping to calm her down.

"Trudy told me about you and that you're staying in the apartment. Do you know when this happened?"

"No. I assume it was sometime last night. I didn't see it when I went out earlier to workout. I only saw the other side, and from that direction I didn't notice anything wrong."

"Did they take any credit cards or anything else of value?"

"No, I think I have all my cards and money upstairs. They may have taken some of my paperwork out of the glove box, but I'm not sure what was in it. This was my gram's car."

The girl wiped a tear away and took a big breath. "I guess I should call my gram. I am on her insurance."

Paige was clearly upset, but seemed to be holding herself together pretty well considering the situation. John was not pleased this had happened on his property. He had cameras and enough lights that it shouldn't have happened, but thieves are rarely intelligent. He would go to the store and see if he could track down any info with the video feed that he then would give the police.

"Paige, I am so sorry this happened. Would you mind if I asked how old you are?"

She looked up and her eyebrows dropped just a little at the question. "Eighteen," she said, unsure if that was going to be a problem for him.

"Insurance is a funny thing. You want to have it, but you don't want to use it unless you absolutely have to. With your permission, I am going to have one of my guys come out and get this taken care of for you." She began to interrupt, but he put his hand up. "No, I insist. You are living here at the plaza and you should not have to be worried about the safety of your car." John was fully aware that there were signs at the front of the lot that said he was not responsible for any theft or damage to cars, but he knew Trudy liked this young woman and John felt the same. Seeing her all alone had pulled on some more heart strings he didn't realize were in him, just like meeting Trudy had.

"Wow. Thank you, but I can pay you back."

"No, no. Think of it as a thank you for all the help you are giving Trudy. She is a sweet woman, and I know she is loving having you around."

Paige smiled and wiped the last tear off her cheek. "What do you need me to do?" She said, motioning to the car.

"Go ahead and empty out anything in it and then give me the keys. I will have my guy fix the tire and drive it over to a shop to fix the window and inside. Do you have a spare tire?"

"Um, I think so," Paige said, as she moved toward the trunk. It was clear she was too upset to process any more info. She seemed confused as to how to check if she even had a spare tire. John wondered if she had a father. A girl should know how to change a tire, especially if she was traveling into other states. But this was not the time to say anything.

"Look, I can verify all that. You go ahead and start clearing things out while I make a phone call. "You are working at the shop today, right?" He knew she was, since Trudy and he had talked all about it the night before.

"Yes. But I need to get cleaned up."

"Good. Go ahead do all that and then Trudy should be here. You are probably scared and don't need to be alone right now."

The girl looked up and over at him. "Thank you so much, John. I really appreciate your help."

"That's no problem. Go on and get started." He watched her go to the other side of the car while he pulled out his phone to call his mechanic. She started removing her stuff and made her way up the stairs to the apartment.

Two more trips and Paige had the car cleaned out. He had his mechanic sending a guy over in 20 minutes, and he had the grocery store manager cueing up the videos from the night before. As he finished up the last call, Trudy drove in and parked by Paige's car when she saw him standing by on the phone.

She got out immediately. "John, what's wrong?"

"Everything is alright, Trudy. Paige's car was broken into last night. I have someone coming to take care of it and fix it, but she is pretty upset by it. She is upstairs getting ready for work. She discovered it when she got back from running. I came in soon after and saw she was quite upset.

"Oh, the poor thing. I am so glad you were here to help her. Did they take anything valuable?"

"No, I don't think so. I am upset it happened at all though. This is the first incident we have had in this plaza. I will make sure I find out who did it."

"I am going to go inside then and get the shop ready. Seth should be here soon, too."

"Good." John watched Trudy go back to her car to grab her purse. Seth and Paige would be there anytime. He didn't want to leave without thanking her for going out to dinner with him the night before. Yet, it also wasn't the time to bring it up. "I am going to run over and grab some coffee, what can I bring you?"

Trudy closed the car door and looked up at him. "Oh, I was going to send Paige over. But maybe that is not a good idea now. Could you pick up something for her as well?"

"Of course, what does she like?" Trudy gave him their drink preferences and John saw Seth make his way into the lot. He parked close by and they filled him in on the morning events. Seth was clearly upset and wanted to go right up to the apartment to check on Paige. "She will be down shortly," he said. "I am going to go get some coffee for everyone. Can I get one for you as well?" John asked Seth.

"Thanks, but if you don't mind, I think I will go with you."

"Sure, let's go."

~

Seth walked across the street to the café with John. He was glad the older man had stopped him from going up to check on Paige. That would not have been appropriate. Not in her emotional state nor as a co-worker, which, he had to remind himself, was all he really was to her right now even after their dinner together last night. It had been a perfect evening. Totally unplanned and without any expectation. They had sat and talked for thirty more minutes after dinner until Patrick came in.

Paige danced her way around the conversation all evening to avoid any personal information as to why she was in Vegas. Seth hadn't pressed her in the least. As the evening had moved forward, Paige relaxed. It was the best non-date he had ever had.

He didn't feel comfortable with Paige walking back alone to her apartment at night, so he excused himself while Patrick ordered his dinner. They joked about their odds of getting run over, considering the number of times they crossed the street in a day, and Seth walked her to the boardwalk of the plaza but stopped short of leaving the pavement. When she put the key in and opened the door, he thought he saw her hands shaking a little. To calm her nerves, he began backing away toward his car and said a quick and final good bye. *Thanks for having dinner with me. See you tomorrow morning.*

She had smiled over to him and said, *You're welcome. See you tomorrow.*

She disappeared into the stairwell, and Seth turned back toward the café. Patrick's questioning look and suppressed grin was the beginning of another great conversation that night. However, this time it seemed to center on God's timing and the cute blond he had walked across the street. He woke early and hoped the fragrance of that perfect evening would last all day. Now, though, Paige would have to deal with her car being broken into. Would she leave? Would she find another apartment? The questions swirled as he entered the café with John.

"Seth, I told Paige I would cover the damage to her car."

"You don't have to do that, John," Seth said, as he approached the counter.

"I know, but I want to do it. For her and for Trudy. Plus," the man said, as he looked back to the plaza through the window, "she seems to need a father-figure in her life. Or maybe I just need to feel like a father-figure." Another statement Seth had not expected from John. He was full of surprises.

"Morning, Sarah," Seth said. John was lost in thought, and Seth wasn't sure where to go with the man's comment. "Can I get three Caramel Lattés?" He turned, "John, what would you like?"

He turned toward Sarah. "Black coffee, please. Large."

"No problem." Seth went to put the money in the box for all 4 drinks.

"No, no. My treat," John said. He went past Seth to put a $20 in the box.

"Thanks."

"This is only my second time in this café. It's a neat concept, everything being donation only. I've never seen it done in a coffee shop."

"Sarah and her husband do a great job with the place. Lots of folks meet here for small group and Bible studies."

"Your mom mentioned she goes to the church down the road. I have never been there. It looks huge."

"It's definitely big," Seth laughed. He leaned his hip on the counter and crossed his arms. "You should come and check it out. Mom goes to the nine o'clock service."

"Your mom also invited me." John relaxed and kept his back toward the counter, as he leaned back to wait for their drinks. Taking his cue from Seth, he crossed his arms, also, but kept watching the plaza out the window across the street. "I've never met anyone like your mom. She is different."

Seth looked down and smiled. He didn't know much about John, except he was a Veteran and a commercial landlord. But there seemed to be so much he did not say, maybe because he wasn't sure how to say it, in the description of his mom. Seth figured the man didn't know Christ personally himself and had never met a woman on fire for Jesus. He looked around at the conveniently empty café, lifted his head, and decided to take a risk.

"Mom is a Christ-follower, John, and she puts Him first in everything she does. She didn't always do this though. God worked in her and myself a couple of years ago when we lost my dad." Seth took a deep thought as he remembered those days, days filled with sadness and then unexpected joy wrapped in realization. "We both learned what my father never did: that we weren't going to spend forever with God in heaven. We didn't know Jesus as our Savior."

John, after several long moments, slowly turned his head and looked at Seth. "I have to admit, Seth; that is a lot to take in. I have known Christians in the past, but none seemed to live the way she does or talk the way you are talking."

Seth smiled. "I know. I used to be one of those people. I thought I was a Christian. I was a good guy and believed in God. I believed Jesus lived, died, and even rose again. But I never made Him my Savior or my Lord. Neither did my mom. I wasn't all in for Christ. It was my Dad's passing, specifically his funeral, that changed everything for us.

"Our church pastor couldn't be there and so we had a pastor from another local church come in. Friends had recommended him to us. It was his message on what really living for Christ looked like that hit us hard. He didn't know my dad, and so his message was general and for everyone who was there. It was not for the man in the coffin. Dad had had his chance to live for Christ. The pastor even said that! Some were offended by it and were immediately turned off by what he was saying, but I was riveted.

"He shared that knowing Jesus, and even believing that He is God, was not surrendering to Him. We may know of Him, but He won't know us because we never really let Him in. He wasn't the leader of our lives. We didn't want Him to interrupt our Monday through

Saturday. We wanted the benefits without complete and total devotion to Him and His kingdom. We wanted to live our lives in comfort and without intrusion. But that substitute pastor had planted a seed of clarity in us. We had to be real and decide if we truly wanted to make Christ our Lord. We had to take a hard look at ourselves and decide if we were all-in. Going all-in for the Army of God is a dangerous and life changing decision I found out, just like joining the military was for us. This world doesn't like hearing that they need Jesus, and so they extend that hate to those who live for Jesus as well. But our Commander tells us to love Him and others."

Seth wasn't sure how much John was hearing. He had turned and was still staring out the window. He was not responding, nodding, arguing, or moving at all. Taking a chance, Seth decided to continue.

"We were lukewarm. Not hot or cold for God. It was hard for me to realize I never was a Christian. I made the decision at my dad's funeral to go all-in for Christ. I didn't want my kids sitting at my funeral one day wondering if I was in heaven. I started attending the church the pastor came from and so did my mom. She had been just as affected by his message. She and I had both been baptized as babies, but this time we were baptized as believers. The first time there was no choice or change in it, just tradition."

John was still staring toward the plaza. Seth looked over his shoulder to Sarah. She had heard the conversation and had been taking "extra care" in creating their drinks so he could speak longer. She gave him a small, knowing smile and Seth nodded in thanks which let her know they were ready for their drinks.

"Here you go," she said and placed their coffees on the counter.

John turned as Seth grabbed two of the four drinks. John looked up to Sarah as he grabbed the other two. "Thank you, Sarah."

"You're welcome. Please say hi to Trudy and Paige for me, Seth."

"I will. If you have an opportunity, Sarah, Paige could use some prayer. Her car was broken into last night and it has shaken her up a bit."

"Oh no, Seth, that stinks. Ask her to stop by later, would you? I will definitely keep her in my prayers."

"Thanks. I will tell her." The two men made their way across the street. Seth didn't want to lose the opportunity to speak to John, but he also didn't want to force the guy to talk. Thankfully, John decided to break the silence when they reached the parking lot.

"Seth, a lot of the things you said back there is stuff I have never heard before. I can see this means a lot to your mom as well. Twenty years ago," John laughed suddenly, "who am I kidding, any time except right now, my pride would have kept me from even talking to someone about God. Because, the truth is, I don't believe in God. I think we just live, then die, and so we should try to live as good a life as we can while we can."

"I understand."

"But I don't understand any of the things you said, and I want to. Not just to talk to your mom," he said, as he looked over to Seth, "but for other reasons."

"I'm sure my mom would tell you anything you want to know."

"I know she would," he said, clearly hinting that he needed something more.

"We can get together sometime, also, if you want," Seth said, reading his hesitation. "But the best place to start is nine o'clock on Sunday morning down the street."

"You're probably right. Thanks, Seth."

"It's the least I can do for all of your help with Mom the past couple of months. " Seth looked toward the shop and then up to the apartment window. "And with Paige."

Chapter 13

After she had taken all the stuff from her car up to the apartment, Paige went into the quilt shop to talk to Trudy. She saw John and Seth walking toward the café together.

Paige was still in shock over her car and couldn't believe how much John was going to help. She was determined to find a way to pay him for the repairs. He didn't know her and wasn't at all responsible for the break-in. God continued to amaze Paige at every turn. Somehow, she knew, even her car being broken into was part of a bigger plan. She didn't know what it was, and would have preferred it not happened at all, but Paige knew it could have been much worse.

When she walked in, Trudy looked up from the computer at the sound of the little bell. "Paige, hon, how are you?"

"I've been better," Paige admitted. "I need to go shower and then I will be down to work."

"Take your time, sweetie. Seth and I can handle things here. He went to get some coffee. Do you want to wait until he returns?"

"No, thank you. I will take it upstairs and heat it up if it's cold. I want to get out of these sweaty clothes."

"John said he is going to help you with your car."

Paige walked over to the counter. "Trudy, he doesn't know me at all. He really doesn't have to do that."

"He knows that, dear. But he wants to help. I have told him about you and he has a sweet heart. Between you and me, I don't think he has much family and there seems to be a part of him that wants to be close to others."

"I am very thankful," Paige said, turning around to see if the men were coming back. She didn't see them yet.

"He knows you are. Now go and shower and come down when you are ready. It's going to be a great opening day and we're not going to let some car thieves ruin it for us, right?" Trudy said with a smile. She made her way around the counter and gave Paige an encouraging hug.

"Right," Paige replied. A few minutes with Trudy and she was already feeling tons better.

Heading back upstairs, Paige knew she would have to start using the bus system for a while to get around. After showering and getting dressed, she pulled out her memories box from the middle dresser drawer where she had left it.

She flopped onto the bed with the chunk of letters and maps from her Aunt Marie. The bus maps were still held in place by the rubber band that her aunt had sent them in. There had not been a need to know the schedule once her gram had let her have the car.

She opened up the main brochure, hoping for an overall view of the bus layout, when a small letter fell out onto her lap. She opened it up and read a hand written note from her aunt.

Dear Paige,

I have not told you this yet, because it didn't matter in the past, but now you need to know some details about your mom for your own safety.

Your mom has a hate for anything relating to God. Before her first mental breakdown, she would not hesitate to tell me how disappointed she was that I was a Christian. She thought I was smarter than to be brainwashed by such nonsense. She was not nice or kind in sharing her point of view on the subject.

After being diagnosed, the only time she was herself with me was when she was angry. And nothing brought out her anger more than

Jesus. The last time I saw your mother, she saw I had a Christian book in my hand (I had been riding the bus and was reading), and it completely set her off. I am not sure if she knew who I was, because she kept asking if I was from the church down the street. The rest of her comments are not important.

She is violent, Paige. I feared for my life that day. She scared me, and I thought for sure I was going to be hit. Since no one has seen her since that day, there is no way to know how she is now.

I hope you find your mother. But be careful, please. Don't mention your faith or anything about God unless you know for sure you are safe. It is a trigger for her anger.

One last thing, Paige. That last interaction with her was 11 years ago when you were about seven. I mentioned you that day and she began talking about how she has your crib and is ready to have you back. It is very possible that she still thinks you are a baby. She seemed to have no concept of time as part of her illness. I am sorry, sweetie. I wish I had good news to give you.

I hope all of these things have changed, and that you don't find them to be true anymore, if you find her. I pray for her always, and I am praying for you. Be safe.

Love,
Aunt Marie

Paige dropped the note and laid back in her bed. She wasn't surprised her mom wasn't a believer, but she didn't know about the violence. Paige had heard her mom was violent in the days when she had lost custody, but nothing about any anger being faith related.

Paige's faith was so much a part of who she was, that it was hard to imagine hiding it—especially in the case of seeing her mom. But she had other relatives that were not Christians, and so it wasn't hard to talk less about her faith. However, she also knew when a sentence included the words "blessed" or "church," they wouldn't freak out.

Knowing that her mom may snap at the mention of God, or if Paige had a cross on or something, was nerve-wracking. It would be a challenge. However, she never, in all the imagined first moments with her mom, thought her own mother wouldn't know her age.

She was grateful for the letter and the warnings. Thankfully, she had not found her mother yet. But what if she hadn't found the letter in time? Her aunt had taken a risk hiding the letter and not telling her before she came to Vegas. It was tempting to get mad, but then again, her aunt didn't have to help or tell Paige anything.

Paige decided to trust the way her aunt had sent the info, as well as the timing God had used to bring it to her attention. After all, with much nicer cars in the area, the thieves had chosen hers.

Yet the events of the morning and the truth of her mom, even with knowing God was looking out for her, suddenly flooded Paige with emotions that she couldn't keep in anymore. She rolled over and sobbed. Hugging her pillow, she felt like a little girl again. Paige felt God put his arm under her head and cuddle up behind her. She felt his free hand comforting her head and his quiet whisper in her ear.

Shh. I'm here.

~

Today was the day.

After years of dreaming, months of work, and days of final checks, the store, her store, was open for business. The open sign was flashing, the door was unlocked, and the computers ready to go.

Trudy wanted to jump up and clap like an awkward, old cheerleader. Over the past two weeks, she had placed signs at shops, churches, and in the local paper. She wasn't sure how the day would go; she was just glad it had finally arrived.

Seth had been a priceless help, and her dear friends had been a wonderful encouragement. With the life insurance money, making a specific amount of profit was not necessary. However, covering the fixed expenses of the shop beyond the cost of goods would be a plus.

This was not a dream about making money. The store was all about bringing people together who loved to quilt. Anything else was simply a bonus.

John and Seth walked in with the coffee. Trudy was pleased to see them getting along so well. Both being veterans, they immediately had a bond when they met. Seth needed a father figure in his life and, after her and John's dinner last night, that thought was even more prevalent. John could fill that role if Seth wanted him to, and only if John felt led to offer it. Both seemed to need each other in ways Trudy totally didn't understand. It was simply a feeling.

However, John was not a man of faith. Trudy had realized that during dinner by the way he spoke and the way he responded when she mentioned natural things such as friends from church. But Seth was not a young, impressionable boy anymore. He understood that folks are in different places in their lives. He could have discussions on a multitude of topics without the fruit of his faith being crowded out by the weeds of the world.

"Sign looks good, Mom," Seth said, as he looked back to the window and then to the parking lot. John made his way to the counter and handed her coffee.

"Thank you, John." She was not going to hide the excitement of the day, yet hoped it help cover the heat that crept up in her cheeks as she thought about dinner with him the previous evening.

"My pleasure. I am liking the café more and more."

"Was Sarah working?"

"Yes. Is she the owner?"

"Yes, along with her husband Tim. They are a cute, young couple. They have wonderful hearts."

"I can see that," John said with a smile. "Are you ready for your big day?"

"I am, but I am not sure how big of a day it will be. We didn't do a massive advertising campaign or anything. We spread the word, hung some flyers, and did only one ad in the paper."

"Opening day is not the best way to gauge how a business will do. It is the regular days in the long run that matter."

"That is very true. I need to remember that." Trudy took a sip of her coffee. "I have never owned a business before."

"I've never had a retail shop, but I imagine much of the same business principles apply."

Seth made his way to the counter and set down Paige's drink. "Did Paige come in yet?"

"Yes, she did. I told her to take her time. She is getting ready and will be down soon. Did she give you her keys, John?"

"She did. I am going to have my mechanic stop by and fix the tire and take the car in to get the window fixed. It should be back in a few days."

"We will need to help her get around if she needs to go somewhere," Trudy said. She knew her son would be more than willing to assist, but Paige was obviously not wanting to share the details of her afternoon activities. She was sure Seth knew that and hoped he wouldn't push the girl too much.

"I will try to have her car back as soon as possible. If you guys aren't available and she needs to go somewhere, she will probably try and take the bus. Although efficient, the bus system is not the safest mode of travel for a young lady."

Seth cringed. "I've never been on the buses here, but I can imagine for someone who hasn't grown up in the area that it would not be the best idea." He didn't know exactly what town she came from, but he imagined it was small compared to Vegas. Most towns were. "Let me know what the cost is, John, and I'll split it with you."

"That's very nice of you, Seth, but you keep your money. I have some to spare and you have a lot of life ahead of you. Alright?"

Seth smiled, and Trudy could tell his like of John just went up a notch. "Sounds good. Thanks."

"I'm going to get out of your hair now. I hope you have a busy first day and congratulations again, Trudy. I will call the shop here when the car is done or just stop by with the news. Would that work?"

Trudy saw him look down at the counter. She wondered what he was thinking. She reached toward the edge of the computer and picked up a business card for him. Trudy handed him the card with a small nod and smile. "Thanks again, John." He took it with reassurance and made his way out of the shop, shaking Seth's hand before he left.

Once John was in the parking lot, Seth looked over at her. "So?"

She smiled, knowing what he wanted to hear. "So, what?"

"How did dinner go?"

"He was a perfect gentleman all evening, if that is what you are asking, dear."

"I never expected anything less. Did you have a good time?" Seth brought forth his most obvious sarcasm and asked, "Or is a grown son not allowed to ask how his mom's date went?"

Trudy could feel her cheeks warming and she laughed...or was it a giggle? "Quit," she said teasingly. "We need to get ready. This morning has already been super crazy."

"That's an understatement." And with that, Seth made his way back to the windows.

Trudy was so tempted to turn the conversation around about his obvious feelings for Paige, but decided one awkward conversation was enough for the day. They could figure things out on their own after all.

~

Seth tried not to watch Paige work. After coming in earlier at about ten o'clock, she received a few words of comfort from his mom and went immediately to checking fabrics. It was obvious Paige was having a really hard time. Seth assumed it was because of her car, but how would he know? She was a closed book when it came to most things so far.

Julie came in just after Paige got to work and Seth knew the sweet lady would keep his mom occupied. Seth saw his opportunity to talk to Paige, and after the night before, hoped she would be more receptive to talking to him. Yet, she hadn't made any eye contact with him when she came into the store. He was concerned that maybe their casual, impromptu dinner had done more harm than good. He had to talk to her. He felt like he would burst if he didn't.

He moved toward her and then he saw her stiffen. "Hey Paige," he said, hoping she could hear the compassion and care in his voice. "I'm so sorry about your car. John told me he is helping you get it fixed. Is there anything I can do? Do you need a ride anywhere today or tomorrow?"

He watched Paige turn slowly. She kept her eyes to the floor, but Seth had already seen the redness that surrounded them when she walked in.

"Thank you so much, Seth. The whole thing was a shock. I never thought about my car being broken into. Maybe staying here is not such a good idea. What if they had tried to come upstairs?"

Seth had already had the same thought. He wasn't a fan of her being all by herself in the shopping center. Not even the grocery store was open 24 hours a day. Yet, could she afford another place?

"You're right. I may be able to help. There are some cheap security systems that can work easily in a small apartment using just a plug." Seth quickly realized what he needed to do. "But better than that is a Wi-Fi system that sends alerts right to your phone. I have internet here in the shop for the credit cards and such, but have not set up any Wi-Fi. That would be super easy to do and it will extend to the upstairs apartment. I have a friend in Virginia who sells equipment and he can recommend something simple that I can get quickly."

"That would be great." She perked up, but still kept her eyes anywhere but connected to his own. "I currently use my phone's hotspot for internet, and I think I could only spend $100-$200 on any equipment. I also need to pay John back, and I don't know how much that is going to cost." Seth could see how dejected she felt. He wanted to hug her. What was it about her exactly that made him feel like battling the world for her?

"Between you and me," Seth said truthfully, "I doubt that John is going to let you pay for the fix. I don't know the guy really well, but there seems to be something in him that wants to be a part of our lives. Even if mom doesn't take to him," Seth said with a smile. "He seems to have a good heart that needs some quality relationships."

Paige finally looked up. Her soft eyes met his and he almost hugged her right then. It took every fiber in his being to hold his hands at his sides, so he moved them to his pockets and gave her a smile.

"I think you're right, Seth. But I can't let him do that."

"Yes, you can. But it's up to you." Knowing Paige loved God helped him to be bolder than he had ever been with other girls. "God's help sometimes comes in ways we least expect, remember? And the giving often blesses the giver more than the receiver."

Paige then smiled like she did the night before, and Seth did his best to not think about her lips. He quickly moved his eyes back up to hers and smiled with her. "And don't worry about the equipment. It is Mom's apartment and the cost of a security system should come out of the expenses for renting the place out. Also, make sure you let me know if you need a ride anywhere," Seth said. He pulled out a piece of paper from his pocket that he had quickly written on when he saw her walk in. I wrote down my cell number, so just text or call anytime."

Paige thanked him and took the paper. "I am going to be taking the bus, but I will let you know if I need a ride."

Seth grimaced inwardly. "I understand the bus system is pretty good here as far as routes go. A lot of folks work on the strip and take a bus every day from all over the city. But it is really not safe, Paige. I can drive you anywhere you need to go. Really, I don't have a lot of stuff going on, especially since the shop is now open."

Paige's eyes seemed to be in a constant state of motion between the floor, Trudy, and Seth. She couldn't seem to focus. "Thanks, but I think it is best if I take the bus. I need to take care of things in the afternoon, and I don't want to bother you."

"You wouldn't be bothering me, Paige." Her eyes met him then. He sensed so much behind them. "But you have my number, and I am here if you need me. Just let me know."

"Thank you, Seth." She seemed to relax once he stopped pushing his offer. But again, it took every fiber to not tell her she was making a mistake.

"Since you are down a car, and there are no actual restaurants within walking distance, would you be interested in having dinner with me?"

He watched her lower her head, but didn't miss the change in her smile and the red blush of her cheeks. He realized he had given her two reasons she should have dinner with him except for the one that underlined his true intention. *God, why can't I just tell her I like her and would like to take her to dinner?*

By her reaction though, she seemed to catch his way around the words. "I'm not sure. It's been a really rough morning. I don't think I would be very good company. Can I let you know later? Maybe around 5 o'clock?"

"Sure. Take your time. Whatever you decide is fine, too. Really. I understand about today and the timing. Maybe it would be a nice break though from a lonely apartment on a hard day." A third reason. "Think about it and text or call me."

"I will. Thanks for the coffee this morning. You saved me a trip over."

"That was John too. He bought for everyone today." The bell rang over the door and they both turned to look. A few ladies, probably in their sixties, made their way into the store.

"I better get back to work."

"It should get busier toward lunchtime. I'm hoping it is a great opening day for Mom."

"I'm sure it will be." Paige smiled, and they both watched the three ladies look around with pleased looks.

Chapter 14

Paige had planned to drive and walk around all of the homeless shelters that afternoon, but not having her car meant changing her plans. In one of her letters, Aunt Marie had told Paige that the bus stops would put her in more dangerous situations because of their distance from most places she would want to visit. She decided to make her way back to Fremont St.

She had been in Vegas less than a week, and finding her mother could take months of her going to the same places over and over again. Searching for one homeless person was a needle in a haystack experience. Paige wanted to stay as long as her funds would last. The hope was to find her mom quickly, or at least by the end of summer.

At some point, Paige was going to have to plan past the summer. She still wasn't sure what direction she was going to go in life. Her family wasn't too thrilled with that, but Paige knew no one could afford to send her to college. Loading up tons of debt when she didn't know which way she was going in the future seemed a waste and financially unwise.

After finishing up at the shop, Paige went upstairs and studied the bus maps. Instead of taking three buses to her destination, she decided to walk to the small hub which was less than a mile from her apartment. She could also pick up a pass there.

The heat was bearable, but she was definitely not used to desert weather in the middle of June. When she reached the hub, her shirt was soaked through with sweat.

She waited in the shade for the bus she needed after getting her 2-day pass out of the machine. Thankfully, she now only needed one transfer to get to Fremont. The bus hub was quiet and clean. There was a current schedule on the board and she would have at least a ten-minute wait. She decided to let Aunt Marie know that she found her note.

She grabbed her phone and brought up Messages. Before texting her aunt, she pulled out Seth's number from her pocket and saved his number as a contact. She wasn't sure if she was ready to text him yet. It would quickly open up a gateway of communication she wasn't sure she was ready to enter. Yet their dinner last night at the café had been amazing. And she didn't want to admit how hard it was to say no to his offer earlier for a ride and dinner.

Even with the car incident and finding her aunt's note, she couldn't stop thinking about Seth Redding. Her mission was finding her mom, but that didn't mean she couldn't get to know him a little more. Or take him up on his dinner invite.

But she wasn't in town to date or find a boyfriend. She had to keep reminding herself of that fact. Yet she also remembered that most things don't work out as we plan, but they do all work out for good for those who love God.

Paige never asked God what He thought about the whole thing. Sitting on the metal bench, elbows on knees and chin on hands, she looked out over the road and down to the park that she ran in just that morning. "So, Lord, what do you think?" she asked softly under her breath. "Could meeting someone be a part of your bigger purpose in urging me to come down here to look for my mom?" Her lips moved silently in her prayer as she released them to the hot air.

No answer came.

"I like Seth, Father. I know I've just met him, but he seems kind—and there is no such thing as coincidence. I know you are sovereign.

This whole week was definitely planned by your hands. Yet, I know that just because something is available doesn't mean it is profitable. And so, is Seth's attention a test or a gift?"

No answer came to her question.

"Maybe I am making all of this more complicated than it needs to be. Can I be focused on finding my mother and have dinner with a nice guy?"

Yes.

Her breath stopped at the small voice in her spirit. In her heart, she knew the answer. She had given herself the rule of not dating while looking for her mother as a way to shield herself from being honest with Seth about why she was here. Dinners led to a lot of talking.

Last night, though, he never asked her why she was in Vegas. He seemed to understand there was some hesitation to share. His consideration was making it almost impossible to fight his invitations. She didn't want to fight them. And going to God about it, on this day, was what she needed to let some of her guard down.

She picked up her phone and brought up his number to message him: *I think dinner tonight sounds good. What time? 7 works for me.*

Paige put away her phone into her backpack and immediately wondered if she was doing the right thing. Yet, the feeling subsided quickly and was replaced with peaceful reassurance and a great deal of excitement now. But was it a date? Or was he just being kind because she didn't have a car? No. There was no mistaking his interest in her and it was done now and the decision made. She smiled and felt refreshed for the first time that day.

Her bus arrived and she smiled at the older driver as she got on. She wasn't sure if she had to show the two day pass she had just purchased out of the machine. When he closed the door, she relaxed and checked her Vegas bus map after she picked a seat.

The bus only had twelve people on it and was very quiet. She had expected more action for a Vegas bus, but she was on the outskirts of the city. When the bus had finished seven stops, and made its way to the next bus hub, the numbers increased and the atmosphere did get as busy as she had imagined. The next bus hub was huge, but easily navigated with all of the signs as long as you knew what bus you needed. Paige boarded the bus that would lead her back to Fremont St.

With most folks out of school, families and groups of college students made up the majority of those living it up on the Fremont St. Experience. Unfortunately, the center walkway of the Experience was lined with numerous half-naked men and women who were ready to be photographed with a willing visitor. The outfits were beyond inappropriate and teenage boys and girls were seeing things they would never forget. Paige couldn't understand why their parents brought them--or didn't immediately remove them once they realized what the experience of Fremont St. was about, or had become.

Paige again, for the second time that week, walked up and down Fremont, in and out of the Golden Nugget Casino, and around the perimeter glancing at every homeless person she saw.

When the late afternoon heat became too much for her, she stopped at an Irish Pub right on the main drag of Fremont. It was a cozy place that made her think of her paternal grandfather. He always sent Paige a card on St. Patrick's Day and reminded her every year that she was part Irish.

The hostess took her to a table and Paige was impressed with the menu. Her mouth watered at many of the options. She quickly reminded herself that she already had lunch and was having dinner that evening with Seth. Her waitress brought her some ice water and asked for her order.

"Is it alright if I just get a side? I just need a snack and a break from walking," Paige asked.

"Sure," said the waitress. She looked slightly older than Paige; long brown hair and beautiful green eyes. "This is the slow time before the dinner rush. Take as much time as you want."

Paige worked her phone out of her bag and went to Messages. Her heart leaped when she saw Seth's reply: *Great. I'll pick you up at 7.*

Dress casually. We'll head down to the local steakhouse, if that sounds good.

She replied with a thumbs up and sent a quick message to her Aunt Marie. *Found your notes with the bus schedules. Thanks for letting me know. All is fine here. No success yet in finding mom. Love you.*

"Here you go. Do you know what you would like to eat?" said the girl, who set down a bowl of popcorn along with her water.

"I think I would just like an order of sweet potato fries, please," and Paige handed the menu back. "This is a really nice place. Have you worked here long?"

"No, just about three months. It is a nice place to work, but the area is not great. You quickly get sick of drunk guys hitting on you all the time. Coming and leaving work is not the safest. Sometimes they have to have a bus boy walk us out to our cars."

"I can imagine. I am walking around during the day looking for my mom, and I am constantly checking my surroundings."

"Is your mom missing?"

"She is homeless somewhere here in Vegas. I moved here to look for her. No one knows where she is or if she is even alive."

"Oh, I'm so sorry. There are so many around here." Paige felt relieved to talk to someone again about why she was here. And the girl looked genuinely heartbroken to hear the news. But it was the truth and there was no way to sugarcoat it. "Do you have a picture of her?"

"I do," Paige said, "but it is about 8 years old. It's the most recent one we have." Paige pulled her phone back out and pulled up her Photos app. She held up the old photo and the girl seemed to study it.

"I'm sorry. She doesn't look familiar. The last time you saw her was eight years ago?"

Paige took a deep breath and put her phone away. "No. I'm told the last time I saw her was when I was less than two, so over 16 years ago. I don't know her."

The girl pulled out a seat and sat next to Paige. "Wow. That sucks. How do you know where to search for her? Have you checked the shelters?"

Paige smiled at the girl's empathy. "The shelters are no help. The privacy laws are so strict that they don't give any info out about anyone who goes there."

"Is she mentally ill?"

"Yeah. She probably won't know who I am even if I do find her. My hope right now is just to locate her, so we know she is alive. Maybe get to talk to her. I really don't know."

"I'll keep my eyes open for her."

"Thanks."

"Let me get your order in. Do you want anything else to drink?"

"No, thanks." Paige watched the waitress go and talk to her co-workers at the bar. She knew she was telling them her story, so she ignored them and got her book out. She took a deep breath and played out, for the umpteenth time, what she would say to her mom in that first meeting. She put the thoughts away and read her book.

When her food arrived, her thoughts went to dinner. And then to Seth.

~

Trudy locked up the shop, and made her way to her car. The shop was scheduled to close at six, but there were still some customers, so she stayed open until they finished looking and buying.

All in all, the day had been wonderful. There had been a constant trickle of customers; some Trudy knew and many she didn't. Three women signed up for the first Beginning Quilter class to be held in two weeks, and all had pre-paid.

Sales had totaled over $250 without the class sign-ups. It was more than Trudy had imagined for the first day, especially with the little amount of advertising they had done. Many women had shared their thoughts on the store and questions about projects she would sell in the future. She didn't have a relationship with any sewing machine manufacturers, and that was one thing she now realized she would have to look into. She didn't want to just carry one line of machines but apparently that was how most stores did it.

She saw Paige walking toward the shopping center, and Trudy met her in the parking lot.

"Hello, dear. How did your afternoon go?"

"Great. How was the rest of the day at the shop?"

"Oh, we did more sales than I expected and a great number of folks I didn't know came in. We had sign-ups for the first class and a lot of fabric was cut. I even had Seth cutting fabric at one point. It was his first time and he had to figure out quickly in his head what a one and one/fourth yard equaled. I think it humbled him for second."

"Most guys, and even girls for that matter, are not used to measuring in yards anymore. We'll have to give him a pass," Paige said with a teasing smile.

"Thank you, again, for all your help these past days. You have really been an unexpected blessing to Seth and me. I don't think today would have been a success without you."

"You're welcome. It was fun. I'm sorry we had all the drama in the morning though."

Trudy waved her comment away. "Nothing we couldn't get through, and John will have it fixed and back to you soon. I'm sorry you had to have that happen right here in the shopping center. Are you worried about staying here by yourself now? I believe John's handyman is coming tomorrow to do something to put more security on the bottom door."

"That will help. I'm more anxious than scared. I don't think tonight will go as smoothly as the past few days."

"Feel free to call me at any time, alright? No matter the hour, I will be right over, but Seth is closer. He lives only a few miles away. You can call him, too." Trudy saw Paige's demeanor change at the mention of Seth's name. She smiled inwardly at the reaction.

"I'll remember that. Thank you."

"Did you have dinner yet? Why don't you come over to my house to eat with me this evening?"

"Oh, thank you. But I, um, well...Seth and I are going out for dinner."

Trudy made sure she didn't react with the glee she felt at hearing the news of the kids going out. "Very good. I am glad you have plans and won't be by yourself all evening." Trudy put her purse back on her shoulder and gave Paige a hug. "I will let you go then, so you can get ready. Have a nice night. Call me if you need me!"

"Thank you, Trudy. I will." A few steps later, the realization of what day it was hit Trudy. She had almost forgotten. She turned and caught Paige before she finished unlocking the door.

"Paige? Tomorrow is Sunday. Would you like to go to church with me?"

Paige turned, and seemed pleased with the invite. "Oh, I forgot it was Sunday." She walked a few steps over. "Would it be alright if I met you there?" It's at 9:00, correct?"

"It is. There is also one at 11:00." Trudy paused for a moment, and watched the girl. "But how are you going to get there? Will you take the bus? It's only about five miles away, but by bus it may take a very long time if there is a transfer."

Paige's face fell and was replaced with a brief look of shame and then frustration. "I completely forgot I don't have a car," she said irritated, and rolled her eyes at her momentary lapse in memory. "And I just got off the bus. That is hopefully my only blond moment of the weekend.

Trudy gave the girl a soft look. "Sweetie, you have had a difficult and long day. Don't be so hard on yourself. When you have a car every day, it is easy to quickly forget that it is not exactly where you left it."

"True," Paige conceded and took a big breath. "I would love a ride to church, Trudy. What time should I be ready?"

"I will pick you up at 8:15, alright? That will give us some time for coffee at the café at church and some food if you are hungry."

"Sounds good. See you then."

"Have a nice evening, hon."

Once in her car, Trudy texted Seth. *Have fun tonight. Be good!* She added a wink to her text and hit send. As she made her way home she thought about the recent turn in events. Last night she had had her first date, and tonight Seth had one. It was certainly ending up to be a very interesting week.

Chapter 15

Seth couldn't believe how nervous he was when he pulled in to pick up Paige. He'd been on first dates before, so his apprehension was confusing. He guessed it was her age.

She most likely had just turned eighteen in the last few months. He was 22 and probably too old for her. Yet it was only four years. The gap was not so large that he should be this nervous or embarrassed. When he talked to her, he found he forgot her age. She was independent, strong, and smart. She was also beautiful and had a love and trust in God he had not seen in anyone her age.

He parked in front of her apartment door and walked over. The shopping center was quiet in the middle. All the activity in the evening happened at the ends in front of the grocery store and the pizza place. He was even more concerned about her being by herself here now after the break-in of her car, but there was little he could do but encourage her to be safe and observant. Maybe he could convince her to carry spray and a knife.

When they had walked back from the café last night, her security had been on his mind. He was angry at himself for not mentioning something to her about taking steps to stay safe. However, he was glad that he had walked her home and saw her to her apartment. If anything had happened to her that night, he would have had a hard time forgiving himself.

He went up to the door. Knowing she probably couldn't hear it, he knocked hard and then texted her. As he waited, he adjusted his belt and plaid shirt. A minute later, the door opened.

"Hi, Seth."

"Hi. How was your afternoon?" He waited as she turned back and locked the door.

"Thankfully, it was uneventful. The bus ride wasn't as bad as I feared, but it did get interesting as we approached downtown." Seth put all his effort into ignoring the first piece of information she had given about what she does or where she goes during the day. He guessed she was either distracted or not caring as much about holding back the details of her days. Seth decided to ignore the comment just in case it was the former.

She turned and they made their way to his car.

"Your mom said that the rest of the day went well. I spoke to her when I got back. She seemed very pleased with how the first day went." Seth opened the passenger door and let her in.

"I think it went great; I'm glad she is happy," he said and closed her door. As he made his way around to the other side, he glanced around the parking lot. He told John he would pay more attention and let him know if there were any problems. He didn't see anything unusual and opened his door. "She made me cut fabric. Did she tell you?" he asked when he got in.

"Yes, she did," and Seth heard the little chuckle and looked over in time to see her try and hide a smile.

"Why do they have to do everything in yards?"

"I don't know," she said with a slightly larger grin. "But your mom said you did well."

"Then she was just being nice. When was the last time you saw a 22-year-old male cutting fabric in a quilt shop?"

"Never. But your mom may get more younger women in there if you keep working the cutting board regularly," she said teasingly.

"I think I'll pass." He started for the restaurant and turned down the next road. He saw Paige staring out the window and taking

146

everything in. "Have you been down this way yet since you got into town?"

"The only place I have seen in this direction is your church, and that was at night. This is all new to me. A few more turns, and I wouldn't be able to tell you how to get back to the shop if you paid me."

"You need a tour then." Paige smiled over at him and he almost forgot to drive with the beauty of it. He forced himself to ignore how sweet her lips looked and focus on the road. "We are not going very far. Over here," he said and pointed over to the left side of the road, "is the movie theatre. I have not been there yet, so I am not sure how they are, but I'm told they are the nice ones with reclining seats that you can choose in advance."

"That shopping center over there has a really good sushi restaurant in it." He looked over to her. "Much better than last night's sushi from the store. There is also a doctor's office that my mom likes. I am not sure who she sees though. You would have to ask her.

"Over there is one of my favorite pizza places. Much better than the one in our plaza. And there is a really good spaghetti house on that side." He paused a moment, trying to look and drive without slamming into another car. "Oh, there is a great micro-brewery down that street and also a Mexican restaurant I go to a lot."

"I am starting to see a pattern here."

"Really? What?"

Paige laughed. "You keep pointing out a lot of places to eat."

Seth laughed. "Sorry. I eat out a lot. I'm not a big cook. How about you?"

"No, I hate cooking, but I can make basic stuff. I prefer to eat out though when my budget allows it." She smiled. "Keep up the restaurant tour, but I did see there was a book store back there that I may have to visit when I get my car back."

"I'm not a big reader, but I'd be glad to take you back to it. I read a lot in the Navy. There's not much to do on a ship but read or lift weights. Given that choice, I preferred to read."

"How long have you been out of the Navy?"

"I got out a little less than sixty days ago. My official last day of active service will be the end of next week. My mom moved out here last year, and I decided to come and help her open the shop while I decide what I am going to do with the rest of my life." He looked over and smiled at her. She was listening to him and seemed calm and happy. If she was as nervous as he was, then she was hiding it well.

"Here we are. This is my favorite steakhouse," he said. He laughed and looked over to her again. She gave him her adorable smile, and he found it was getting harder and harder not to look at her lips. He definitely didn't want to start this date with her thinking he was some creepy guy who couldn't find her eyes. He brought his attention back to parking the car--hopefully without hitting anything.

~

Paige couldn't believe the military stories Seth told her over dinner. She was stressed just thinking of the things he had to go through while on active duty. He had lived in Asia, served on various ships, and also worked counter-drug in the Caribbean. She couldn't comprehend the responsibilities he'd had every day.

"I flew in once onto an aircraft carrier, and it felt like it crunched your whole body together with the force of it. Thankfully, I only had to do that once."

"I would have been sick, I think."

"I kept my lunch down, but barely." Seth cut another piece of his steak and looked up at her. "Have you ever thought of going into the military?" She put her soda down and looked over to Seth.

"I have a lot of family that were in the military, but, no, I never had any interest in going in. Not yet anyway." She picked her fork up and started pushing her mashed potatoes around. She really had no clue what she was going to do with her life yet. Searching for her mother was the only thing God had put in her heart.

"How about college? Do you have a degree you want to pursue?"

"My grades weren't good enough to get into any school but the local community college, and my gram didn't have the money to send me. I didn't want her to pay for it anyway. I wasn't ready to go, and I had no clue what I wanted to study."

Seth picked up his own soda and looked over the rim before drinking, "Did your gram raise you?"

Paige took a deep breath before putting a full fork of mashed potatoes in her mouth. This was the moment in the evening she knew would come, but it scared her nevertheless. She didn't want to share about her mother. What guy wants to hear on a first date that the girl has a crazy mother? Or on any date for that matter. She wanted to avoid that conversation.

Deep down she knew it was dumb. Her mom's mental illness was not something Paige needed to hide. However, the fear that she could end up just like her mom someday terrified her. What if she had inherited whatever had contributed to her mom being in the mental state she was in? It had become a habit to hide the truth as long as possible when she met new people, and it gave her the illusion of a more normal life. She tried to never lie; she also tried not to volunteer information. And now, in a new town where no one knew her, she wasn't the orphan who had a crazy, homeless mom somewhere. She was just Paige and on a first date with a great guy.

Now, with his last question, the normalcy she craved and currently had was going to shift. She definitely did not want to lie to Seth. She looked over at him as he put his drink down and picked up his fork and knife again. He was relaxed and waiting patiently.

As she finished her bite, she adjusted the napkin on her lap. "Yes, she raised me since I was about two. She is great. She would love your mom's store. She taught me how to quilt a little when I was growing up."

Seth was listening and looking interested. He didn't say anything and seemed to be waiting to see where she wanted to take the conversation. She wanted to pour out her whole history to him.

"That's great. Is she happy about you being in Vegas? Is it your first time here?"

Paige felt the tension begin to slowly melt off of her. This guy wasn't like the annoying boys at school she grew up with, and besides that, he had a relationship with God and was older and kinder. She had never really known any guys who obviously loved the Lord. She was keeping herself from being honest and open out of fear. It wasn't fair to him. Paige had felt led to be here, and she needed to take the next step.

"She understands why I am here, but I would say she is not happy about it." Paige smiled, and tore off a piece of bread with her fingers. She was nervous. Her heart was beating faster and she felt she couldn't eat at that moment. "She is not thrilled that I am here alone. I told her all about Trudy, the shop, and the folks I have met. Her concerns are far less than they were a week ago."

Seth had a small smile on his lips. "Your arrival was perfect timing. Mom needed your assistance and you needed a place to live. It's interesting to watch how God works."

Paige felt her heartbeat settle down a little. "God has definitely been with me every step of the way. Meeting your mom outside her shop when I had only stopped to get something at the grocery store was beyond amazing. I was in awe of what God had done."

"When we first talked at the coffee shop that day, I never thought you would be working for my mom, living above her shop, or coming to dinner with me. Had I known, I definitely wouldn't have made such a mess of our first conversation."

"You were very funny," Paige said with a smirk. "But I do have a confession. I knew who you were when you came and talked to me that day. I had overheard your conversation with Sarah, and so I knew you were Trudy's son. But I was trying to stay low key. Plus, I never expected your mom to hire me."

"I almost fell over when she said she had hired you," he said as he finished up his meal. "When she told me she was letting someone she just met stay in the apartment, I thought she had lost her mind." He put his arms up on the table and leaned over toward her from across the table. He had a mischievous grin on his face. "But I have a confession too."

"Really? What?" Paige found herself so excited. She was shocked that she wasn't nervous about what he might say. She waited with a grin as she leaned forward to hear what he would say.

With all the space between them gone, Paige could see every detail of Seth's face. Good looking didn't begin to describe him. He had a bit of stubble on his face. If she had to guess, he had shaved the day before. He smelled wonderful. All the windows had been down a little in the car, and she hadn't noticed his cologne before. She didn't want to move. She could talk to him like this for the rest of the meal.

"I was excited that she hired you."

"Excited that she hired someone she didn't even know?"

"As soon as I met you in the coffee shop, I knew I wanted to see you again." He slowly leaned back. "I played 'concerned' for my mom, but I was actually very happy once I knew it was you. You're working there would give me the excuse to see you more."

Paige couldn't believe it. Just a week ago she was in Washington, planning a trip to an unknown city, and packing for an unknown amount of time in hopes of finding her mother.

"I see," she said with a grin and then scrunched her eye brows down into as much of a serious look that she could create. She leaned back and folded her arms and teased, "What if I didn't want to see you? Or what if I had an amazing boyfriend somewhere?"

Seth laughed. "I knew you didn't have a boyfriend—at least not a good one."

Paige's look morphed into shock and confusion. "How?"

"Well, if you had a boyfriend, I don't think you would have come to Vegas without him. Especially in the summer when school is out and college hasn't started. If he was a good boyfriend, he would have come with you. Vegas isn't the safest place to travel alone." Seth smiled. "So, do you have a boyfriend?"

Paige pinched her lips as hard as she could to keep from smiling. He was certainly very sure of himself. She didn't know what to do with that, but it was a nice change to the uncertain and fumbling guys her own age. "No. I don't," she admitted.

"Great. Now that that's all out of the way we can enjoy some dessert." He motioned to get the waitress' attention. Paige took another couple of bites of her food and pushed her plate forward a couple of inches and put her arms up on the table. Her heart felt like it was going to beat out of her chest.

She was falling for this guy and she didn't know him at all. More importantly, he didn't know her. He didn't know she was an orphan or a daughter of a crazy, homeless woman. He didn't know that she had average grades, and even if a college wanted her, she couldn't afford it. And he didn't know she didn't have any future plans and that she was clueless as to what she wanted to do in life. Honestly, she didn't even know what she was going to do next week.

"Paige?"

She looked up suddenly. "Yes?"

"You alright?"

"Yeah, fine. Why do you ask?"

"Your face looks serious, and your whole body and mood seemed to change. Are you upset?" Paige didn't realize she had got lost in her thoughts. He was right. She had gone from thrilled to fear and sadness in only a few moments.

"Oh, no," she said honestly. "I was just thinking."

"Anything you want to talk about?" He rested his arms on the table to match her own.

Paige looked down. How should she answer? She wanted to tell him everything. Tell him why she was in Vegas. Tell him about her family. But she wasn't ready. She just wanted to enjoy the evening and not think about her family or the future. Just one night of relaxation. Yet, she still did not want to lie. "No. Not really. Just a little overwhelmed with stuff."

"I'm sure. I remember being eighteen and there was nothing easy about it. I do have an idea about how to make it a little better though."

Paige smiled. "Really, what?"

"Crème Brûlée."

Paige laughed and the evening was quickly back to where it started. "That sounds perfect."

Chapter 16

Seth handed the bill and his credit card to the waitress. This was the first time a date had paid for her meal—a real meal—and didn't ask if she had any money. Granted, she didn't date much in high school, but it was more common to split the bill or go to a fast food restaurant. The few guys she had gone out with didn't have jobs and were not taught how to properly take a girl out.

It was so refreshing. It felt unreal. The entire night, maybe the whole week, felt like a dream. A wonderful dream.

Her purpose for being in Vegas was not wonderful. Yet, at the same time, it was wonderful. She had the opportunity to come and look for her mother. She had amazing family that were helping her do what she could to find her. And she had hope that her mom was alive.

"What would you like to do after dinner?" he asked, bringing her out of her thoughts—again.

A little shocked, she looked up and smiled. "I don't know. This is all pretty new to me, not to mention the area as well."

"I have a few ideas." He brought up his hands to count them off. "One, we could go bowling. Two, we go to the closest mall and do some random shopping for your apartment. Mom said you need a few things up there. Or, three, I could take you home so you can get some sleep after a hard day." He leaned forward. "My least favorite option is taking you home, but I don't mind which one you choose. I'm hoping I will get to see you tomorrow. Maybe at church?"

Paige found that she could not pass up an opportunity to get close to him, so she leaned forward and met his gaze with a grin. "I love bowling, but I stink at it. And your mom is picking me up tomorrow morning for church really early, but I think we could have time for a couple of games."

"Well, I haven't bowled in about four years so we are probably at the same level. Getting a lane on a Saturday night may be difficult, but we will definitely try." Their moment was interrupted by the waitress with the final credit card receipt. Seth signed and looked over to Paige. "There is an alley just down the street. Let's go check it out."

"Sounds good." Paige got up, pushed her seat in, and grabbed her purse. Seth was there, patiently waiting, and put his arm out toward the exit so she could go first. Paige whispered her thanks. She didn't know these types of guys even existed in real life.

The bowling alley was very close and the parking lot was full. Seth found a spot and turned off the engine. He looked over at her. "I need to open the trunk really quick, and then I'll open your door."

"It's alright, Seth. I can get my door one time tonight. It won't ruin my evening or my impression of your first date skills," she said in a teasing tone.

"Oh, good," he said with a smile. He opened his door and jumped out. She guessed he was still trying to be at her door as soon as possible still. By the time Paige had gotten out of the car and was ready to go in, Seth was already by her side and softly put his hand to her lower back. Paige's heart seemed to be linked to his touch because it started beating faster when she felt his hand lead her through the parking lot.

One thing that Paige noticed was Seth's awareness of his surroundings. He always seemed to be looking around and noticing everything.

"You're not a big fan of parking lots?"

He looked over at her, and gave her a questioning smile. "Not at night. Why do you ask?"

"You look around a lot."

"Habit. I just try and be aware of what's going around me. I picked it up in the Navy when we were in bad ports and dangerous cities."

"This is my first time out of Washington state. I don't have even have a passport."

"Well, you can fix that easily. A small fee, some pictures, and an application at the Post Office and you will be good to go."

Paige laughed. "I never even thought about getting one before tonight. But it does sounds like something I should have."

"You can't even go into Canada now without one, so it is a good idea. Before 9/11 happened, you could."

The bowling alley was packed and there was not a lane open that they could see. "Should we go or would you like to see how long the wait is going to be?"

"Let's see what they say."

Paige turned toward the counter, which was being managed by a woman, probably in her mid-twenties, who was obviously overwhelmed and struggling. She had a well-worn sweatshirt on with the name of a college that Paige did not recognize. Her long hair was quite disheveled. Paige felt bad for her. It was Saturday night and it seemed she was all alone.

Almost on the verge of tears, the woman barely looked at them when they approached the counter. "I'll be with you in a minute." She quickly checked out four bowlers who all paid individually. Paige was impressed with her speed despite her apparent stress. The phone rang and she picked it up. "Nope, we are full until 11." Paige and Seth looked at each other. It was not even 9 yet. She hung up the phone and looked at them. "Do you have a reservation?"

Seth spoke up. "No, we don't. So, the next free lane is not until 11:00?"

"Officially, yes, but let me see." She checked her computer and looked down the lanes. "How many games do you want to play?"

Seth looked over at Paige. "I don't know. One? Two?"

"Whatever we can. It would be nice to play one game, since waiting until 11 is not going to work."

"Well, I've got a lane that was booked for two hours and the folks are packing up right now with a little over a half an hour left on their time. You can have that lane and just pay for your shoes. Sound good?"

Seth pulled out his wallet. "That'd be great. Thanks. Size ten for me.

"Size 7 1/2 for me, please."

The woman got their shoes and placed them on the counter. "Lane 10 then. They are packing up now. By the time you find the ball you want, you should be good to go."

"Thanks so much. I hope you have a nice night."

"Thanks. The other guy cancelled so it is just me and the tech guy in the back this evening. Very hectic."

"I can imagine. Thanks, again." Paige grabbed her shoes. They walked toward the middle of the alley and found a free table. They put their shoes on and began looking for balls that fit. Once found, they walked back and Seth looked over at her.

"I think the girl really appreciated you being kind to her."

"She looked so overwhelmed. I felt bad for her."

"It was really nice of her to let us have a lane and not to charge us for the remaining time. She could have easily ended the prior session and put us in for thirty minutes at the regular rate."

"It was nice a surprise. Maybe we were the only ones who waited patiently without huffing and puffing until she could come to us. I'll give God the credit for the blessing."

He looked over at her again. "Absolutely."

~

Seth watched Paige bowl and could tell she enjoyed it. They were at about the same skill level. Paige was on her third frame and just got a spare.

"Looks like I am in the lead," she mocked as she came back to the table. She had a competitive edge to her that just attracted Seth to her even more.

"Not for long. I'm up." He threw the ball and got a split. He grabbed his head in mock terror and looked back at Paige. "That's not good."

"Nope, not good at all," she teased. He threw his second ball and got half the split. They passed each other as she came up for her turn. "Get a few more of those, and I will definitely stay in the lead."

He laughed. "When did you learn how to play?"

She picked up her ball. "High school gym class. They took us to the bowling alley twice a week for 8 weeks."

"Wow. They never did that for any of our gym classes." Paige threw her ball. Seth laughed as she tried to guide the ball with her hips. Nine pins down, she turned around frustrated. "You know that doesn't actually work, right?"

"What?"

"Moving your hips. They are not attached to the ball; at least I don't think they are attached." He exaggeratedly tried to see an imaginary line coming from her hips as she approached their table.

She lightly slapped his arm with an equally exaggerated look of mock anger and took her seat. "I know. But it sure feels like it helps. It's a bad habit. Getting only nine pins and getting irritated is also a bad habit." She smiled over at him and she had no idea how hard he was fighting back the desire to grab her hand. It was clear by her "slap" that she was getting more comfortable around him. After the day she had, he was glad that she was having a good time.

"There are worse habits, I am sure." He looked over at the bar. "Do you want a coke or anything?"

"Yeah, that would be great."

"Let me take my turn, and I'll go get some." He got up and grabbed his ball.

He took a step and heard Paige say, "You're doing great." He fumbled and threw a gutter ball. He slowly turned and watched her pretending to look around for something. She looked so cute trying to seem so innocent. "Oh, a gutter ball. That's too bad."

"Careful now," he teased, "two can play at that game." He smiled and she raised her hands in surrender. He threw his second ball with no "encouragement" and got a strike. "Now I get a strike and it only counts as a spare," he said to her in the most fake accusing tone he could muster.

"Well, we don't want that." They passed each other and she gave him a high five.

"I'll be right back with our drinks. Want some popcorn?"

"I'm good thanks. I ate a lot at the restaurant."

She got her ball and was preparing to shoot as he approached the bar. He took out his phone. He replied to his mom's text. *Having a great time, Mom. Thanks."* He was close to his mom but not close enough to share that he was loving every minute of his time with Paige. But he still felt he didn't know anything about her. What he did know he liked; and for now, that was all that mattered.

~

"Why do they do that? Why do they throw them all over the street?" She looks up the block. "Did he just throw one? Hey! Hey!" Throwing her black shawl over her shoulder, she walks quickly to a young man and his wife. She doesn't see the folks around her trying to get into the casino and giving her strange looks. Her boots click loudly and are fast enough to get everyone out of her way as she approaches the man.

There is a slow, easy going pace for most visitors to the strip. She stands out easily with her quick steps, loud shouting, and her shiny, rhinestone embossed bag hanging from the crook of her arm. Her baseball hat, also embossed with rhinestones in the shape of the Playboy bunny logo, is pushed low over her tangled, shoulder length, light brown hair. "Hey," she shouts again, and the man looks over as he quickly grabs his wife's hand.

"You just threw that cigarette butt." Her accusing and loud comments bring everyone's attention to her presence. "You need to pick it up. It's trash." She points down at the ground at the still smoking cigarette.

She walks a few feet toward the trashcan where the butt needed to go and looks back. "What is he doing? We don't have time for this." She looks back over her shoulder at the guy. He gives her a nasty look and turns to leave. "Hey! He is leaving. Hey! You need to pick this up. Why is he just looking and not cleaning it up?" She laughs unexpectedly, startling the guy and his girlfriend. "Is that your girlfriend. Does your wife know you are with her? Hey! Do you know he just dropped a cigarette?" The couple ignore her comments and pick up their pace.

"Where are you going?" She sees them talking together. "What is she saying to him? Is she...do we know her? We're going to be late." She begins to turn, and sees more trash on the ground. What is this?" She leans down and picks up a small flyer with a naked girl on it. "Yuck. Did you put this here?" She asks, whipping back to look at the man and the woman, who are quickly trying to get away.

"Where are you going? Did you put this here? We have to go. We are not cleaning this up." She looks down at the plethora of flyers of naked women. "Where are these coming from?" She explodes in laughter again and draws the attention of more people walking by. She waves at them mockingly. "Hi. Did you put these here? We're going to a better casino. No one sees all this trash. Why do people come here?"

Frustrated that everyone is not doing anything useful, she grabs a joint from her bag and lights it. Looking over her shoulder, she waits to see if the couple are coming back. "We have got to go. We can do the slots at Circus Circus and the smoke shop is around the corner. We can get some there."

Taking a few steps over the advertisements, she takes another drag from her smoke and erupts in laughter. Her body movements are over exaggerated and wild and pedestrians give her a wide birth, as if they will catch whatever is making her act crazy.

"We should take the bus. We can avoid all these pictures then. Wow. We need to get on the bus. We have a ticket." Smoke in hand, she rummages through her bag and checks the dates on the numerous bus passes she finds.

She sees another man throw something down on the sidewalk and yells at him—quickly and repeatedly moving her outstretched, accusing finger from him to the item on the ground. "You need to pick that up. We're going to the bus. You need to clean that up."

"Get lost." He gives her a nasty look and keeps walking.

"What did you say? You need to pick this up right now." She begins to go after him. "Where are you going? Don't you care?"

"Ma'am?"

She looks over at the man suddenly standing next to her. "Great. Perfect. The cops are here." Being shorter than the officer by a foot, and the brim of her hat pulled down to her eyebrows, she has to put her head back to look him in the eyes. "Did you see that guy throw his cigarette? You need to do something." She points down the road to the long-gone couple and catches a glimpse of someone spitting. "There. Did you see him? He just spit. That is super gross. Isn't there a law or something about that? Now look down. Do you see all these nasty pictures on the ground? What are you going to do?"

"You seem to be causing a lot of problems out here. Do you have any I.D.?"

"Are you kidding? You're kidding right?" She laughs. Almost yelling, she looks the officer up and down with disgust. "Why are you bothering us? They are littering all over the place." She points to the people walking up and down the strip. "Let's go. This place sucks." She takes a step.

The officer blocks her way. "No. "You need to show me some I.D., if you have any. You're disturbing the peace out here."

"What??" Her laughter is louder this time and comes so suddenly that everyone around her reacts as if she is a Jack in the Box toy that just popped. "We are allowed to be here. This is a free country."

"Yes, it is. But you are causing problems. Where are you staying here in Vegas?"

"Why do you care? We're leaving."

He grabs her arm. "No. I need you to stand right here. You need to show me an I.D."

"No. We're allowed to be here." She puffs from her joint and stares at him—knowing she is smoking a legal substance. "Are you going to take this away too?" She waves it close to his face. "We don't have time for this." Her anger begins to boil over and her voice is heard easily over the music coming from the closest casino entrance. "You have nothing better to do, do you? You see all these people littering, and yet you don't do anything. Do they actually pay you to do nothing?"

"What are you smoking, Ma'am?"

"We're allowed to smoke this." She pulls the bag of stuff from her purse. Annoyed, and confident, she holds it up to him and laughs. "See? We bought this and can smoke it if we want." She pushes the bag of man-made marijuana back into her purse and folds her arms.

The officer leans down to his shoulder and says something into the radio.

"What are you doing? Are you calling someone? We are late. You need to leave us alone." She starts walking away. He grabs her arm again.

"No. You're going to stay right here and get your I.D. out." Another cop approaches and stands behind her.

"Fine. Since you're obviously not going to do your job, why not bug people who aren't doing anything? Don't you have a donut you can go eat or something? Isn't that what you should be doing if you're not going to keep people from littering?" She reaches into her purse and pulls out her wallet. Buried beneath numerous slot machine slips, she pulls out her I.D. and stands with one hand on her hip. "Here. Since you have nothing better to do, you can look at our I.D."

She jams the card into his hand and watches him turn it over and look at her face multiple times. "Yes, that's my picture. You don't need to keep looking at us like that."

"Alexandra Hanson." He turns her I.D. over and looks back at her. He calls in her name and I.D. number as the other cop waits to catch her if she tries to run. She takes a hit and then laughs. She notices the people watching her. "Do you see what these pigs are doing? We have every right to be here and have not put anything on the ground." She looks over at the second officer. "Do you see all the litter on the ground? Your buddy here doesn't seem to care at all."

"Ms. Hanson." She looks over at him. "Seems you have a court date you never showed up for years back and there is a warrant out for your arrest. Your I.D. is expired and you have no current residence in Vegas. Is that all correct?"

"Whatever. We need to go." She snatches her I.D. from his hand and moves toward the bus stop. Her arms are suddenly locked behind her, and she looks back in anger at the officers.

"What are you doing?"

"You are coming with us."

Chapter 17

Paige laughed again. She smiled over at him and struggled to catch her breath.

He was unable to hold down his own chuckle while hearing her contagious laughter. "My ideas are not that funny."

She turned toward the window, holding her stomach which ached from laughing. She tried to remember the last time she had laughed so hard. When she looked back over at him, she felt warmth and joy flood her.

Seth loved how her eyes disappeared when she laughed. He never thought of himself as a funny guy, but found himself hoping he could make her laugh all day. "You lost, so you don't have a choice about what we do."

At the end of their first game, they had made a bet about who would win the second. The bet was simple: the winner got to decide what they would do together on Sunday afternoon. Paige thought for sure she would win. She had won the first game, after all, by thirteen pins. She decided once she won, she would choose a nice lunch after church. However, her lead was gone when she got a split in the tenth frame—he won by two points.

His victory brought out a litany of ideas on what to do the following day that had her laughing still.

His ideas were simple to hilarious. They could have lunch down at the strip, go to the top of the Stratosphere to experience the rides, go

Lilly Horigan

to the Hoover Dam, visit the Pawn Stars shop, or take a donkey down into the Grand Canyon.

"No one wants to see me try and ride a donkey up a hill in this heat," she stated, with as much seriousness as she could muster in the moment.

"Oh, I think I would love to see you on a donkey. Have you ever ridden one?"

"No. There weren't a lot of donkeys where I grew up. Have you ever?"

"Not that I remember. Maybe once at a fair when I was little." He was watching the road and glancing over at her. She could tell he was enjoying his evening. Neither one wanted it to end. "But it's probably about time I did."

"I did lose...somehow." She loved teasing him. "Whatever you decide, I'll be ready. But I need to be back to the apartment around three in the afternoon so I can catch the bus." She looked forward, still smiling. Three would give her enough time to do some searching before it got dark.

"Three? Where do you need to go on a Sunday afternoon in Vegas?"

The tension came like a lightning bolt. Suddenly everything changed. She had messed up and the reality of why she was in town came rushing back to her. She had completely forgotten, in the joy of evening, to cover up why she was there and what she was doing. She shut down and looked straight ahead. Her laughter vanished.

He waited and looked over a couple times.

She needed to say something. The longer she waited, the harder it would be to get back to where they were a minute ago.

"Paige?"

She looked over at him. Sadness filled her eyes. She wanted so much to tell him why she was in town. Would he understand? Would he run--concerned she would also end up crazy? She looked over one more time and saw nothing but compassion and confusion.

166

"I'm sorry, Seth. But I am here for a reason, and I never expected to tell anyone why. I never expected to even want to tell anyone, or be so afraid to do it if I had to."

Seth glanced over every few seconds to her. He was giving her the time she needed to process what she was thinking. He really was a nice guy. He wouldn't leave because there was mental illness in her family, would he?

After a long pause, and a lot of awkwardness in the air, Seth looked over at her with a soft smile. Faster than she had expected, they pulled into the parking lot of the shopping center. Their evening was at an end—and it was ending badly. He parked in front of her apartment, turned the car off, and turned toward her.

"Paige, you have something going on in your life that has made you come all this way on your own. I don't know what that thing is, and I admit my mind is going a little crazy imagining, but you don't need to tell me anything you don't want to tell me. I promise, though, that whatever it is will not alter how I feel right at this moment.

"I had a great evening, and I would love to do it again. If you need to be back by three tomorrow, then we will be back by three. I will even wait and take you over to the bus stop if you want to save time. Mom is going to pick you up tomorrow morning for church, right?"

Paige stared at him, shocked and amazed at his understanding. She had never experienced kindness of this magnitude beyond her family members. She needed to say something but tears came, not words.

As a tear fell down her cheek, he reached over and wiped it off. He smiled another one of his handsome smiles that made her heart ache for good, instead of for sorrow, and then he grabbed her hand.

"Come on. I'll walk you over and make sure you get in alright." He let go of her hand after squeezing it, and got out of the car. Paige wiped her tears and tried to collect herself. He opened the door and they made their way to her apartment.

She unlocked the door. "Thank you, Seth, for a wonderful evening. I've never had such an amazing first date."

"Neither have I," he admitted. His hands were in his pockets, as if he wasn't sure what to do with them if they were free. He looked down and then up to meet her eyes. "I will see you tomorrow morning at church?"

"Yes."

"Wear jeans tomorrow, alright?" He smirked a little. "I think I know where I am taking you after, and you won't want to wear a skirt there."

She laughed a little and the tension released. "Now you have me wondering what you are thinking."

He smiled. "Go on. It's late and my mom will be here before you know it. She'll probably want to hear all about your evening, too. You will need to be rested," he said jokingly.

She laughed. "Thanks for the warning." She opened the door and looked over at him. "Inquisitive mom-types are not new for me, so I should be able to deal with it."

"Did you go out to dinner with the only child of one those inquisitive moms and then be stuck in the car with them the next day?"

The question caught her off guard and she glanced over. "No. Why?"

He raised his eyebrows and smirked at her surprise. "Good night, Paige. Get some sleep."

She smiled back at him as she closed the door, locked it, and made her way upstairs.

He hadn't tried to kiss her. Yet it was his lips that Paige imagined until she fell asleep that evening.

~

Trudy turned into the parking lot and took a spot in front of her shop. She couldn't believe one of her life-long dreams had come true. The reality of her new shop was bittersweet as she remembered again that it was only because of her husband's death that it had been possible. She could not have afforded it otherwise, and without Seth's help it would never have happened either.

The timing of it all was overwhelming to think about. She knew God was sovereign and nothing happened without his permission. Sitting in her car in front of her new shop, and thinking of how she got to where she was, only confirmed in her heart that everything really did happen for a reason.

She didn't know why Bruce had to die when he did, but Trudy couldn't ignore all the events that had happened afterwards. Only God knows the why of everything. She saw only a speck of what God's purpose had been in allowing her husband to pass away when he did. At times she wanted to wail and question why God hadn't brought her husband along for this journey. Yet, this tangent in the timeline of her life wouldn't exist if Bruce had not died.

That truth, as she saw it now, was sobering. Looking back, she saw that God had tried to get her family's attention before in hundreds of different ways. Together, as a family, they sat in church and listened to God's words year after year on Sunday mornings. They nodded their heads and sang the hymns. Then left to finish their weekend and live life as comfortably as possible until the next Sunday.

She had raised Seth to play the part--attend, leave, and live like everyone else—perhaps not as badly as everyone else. She still taught him right from wrong but never what, or more specifically Who, defined right and wrong. Their apparent relationship with God had been shallow and without heart. They were not against Him, but they were definitely not all in for Him either. They had gone to their church almost consistently for years and years and never heard the hard and sobering truth: they were most likely not Christians at all.

She had never volunteered there. She thought about it, but there was no interest in going beyond the same seat she sat in each week. They had always put some money into the offering basket when it went by-- maybe five or ten dollars.

She had quickly learned, after her husband's funeral, that all of it had been a waste of time. She was sure that their church had probably spoken of the characteristics of a true Christ-follower, but if they had, their family had ignored it. Then again, she couldn't remember one adult ever choosing Christ and getting baptized at their church.

Now she couldn't get enough of learning how to love God more each day and how to truly love others. Loving others wasn't easy. Living sacrificially in the current culture wasn't easy. She was still learning.

With all the poor and suffering in the world, it seemed crazy opening up a quilt shop with the insurance money. Yet she felt led to spend it wisely, grow it, and not only help others across the world, but those in her local community as well--all with fabric and thread.

Trudy pulled herself out of the memories when she saw Paige come out the door from her apartment. She unlocked the door and Paige put her purse on the floor before settling in. She grinned at Trudy and motioned toward the shop. "I bet it's really exciting to see your shop open after all your hard work."

Trudy put the car into gear and backed out. "It is. The whole experience has been amazing. But I was also thinking about how it came to be. Did Seth tell you his dad passed away a couple years ago?"

"He did. I am so sorry."

Trudy could hear the sincerity in Paige's voice. "It was a hard time and so unexpected. He didn't smoke and ate reasonably well. He was a little overweight and went to the doctor when necessary. He had lab work done every couple of years. He worked for Pepsi restocking the vending machines in the area. The company paid well and we had great health insurance. His job allowed him to meet and get to know all kinds of people. He very much enjoyed his job.

"When Seth was six, we bought twenty-year term life insurance policies for both of us. We were still young and in good health, so the total rate was less than a thousand dollars each year. My husband also got a small life insurance plan from the company. When he died, I didn't need to work at the doctor's office anymore—I was in charge of patient records. So, I quit my job soon after the funeral and took time to mourn, weep, and slowly give his items away. I didn't miss my job, but I missed the ladies I worked with all those years. Thankfully, they spent time with me and got me out of the house once in a while."

Trudy turned her turn signal on and began navigating to a parking space at church. They had arrived so quickly, that she couldn't recall seeing anything on the way over.

"Seth took it hard, being the only child and very close to his dad. He got emergency leave and was able to stay home a couple of weeks. We did a lot together during that time, including coming to know Christ. Here we are!"

They got out and made their way to the entrance. "Sounds like you and your husband did a great job preparing financially for each other."

"Thank God we did. I don't remember who said it to me, or if I overheard a conversation somewhere, but I came home one day from work and told Bruce we needed to do something so that if one of us died the other could afford to take care of Seth."

Paige opened the door and they said hello to the greeters. "So many parents don't prepare like that for their kids, even if they have the financial means to do so."

Trudy looked over to Paige who was staring ahead toward the hallway. She looked sad and lost in her own thoughts. Trudy knew someone had not prepared for their death in Paige's life.

Trudy put her arm around Paige's shoulders. "When you are ready to share who you've lost and the pain it's carved into your heart, sweetie, I would love to listen. I am sure it must be so hard to live with at times."

Paige batted away the shimmer of tears filling her eyes as she nodded, unable to speak.

"Let's get a fancy coffee, hmm?" She gave a quick squeeze to Paige's shoulder and let go.

A little smile of comfort began to grow and eventually reached all the way to the young girl's eyes. Trudy felt blessed to have a young woman to help and comfort. It was a unique answer to a long-ago prayer of having a daughter. "Have you eaten, yet? I think I am going to treat us to a cinnamon roll," Trudy decided. "I will take an extra-long walk tonight to work it off."

"Maybe John will join you on that walk?" Paige grinned as she bumped Trudy in the shoulder a little.

She couldn't hide the shock or the blush that suddenly appeared. "Oh, I see Seth has shared a little bit about that recent and unexpected dinner invitation," she exclaimed. Now it was her time to look down, this time with embarrassment.

"Only that he asked you out. He seems like a great guy--handsome too."

"Like Seth?" Trudy asked with a quick turn of the table.

Paige laughed, somewhat awkwardly, as her own cheeks got a shade rosier. "Yes, like Seth".

Trudy laughed with her as if they had known each other for years. They made their way to the line at the café where Seth spotted them. He wore a look of calculating nervousness, mixed with wonder, as they approached.

She leaned over to Paige. "I'm not sure if Seth is pleased we are laughing, or nervous we are scheming."

Paige didn't seem to hear her.

"Don't forget to breath, sweetie, or you will pass out."

~

With her coffee finished, Marie logged onto her computer for her next daily task. After doing this for years, she always contemplated giving up. Alex could be anywhere, but her gut still led her to the Las Vegas Detention Center Inmate Search webpage every day.

The only way to know if Alex was alive and living in Vegas was to track her arrests. The humorous irony of hoping her sister would be arrested was long gone. Marie knew that the only hope Alex had of getting on the road to recovery, beyond her own choosing, was to get arrested and have someone observe and evaluate her mental state.

Every morning she typed Hanson into the search engine of the site. Marie battled the nagging thoughts of what else she could do if her sister's name didn't appear. She always said a little prayer when she hit submit, and the prayers intensified when she moved to the next step of her morning ritual—searching the Las Vegas Morgue.

Everyone had given up trying to find her. Marie couldn't. She believed God still had his hand on Alex, despite her hate for Him. If she was still alive, it was by God's amazing grace. If she wasn't--only God knew that too.

With a slow blink and a deep breath filled with all the prayers of hope she could muster after years of the same *There is no inmate that matches that search criteria* message result, she typed her maiden name in and hit submit.

She sucked in a breath of astonishment and felt the sting of tears rush in.

One match found.

Alex was alive!

Chapter 18

John sat in the back row and listened to the sermon. The last time he sat in a church was at boot camp when he was eighteen. It was the only authorized escape from the intense training.

He never paid attention when he went. He knew he was at the Protestant service since the Catholic service was earlier, and he preferred to be a little more awake before arriving. Sleeping in church would draw negative attention to him.

He stayed awake and stared at nothing in particular as he thought about what he would be doing if he hadn't joined the Air Force three months prior. He came away from church, not with any knowledge or interest about God, but with confirmation that he was doing the right thing at the right time in his life.

Every Sunday he came to the service physically exhausted and uncertain about his decision to join the Air Force. The hour always passed quickly as his mind raced with the what-ifs and past memories of friends and fun. Yet, he knew those same friends now struggled through college and collected debt they would be paying back for years. He always left service with a stronger resolve to see his commitment through.

Now, however, he had come into this service with an actual desire to hear and try to understand what it was that gave Trudy such fire for God. He found that being around her was intoxicating, and it put a sense of wonder in him he had never experienced before.

He hadn't told Trudy he was coming this morning. He snuck in right at the beginning of the service and sat in the back. He saw her toward the front with Seth and Paige. It was tempting to go up and say hello, but he wasn't sure he was going to want to come back next week. In his heart, he knew that Trudy wouldn't begin a romantic relationship with someone who did not believe as she did.

That was hard to comprehend, but he loved her commitment.

He listened and tried to understand what was being said. It was like they were speaking another language at times. The sermon was practical and full of different verses from the Bible. John didn't know much of anything about the Bible, but he was sure it wasn't useful for everyday living.

Apparently, he was wrong.

He was also wrong about what he would experience when he entered the building. He was ready for a hallway lined with photos of Jesus and crosses, like guideposts, leading toward a quiet sanctuary. Instead, he passed a café and a large children's park. He was expecting an altar, flowers, and pews; and instead entered a giant gym with rows of chairs, a few carpets in the aisles, and a stage. He looked for the hymn book and instead got semi-rock music with words on a screen. He was expecting suits and ties and saw jeans and shorts. He had prepared himself for a big speech about money, but they didn't even pass buckets and briefly mentioned that folks could drop any giving in the boxes at the doors.

What else am I wrong about? he thought. *God?*

The sermon was primarily about being the church in the world. It was obvious this sermon was for those who believed in, whatever exactly, this church believed in. The pastor, which John learned was the correct title for the man via the church brochure passed to him when he entered, was teaching about being everything to everyone in order to love them where they were in life--as Christ had loved them before they knew Him.

No one got up and left. The bulk of the people, less a few groups of teenagers scattered throughout, seemed genuinely interested in learning how to be like Jesus. They took notes and seemed to be 'learning.' Maybe, had he met Christians like this in the past, he wouldn't have had a negative view of them all these years.

John felt a sudden hopefulness. That hope is what kept John in his seat and intently listening to the man on the stage. He had seen Trudy and Seth aiming to live like Christ, yet he didn't know how to put what he saw into words before now. What a refreshing contrast to the anger and hypocrisy he had witnessed in the world.

John followed along and took mental notes of all the questions that he would ask Trudy or Seth sometime. He wasn't sure he understood how a person could be everything to everyone and not break the Ten Commandments. Did the Ten Commandments still apply to Christians? He only knew a few of them, but he assumed they were still important.

As the sermon came to a close, everyone stood and the pastor prayed. John decided it was his opportunity to sneak out. With all heads down and eyes closed, he slipped out of the aisle and an usher opened the door for him. He made his way through the lobby to the exit where another man was standing ready to open the door for him.

"Hi, John." John hadn't paid much attention and suddenly looked up when he heard his name. A young man was on his way in and was dressed for a concert and not a church service.

"Patrick? I didn't know you attended church here." They moved off to the side to talk without getting in the way of those leaving. People were starting to trickle out.

"I grew up here coming here." Patrick crossed his arms and smiled broadly—he stood a little straighter too. "My family has been coming here since before I was born."

Although John didn't know Patrick well, and had only met him a few times at the grocery store, he knew Patrick was Mike's younger brother and together the boys ran the store for their parents who were now retired.

"Did you see Mike in there? He comes to the early service. I go to the late one so if there is any trouble at the store one of us is available.

"No. I didn't. I came in just after it started and left during the prayer at the end." John took a deep breath and put his hands in his pant pockets. "To be honest this is my first time here."

"Great," Patrick stated with no shock or surprise. "Think you'll come back?" John looked in and saw the doors open and a mass exit of the early service on their way towards the two men. He quickly thought about Patrick's question and was surprised by the answer he had unknowingly already chosen by the end of the service.

"Yeah. I think I will. Some of my other renters go here and they invited me to try it out. Trudy and Seth Redding. Do you know them?"

Patrick grinned and nodded, "I mentor Seth. We meet every week or so to go over spiritual matters and such. He's also in one of the worship bands here."

John looked in and wondered if Trudy had already spotted him. There were multiple parking lots and probably different doors as well. It was probably unlikely that she would see him. He felt anticipation filling him—he actually wanted to be discovered now that he had decided to come back.

"I was thinking I might need someone to go over a few things with me as well. This is all new to me."

"Everyone has to start somewhere. Seth would be a great person to talk to and if that doesn't work out, you could always come over and chat with Mike or me at the store. We'd love to schedule a get together and answer any questions you might have."

"Thanks, Patrick. I will keep that in mind. Have a great day." John reached out and shook the younger man's hand.

"Thanks, John. You, too."

Patrick looked a little older than Seth; probably in his young thirties. They seemed like a good match for mentoring. John wondered if he would be comfortable having a twenty-something mentoring him. Any pride he might have would have to take a back seat if he was going to learn anything about Trudy's faith.

John made his way to his car, amazed that he was excited about coming back next week. But first, he would talk to Trudy and Seth. He wanted them to know he had been here.

He wanted to start asking questions.

He wanted to hear the answers he would've never entertained before.

~

Seth walked out of the sanctuary with his mom on the right and Paige on the left. A feeling of completeness swelled up in him. He was sure the excitement was written all over his face. If so, the girls didn't notice or say anything about it.

Paige had sat in the middle, between himself and his mom, for the service. The whole experience felt so right. It was almost scary, or too good to be true. He pushed his fears down. He would not let the fear of losing another loved one keep him from loving again.

After stepping out into the hallway, Paige pulled out her phone that he could hear vibrating. She went to answer it and held up her finger for them to wait as she stepped over to the wall to get out of the way of the hundreds of people making their way to the parking lots.

Seth grabbed his mom's arm and pulled her in Paige's direction, while also giving Paige room and privacy. "Paige is on the phone. Let's wait over here for her."

"Oh, ok." Having his complete attention, she didn't wait to start asking questions. "Do you two have any plans together today?" Seth smiled to himself. His mom could not help wanting to know every detail of his life. That was the joy of being an only son to a very inquisitive mother.

"I think I am going to take her down to the range after lunch for some shooting."

Seth waited only an instant before the expected concern appeared on her face. "Does she know how to shoot? Isn't she too young? Has she ever touched a gun? What does she think about that?"

Ignoring most of the questions, he answered only the last one. "I haven't told her yet."

"Told her? You mean ask her, right?"

"Nope. We went bowling last night and the winner of the last game got to pick what we would do today. I won." He looked over to Paige who had answered her phone with a smile. What followed was a roller coaster of facial expressions—shock, joy, worry, and hopeful resignation. Seth couldn't imagine what she was hearing. Paige said a few more words, nodded, and then hit the END button on her phone.

"Everything alright?" he asked.

"Sort of," she stated cryptically. Seth found his patience with her secrets starting to wear thin, but he remembered this wasn't about him or any of his business. "That was my Aunt Marie. She had some important information on one of my family members and called to tell me about it."

"Want to talk about it, hon?" Seth had forgotten his mom was standing right there. He was grateful for her compassion. Although his patience was also very limited with her thousands of questions over the years, she was always willing to listen and help if she could.

"Not right now; but thank you, Trudy."

"You are always welcome to come sit and chat with me, sweetie." Paige smiled her appreciation and looked to Seth.

"I'm not sure I'm going to be great company today, Seth. But I don't need to get back to the apartment by any specific time now. I may space out in thought, but if you are still up for going out, we can."

"I think what you could use right now is a good lunch and a stress-relieving activity." His mom suddenly looked over at him with shock.

"Are you still planning to go where you said, Seth?"

He looked over with a grin. "Absolutely. It's an even better idea now."

Paige looked from one to the other. "What are you guys talking about?"

"You'll see." Seth gently grabbed her elbow and guided her toward the door. He glanced over at his mother. "I was telling Mom about our bet last night."

"Ah, I see." Paige looked over to Trudy. "Should I be nervous?"

Trudy laughed and put her arms around the girl. "I am."

~

Paige expected lunch to be very difficult after hearing that her mom had been arrested. Yet she found herself excited and thankful. Her mother had gone years without being arrested and now, finally, the family knew she was alive.

While on the phone with Aunt Marie, Paige mentally went over what she might do, how she would see her, and if this was the event that would change both their lives forever. She thought for sure she would be horrible company and was tempted to ask Seth or Trudy to take her back to her apartment.

But Aunt Marie's joy had been contagious and Paige found herself smiling and laughing more than thinking and planning. Trudy's response to what Seth had planned also left Paige feeling apprehensive, but adventurous.

They said their goodbyes to Trudy and made their way to Seth's car. "Are you in the mood for anything particular for lunch?" He opened the passenger door for her.

"Nope. Winner's choice."

He looked down at her after she sat and rested his arm on the door. His smile thrilled her. If anyone could get her to share her concerns about how to see and reach her mother, it was Seth. She felt lost in the depths of his dark, sea-blue eyes. "Anything? Are you sure? It could go way beyond a simple California roll if I pick."

She made herself focus on something else. His teeth. Clean, straight, and just behind his perfect lips. Losing the battle of her thoughts she shut her eyes and shook her head fast to wipe out the images as best she could. "Sure. I think you'll be kind and not go food crazy on me--not too quickly anyway."

He smiled at her trust and leaned down before closing the door. "I think you're right. Don't want to scare you away."

~

Sergeant Lisa Kennedy had processed a lot of women through the night. The line seemed like it would never end. They were prostitutes and trouble makers who were not shocked by their arrests and gave little trouble during the process. Occasionally you got the homeless person that was causing a scene of some sort. They felt they could be anywhere and do anything they wanted. To them, the police were the enemy—there to keep them down and they were not shy about letting everyone know. Those bookings were the most exhausting. She was mentally and physically ready to go home and rest.

She was rushing through the reports a little faster than was wise. When she arrived tomorrow, she didn't want to be welcomed by a list of errors found by her superior officer. She slowed down and took her time with the final one and was glad when she finally hit the submit button.

Lisa went to logoff the program, but her thoughts kept sliding back to one of those angry, homeless women early in the morning hours—Alexandra Hanson. She was beyond normal rage, and probably on some type of drug. Yet she also talked to herself and seemed to be trapped in the past. She had no idea what year it was, or where she lived. She was also a Veteran, it seemed.

Expired IDs were checked in with her personal belongings earlier in the booking, as well as random names and numbers, receipts, and strange items most likely stolen or found over time. A quick search revealed she had not checked into any homeless shelters in years and Lisa was amazed the woman was still alive. She was skin and bones.

Homeless Veterans were not uncommon; however, female homeless Veterans were. Having a brother serving in the Air Force may have been what led Lisa to keep thinking about the woman--or maybe it was that the woman was about the same age as her mom. Whatever the reason, she could not ignore that the woman's sunken, acne-scarred face, rotting teeth, and extremely dirty hair kept coming up in her thoughts.

There was so little that could be done for the homeless that came in. She always felt her hands were tied and wished she could do more. There was only one thing she could do, and she decided to do now. She pulled up the report and re-read what the arresting officer had written.

She went down to the booking area of the form and checked the box for *Mental Health Check*. It was the only thing within her power that she could do to try and help the woman.

Maybe it would be enough to start the process for getting her some real help. Otherwise, she would likely be another nameless, homeless woman found dead on the street.

Chapter 19

Despite the sudden blast of intense heat of the day, which almost made it hard for Paige to breath, she laughed as she exited the gun shop. She still couldn't believe that Seth had taken her shooting. The shaking had calmed down, but her hands were still trembling. They also hurt. She didn't realize it would take so much hand and arm strength to shoot a pistol.

Seth was prepared for their outing and had brought his own guns and ammo. He hadn't let her know where they were going until they had left the restaurant, which thankfully was just a simple burger joint down the road from church. She had begged, and he had let her try and guess, but he never gave up what activity they were going to be doing.

By the time they had arrived at the gun shop, which also had an indoor gun range, she was a ball of excitement and nerves.

Seth was a great teacher and super patient with her. For safety, he loaded the pistol with only one bullet at a time until she was comfortable and had the basics down. He didn't laugh at her questions or her terrible shots. Most of the laughing had been when they paid for the lane. He had been there before and didn't need to sign the liability forms again. Since she was new, she was required to sign. The thought of what had happened next still made her smile at the awkwardness of it all.

"Hi. Here to shoot?" asked the young man at the register.

"Yes."

"Have you been here before?"

"I have, but she is new."

"Great. We just need to get some papers signed." He laid a liability form in front of Paige. "Are you 21 or older?"

Paige's eyes widened a bit and she looked over to Seth and back to the man. "No, I am 18. Is that alright?"

"You just need a guardian to sign for you." He looked over to Seth. "Are you over 21?" Seth nodded. "Great. Will you be signing for her?"

"Sure."

Paige looked over to Seth. "You're going to be my guardian?" Seth squeezed his lips tight to try and control his laughing. Paige turned to back to the guy at the counter. "Is that allowed?"

"Yep. Not a problem." He flipped the form over and pointed down through the additional sections showing that she would be the minor and Seth would be her responsible adult while on the range. "You just need to sign here, and he will sign here."

Paige stared down at the form and glanced over to Seth. He had his arms crossed, and he was looking down at his feet. He was laughing.

"You think this is funny, don't you?" Paige couldn't help but smile and start laughing with him. "You knew you were going to have to sign for me, didn't you?"

He looked up with a twinkle in his eyes. "Of course. You can't shoot a pistol without someone over 21."

She squeezed her own lips and tried to give him her best, fake angry face she could muster. "We are definitely going to have to have another bet soon, so I can repay you for this." She turned and quickly read over the documents and then signed. She leaned one elbow onto the counter and handed him the pen. "Your turn."

He grabbed the pen and looked into her eyes. Paige couldn't believe it was possible, but he was getting better looking by the day; and it was getting harder every day to look away from him.

Paige was still amazed that the shop had allowed him to be her guardian. Yet, despite the embarrassment, it had felt right and the awkwardness was short-lived. Seth let her pick the targets and helped her get ready with eye and ear protection. He smiled at her when she was ready, and he began patiently instructing her on how to shoot for the next 30 minutes or so.

The entire experience was a great distraction from thoughts about her mom. As Paige walked to the car next to Seth, she found herself wanting to talk to him about why she was in Vegas —and Aunt Marie's call. The thought of talking to him about it though created more butterflies in her stomach than shooting for the first time had just moments before. She decided to distract her thoughts again.

"Where did you learn to shoot? In the Navy?"

"I didn't shoot much in the Navy, actually." He opened the car door for her. The heat radiating from the parking lot blacktop made it hard for Paige to breath. She couldn't understand how people survived in this heat. If it bothered Seth, he gave no indication of it. He closed her door after she was in and she thought she could definitely get used to his attention.

"I was introduced to guns very young," he continued, after he turned on the car and the A/C. He lowered the windows and then pointed the vents toward her. "I grew up with guns and knew how to use a rifle since I was seven. I always had a loaded gun in my room. It was never a concern." He looked over with a look of irritation. "Today that would never happen. You would probably lose custody of your kids or something."

He backed out and then rolled up the windows when the air conditioning kicked in. She loved hearing him talk so easily with her. She didn't want the day to end.

"My dad taught me how to shoot, and I walked the woods alone for hours hunting small animals. He also taught me how to skin and eat them, but I have no interest in hunting anymore. In the Navy, I qualified with a pistol and thought I knew how to properly shoot. Once I got my concealed carry license; however, I looked into getting some real training beyond what was required to carry my gun legally concealed."

~

He looked over to her and stopped talking when he saw her wide eyes and slightly opened mouth. "What's wrong?" He put his eyes back on the road for a moment before looking at her again.

"You carry a gun?"

He suppressed his laugh and smiled a little. "Yes."

"Loaded?"

He laughed. He hadn't planned on telling her yet that he carried a gun every time they were together, but she had handled shooting so well. Plus, the more time they were together the safer it would be if she knew. "Well, what do you want me to do? Throw it at them?"

She looked straight ahead, her mouth still hanging open a little fish-like. She really was beautiful. He reached over and put his finger below her chin and closed her mouth. She broke into a grin. "Sorry. I am just shocked."

"You've never known anyone who had a concealed carry license?"

"No. I mean, I've heard of it a lot, of course. But I've never known anyone who actually did it."

"Maybe you can be the first in your family someday to have one."

Her shocked face was back, and he couldn't hold back a small laugh at her reaction. "Me?"

"Yes, you. Why not?"

"Um," she looked forward again while she tried to come up with a reason. Seth sensed she was deciding how to say what she thought without offending him. "It's not safe."

"Sure it is. You just need training."

"It's dangerous."

"Not if you know what you are doing." He leaned over. "And *the world* is dangerous. Plus, a gun levels the playing field for girls."

She gave him a questioning look. "What do you mean?"

"You are most likely going to be physically weaker than any attacker. Having a gun puts you on equal footing. Awareness of your surroundings and making wise decisions about going to your car, using your phone, and the like, are important, but having a weapon makes you a stronger and harder target."

"Oh. I never thought about it like that."

"What would you do if you came out of your apartment one evening to go to your car and there was someone waiting for you? How would you protect yourself?"

He could see her mind working. "Maybe stab them with my keys? I remember a teacher in high school telling me to have my keys out and ready when I went to my car after school. She even told me to put them between my fingers so I could drive them into the attacker's throat, if need be.

"Well, that's a good backup plan if you're in a 'gun-free zone.' The problem is the bad guys don't care about the sign that tells them to keep their guns out. That only keeps good guys with guns out." He looked over to her. "You never want to get to the point where you are close enough to need your keys in those situations. Keep an eye out, look for suspicious behavior so you can avoid it, and yell at them to stop if they are approaching. It's also a good idea to always have a knife on you and know how to use it."

He didn't want to scare her, but the image of her car being broken into kept nagging at him so he went on. "Since you can't carry a gun until you are 21, you are going to have to use those back up methods. They also include keeping your head up, staying off your phone when alone, and checking in and around your car before you get in."

He didn't want her to be another statistic. She was deep in thought so he kept quiet to let her process her thoughts. After a minute, she turned to him, putting her leg up on the seat to get a better angle. She leaned her head on the head rest and looked at him as if the world were upon her shoulders.

"I was taught that Christians didn't need guns or even alarm systems because if we had them then we didn't really have faith in God."

Seth was flabbergasted. "Really? Having a line of defense is a lack of faith?" He had never heard that type of thinking before. "What about going to the doctor for a checkup? Is that a lack of faith?"

She gave a quick jolt back of her head and her eyebrows curled down into a questioning frown. "No. It's a way to catch a problem before it becomes worse, but you think it's the same?"

"Well, it was just the first thing that came to mind. How about calling 911 if there is an emergency? Wouldn't that also be a lack of faith? What about the fact that many of Jesus' disciples carried swords? Or, bringing it back to this century, wearing glasses to see when your vision goes bad? Or taking preventative medication for an ailment? Or having an emergency fund? Wouldn't that thinking, if it's not being hypocritical, also mean that doing your part to take care of what you have or to prepare for what the future holds—which *is* in God's hands—is also a lack of faith?"

Paige wrapped her arms around her knee and looked toward the road again. "Those are good questions and your argument makes a lot of sense. Especially with God saying that our body is a temple of the Holy Spirit. But I hate that a lot of what I was taught may have been wrong."

Seth's heart went out to her. She was living the best life she could for God and she never considered the path she was on had a lot of unnecessary stumbling blocks. "If anything, it will help you to be more patient with others in the future who are also learning. Don't look at it as a fail, but as an opportunity to grow and to remember to question everything based on God's words and not man's."

Her smile was back, although a little sadder than before. "Plus," he said teasingly, "maybe that is why God had us meet. You needed to see how good lookin', gun-totin' guys think."

They both laughed as he pulled into the parking lot of the shopping center. Seth found himself disappointed that he had made it to her apartment so fast. Their day had been perfect.

"What are you doing for the rest of your Sunday?"

Paige paused and stuck out her lips as she thought. Seth knew he was falling hard for her when he found every facial expression adorable.

"I have some research to do, and I think I'll take a hot bath," she stated after some thought. She grabbed her purse from the floor and placed it on her lap. Seth wondered if she was as sad as he was at the moment to see the day end. "You?"

"Every other Sunday night there is a young adult meetup at the church, but that isn't going on this evening. On Sunday's when there is no meetup, I always have dinner with my mom. Would you like to join us?" He wasn't sure if that was the right move or not, but he knew his mom would love to have them both over for dinner.

"Aw, that is sweet--you having dinner with your mom every week. I wouldn't want it intrude."

"Have you not met my mother?" Seth joked. "She adores you."

Paige genuinely beamed at hearing his words. "Dinner sounds great, but can I take a rain check? I have some work I need to do tonight."

"Sure, a rain check would be great. It's an open invitation."

"Thanks." She opened the door and made her way to her apartment again with Seth coming up behind her.

Don't even think about kissing her!

He tried to reign in his thoughts, but they were going crazy. There would be plenty of time to kiss her in the future, he hoped.

Paige looked over at him, as she opened the door. He noted that she now had a bell on the side of the door. John had taken care of that quickly. It was one more reason he liked Mom having John as her landlord. "Thank you for a great day and for teaching me how to shoot. It really helped take my mind off some stuff."

He purposely kept his hands in his pockets, which seemed to relax Paige since it took the unknown out of what he was going to do with them. Her eyes; however, told him she wouldn't mind if he took a few steps closer or if his hands were out of his pockets.

"You are a good shooter. I had a lot of fun. We'll have to do it again." He started back toward his car. "Don't forget to lock your doors. I'll see you tomorrow at work."

"Great." He saw her hesitate and look down at the ground. "Seth?"

"Yeah?"

"I'm not sure when I'm going to have my car back, and I need to go downtown tomorrow after I work. Would you be willing to take me? I may need to stay there an hour or so. I am very nervous about it, and would like some company. I prefer not to take the bus."

Seth put all his effort into looking natural and not giving voice to the thousands of questions her comment just raised.

"Sure."

"But you will have to leave your gun at home, or in the car, I think."

"Now my curiosity is super peaked." He started toward his car again. "Whatever you need, Paige. See you tomorrow."

"Thanks, Seth. Bye."

~

Trudy strained the noodles and poured them into the bowl she had just washed. She had found the silver-lined, porcelain dish in the back of the cabinet and knew it would be a way to spruce up the meal a little. She went back to stir the meat sauce on the stove. Seth loved spaghetti and she made it at least once a month when he came for dinner.

She never spent any time picking special bowls though on those nights. She used her everyday dishes that had survived the move across country. Prior to the move, her friends had helped her do a large garage sale to scale down the house goods as much as possible. Her new home in Vegas was a third of the size of their Ohio home.

Letting go of items that made her think of her late husband-which was almost everything—had been excruciating. A friend had suggested she take a box and fill it with the things, beyond pictures, that brought to mind her most precious memories.

Trudy had picked out a large boot box and did just that. Ticket stubs, one of his morning mugs, his best watch, a shirt from his favorite band, a knife his father gave him, and some other items now sat in that same box in her closet. Occasionally, she took it down and went through the items. The shirt still held his scent.

She poured the spaghetti sauce into a separate bowl and brought it to the dining room table. Usually Sunday nights were on the back patio; relaxed and without much prep work. Tonight, with John coming by, she decided to go a little fancier. As time passed and dinner approached; however, she felt her apprehension increase. Seth had no idea he was coming. Maybe causal and relaxed would be better.

She felt like a schoolgirl with her wishy-washy feelings. When John had called asking if he could stop by and talk, inviting him to join them for dinner seemed perfect. Now she was questioning that decision.

Setting down the meat sauce and looking at the set table of three of her best plates, mats, and folded linen napkins; she shook her head and decided she had gone too far.

Keep it simple, Trudy.

She picked up the spaghetti and meat sauce and moved it to the patio. She transferred the plates but put the table mats and linen napkins away.

She brought out simple paper napkins and put one on the right side of each plate under the fork. Even putting a napkin under a fork was more than she usually did when Seth arrived, but she did want to do a little something special. After all, it would be the first time another man, besides her son, sat at any table in her new home.

She decided against putting any drinks out. She never did that either. At least that would keep a thread of continuity for Seth, since he always got his own drink. Plus, she wasn't sure what John would want.

She covered the food and looked at the clock. They would arrive soon and she still needed to get the garlic bread out of the oven. She opened the oven door and heard the front door close. Her new home, although cozy, was small It wasn't hard to hear anything from one room to the other.

"I'm here, Mom. I'm going to grab a beer out of the fridge."

"Alright."

Seth had stocked her small refrigerator in her garage with his favorite beer, so she never had to buy any. The system worked well since Trudy never knew what to get for him. He had developed new tastes and interests in the Navy. He had grown up and matured well beyond his years. She had a hard time not telling him how proud he made her every time they saw each other.

Walking into the kitchen, Seth breathed deeply. "Smells good. Need any help?"

"Everything is done. I'm going to cut up the bread and we'll be ready to eat soon."

Seth made his way to the patio. He looked out over the rock garden and stared at the mountains. He placed his beer on the table. "Mom? Someone joining us?"

Trudy smiled and prayed he would be okay with another guest. "Yes. John wanted to talk about something, so I asked him to join us. Do you mind?"

"No." Trudy heard him drop into his usual chair at the head of the table. Trudy had placed John across from her spot. Since his father's passing, Seth had taken the head of the table spot in more ways than one. He had been a rock during the hardest of times. "Do you know what he wants to talk about?"

"Not at all."

Chapter 20

John took the bottle of wine out of his trunk. He wasn't sure if Trudy even drank wine, but he was not about to show up for dinner without something.

He had come home after church unsure of what he was going to say or do about his attendance that morning. He felt a longing to talk to Trudy, and remorse that he had not told her of his plans to try it out, since it was she who had initially invited him. John also battled the excitement he had felt while there with the years and years of indifference toward anything God related.

He was pleased that she had let him join in on their Sunday evening meal. Knowing Seth was going to be there brought on feelings of nervousness, but also relief. He liked the boy, and being Trudy's only son, and his father gone, Seth had a role and responsibility unlike many other kids his age.

John went up the walkway of the small house. It looked similar to all the other houses in the neighborhood with its red sandstone, but Trudy added little touches that set it apart: hanging baskets, cute animal figurines among the stones, and randomly placed painted rocks in pastel colors and patterns.

John rang the doorbell and waited.

Trudy opened the door with her apron in her hand, obviously quickly removing it before welcoming him. She gave him her sweet smile.

"Hello. Come on in."

John stepped in. "Thanks for the invite. This is for you. I wasn't sure if you liked wine, but this is one of my favorite reds."

She took the bottle with her thanks and looked at the label. "I do drink red wines occasionally, but I don't think I've had this. Maybe I will try it tonight with our dinner. Thank you."

"My pleasure."

She closed the door behind him. "Seth is on the porch. We usually eat out there on Sunday evenings."

"Sounds good." She led him through the foyer and then into the kitchen. The smell of a home-cooked meal brought on a slew of strange feelings inside him--most centering around the hole that a lack of family in the house had created in his life. He missed having someone to share his every day with, but he didn't miss the fighting that always seemed to be a part of it.

Trudy went straight to the counter and pulled a wine opener from the drawer. John took a step toward her. "May I help you open that?"

"Sure. I usually mess up the cork trying anyway. Would you like a glass?"

Before he could answer, Seth entered.

"Hi, John. Glad to have you here." The young man shook John's hand. "Can I get you something to drink? I've got beer in the garage."

John felt a sudden awkward moment. "I'm about to open a bottle of red for your mom, but I think, with this heat, it feels like beer thirty." He looked over to Trudy. "Still want me to open it, Trudy?"

"Yes, please. I'm not a big beer drinker mysef."

"Sounds good. Want anything in particular?" asked Seth.

"Whatever you're having will be fine." He grabbed the wine opener and set to opening the bottle. He was only a couple feet from Trudy as she pulled out bread from the oven. "Something smells great."

"That would be the garlic bread. We are having spaghetti tonight."

"I haven't had homemade spaghetti in years. It sounds *and* smells wonderful." She shot him a quick grateful glance with a bit of red in her checks that was definitely not from the heat of the oven. He was pleased she was happy to see him. She was a sweet woman that had caught him off guard the past couple of months. He never thought he would date again.

The cork popped when Seth came back in the kitchen. "Here you go. You'll need the bottle opener on this too," and he handed John the beer. John turned the wine opener over and popped the bottle top. He took a sip and found himself enjoying the moment of being around Trudy and her son.

"This is good." He looked at the bottle. "I don't think I've had this."

"It's made at a local brewery in the area. It's on the other side of town but worth the trip. They are starting to sell it in the local stores though."

"Alright. Enough beer talk," Trudy interrupted with a smile. "Seth, will you take this bread and put it on the table?"

"Sure."

Seth turned and led the three to the patio. Trudy motioned for John to sit on the other side of the table and took the seat closest to the door. Seth took his seat at the head of the table.

"Seth, will you pray please?"

Heads dropping, Seth led them in prayer. John quickly closed his eyes and bowed his head as well.

"Father, thank you so much for this meal Mom has made. May it nourish our bodies. And thank you for bringing John over to share the meal as well. We are thankful he is in our lives, not only as a great landlord, but also as a friend. We also lift up prayer for Paige, Lord. Give her strength and peace in whatever it is she is going through. Thank you for bringing her into our lives. In Jesus' name, Amen."

"Amen," echoed Trudy. John mouthed his Amen and opened his eyes. Both mom and son had their eyes on the food and were not paying attention to him at that moment. He was honored to be mentioned in Seth's prayer and grateful they were not staring at him like a lab rat ready to be studied. He wasn't quite sure what his look was saying at that moment. He decided to be honest.

"Thank you, Seth. I'm so glad your mom found my little shopping center and gave me a call. Your store fits well in there and your friendship is a rare bonus in the world of commercial renting."

"I imagine it's hard being a landlord to all the shops in each of your centers," said Trudy as she reached for the noodles. Seth picked up the bread and handed it to him.

"It is. Unfortunately, it is also getting harder with more and more people shopping online. To keep shopping centers up and operational, owners need to be creative with what they bring in, since most stores don't survive past a year anymore. When stores do fail, and units are left vacant, it tends to bring down the entire center since it leads to vandalism and an overall unsafe feeling for any potential customers of the shops still open."

"I was shocked Paige's car was broken into. Our center only has one vacant slot and its whole atmosphere is cleaner and safer than surrounding centers."

"The criminals are not totally stupid. They were able to see that the cameras in the center, put in by the grocery store, don't extend far past their unit. Her car was just outside the reach of the last camera. I am planning to fix that." He poured spaghetti sauce over his noodles while he recalled the moment when he'd made the decision not to put cameras in. He was angry at himself now. He had thought the classier look and feel of the center would keep the thieves and vandals out. Apparently, he was wrong.

"I appreciate you doing that. I know I will feel safer working there and now, with Paige living upstairs, it's very nice to know she will be safer, too."

"She and I had a long conversation about safety today," Seth said.

Trudy quickly brought her napkin up and wiped her lips. "Oh, that's right," she said excitedly. "How did she do at the range?"

~

Seth smiled thinking about the day and how Paige did with her first shooting experience. She was a quick learner and also open to trying new things. It was obvious she came from a less-than friendly gun background, but most of her conclusions were based on inaccurate assumptions she had grown up hearing.

"She did great. She was really nervous, but coachable. I started her off on my .22, and then moved her up to the 9mm by the end. She was hitting the target pretty well during our 30 minutes there."

"Did she ever figure out where you were taking her?"

Seth laughed. "No, but she put a lot of effort into trying to figure it out."

"Sounds like you both had fun. She is a sweet girl. I am hoping to have her car back to her by Monday afternoon."

"She'll be happy to hear that. She asked if I could take her somewhere downtown tomorrow after work." Seth silently hoped her car would not be ready by then. He wanted to spend more time with her.

"It would probably be late in the day if not Tuesday," John stated quickly, as if he could sense Seth's concern.

"I'll let her know. Thanks, John, for taking care of all that."

John reached for another piece of bread. "My pleasure."

Seth wondered what made the man ask to come to over. One would have to be blind not to see that John and mom were both excited to be in the same room together. They were trying hard to hide it, but the little glances and the small smiles were like amateur fireworks on the porch—small, but loud! It made Seth a little uncomfortable, but he was determined to get through the dinner and excuse himself as soon as possible.

His mother lightly touched his hand resting on the table. "Do you know anything about where you are going with her tomorrow? Also, what time you are leaving? I could have one of my friends come in and help."

Seth knocked his head with his palm. "Oh, Mom. I'm sorry. I forgot that you would be by yourself at the shop. Yes, could you get someone to come in?"

His mom smiled and patted his hand. "Of course, sweetie, and I am sure I would be fine by myself for a few hours."

"No, I think you're going to need two people all the time for safety as well as practicality. Eventually you may need to get stuff out of the back, use the restroom, get food, and the like."

"True," she said as she twisted more spaghetti around her fork. Plus, I am still nervous without you there. What if I mess up the computer or something?"

"Do your best and we'll work it out later. Worst-case scenario--just do it by hand and we'll fix it when I return."

She nodded and gave him one of her thankful, motherly smiles.

Seth grabbed his beer and took a sip. He was angry at himself for not thinking about his mom and the shop. His heart was leading his days now it seemed, which could lead to all kinds of trouble if he wasn't careful.

John took a deep breath and pushed his plate in a little to give himself some room to rest his arms. Seth looked over to the man's empty plate and then to his face. He saw a mix of determination and sadness in John's look and demeanor. Seth knew they were about to find out the reason for his visit.

Looking over to Trudy, John smiled. "Thank you so much for having me over at the last minute. I really appreciate it."

Seth's mom returned John's smile with one of her own, which held way too much hidden meaning for Seth's comfort level—the motherly smile had quickly disappeared. He decided to listen to John while still eating in hopes of lowering the strange tension in the room. The man had only been out with his mom for dinner and Seth found himself suddenly concerned their relationship was going to go to a new level at lightning speed.

"I have a confession to make," John said.

Seth glanced over to his mom whose face seemed to fall a bit. She obviously wasn't sure what his confession was going to be about, and a flash of fear crossed her face. Seth grimaced inside.

"You invited me to your church, Trudy, and I went today." His head dropped some as his eyes went to his plate in front of him.

Seth and his mother quickly exchanged a look of confusion as to where John's comments were going to take them in his confession. Thankfully, his mom's face seemed to perk up a tad--apparently her fear had nothing to do with him going to church.

"I know your faith is a major part of your life, and I can see it in the way you live." His comments were directed toward his mother, but his eyes included Seth when he raised them for an instant. He lowered them again and took a deep breath. Whatever John wanted to talk about weighed heavily on his mind. "Thank you so much for inviting me to come." He raised his head and looked at Trudy. "I am ashamed to admit that I went today without telling you so that I could see what it was all about. I planned to sneak out and not tell you I had gone until I was sure what I thought about it all."

Seth sat back and took another quick glance towards his mother. She had a soft smile of understanding on her face. Seth would not have expected any less. He wasn't sure why the man would hide his going to church, but he was glad John had taken the time to come and investigate. Maybe their conversation at the coffee shop had more impact than Seth had originally thought.

"I understand, John. It's fine you went without telling me. It doesn't upset me at all. It's new to you and probably a lot to take in."

"I saw you all sitting up front. I was in the last row. It was," the man paused as if searching for the right word, "different than I had expected."

"Good different?"

"Yes."

Seth joined in the conversation. "Had you ever been to church before?"

"Over 20 years ago while in Boot Camp. I never paid attention there."

Seth nodded, "It was an escape."

John smiled at the young man's understanding. "It was. By the time I left today; however, I was very excited to talk to you both and even ask questions. On the way out I ran into Patrick from the grocery store. He's been going to that church since he was little. He said he mentors you, Seth."

"Yeah. I met him just after coming to Vegas. We meet once a week usually. He's been a great help."

"Do you talk about the Bible?"

"We do. We also talk about how to live like Christ in this world." Seth took another sip of his beer and didn't want to overwhelm him. He was thrilled John was asking questions though. He could only imagine the glee his mother was holding in and took a quick look-- she was glowing!

~

"How did it go today?" Paige's grandmother asked over video chat.

"It was a great day, Gram, and I have good news." Paige leaned back and pulled her feet onto the chair. Hugging her legs, she settled in for a long conversation. "My mom was arrested yesterday and is in the local jail."

Paige waited for what she said to sink in.

"Wow, I didn't expect that."

She knew Gram was worried. Although Paige didn't remember anything of her mother, or the events that happened when she was a baby, her grandmother never forgot. The pain and difficulty during that time was always fresh, it seemed. Yet she rarely wanted to speak of it. "I guess that is good news."

"Think of the timing, Gram. Mom hasn't been seen or heard from in years and she is arrested within the first week I am in Vegas. How can that be anything other than God's awesomeness at work?"

Throughout the day, Paige found her emotional roller coaster wouldn't let up and continued to surprise her. She bounced from shock, to fear, to dread, and then excitement.

"That's true. It's remarkable," conceded her grandmother. "I am very thankful for God's hand in all this. I just worry you are going to get hurt, sweetie."

"I know, Gram, but wouldn't it be hypocritical to trust God through all that has led me to this moment, but not trust him in what's going to happen in the future?"

Her grandmother smiled. "You're right and don't forget that in the days ahead. So, what is your plan?"

"I'm going to the jail tomorrow. Aunt Marie sent the address and visitation hours to me. Seth is going to drive me down after work."

"You told him then about why you're in town?"

Paige looked down at her toes sheepishly. "No, not yet."

"Have you seen him lately?"

"Yes, we went bowling last night, church this morning, and then shooting this afternoon after lunch." Paige patiently waited for what she knew was coming.

"Shooting? What does that mean? What did you shoot? Not a gun?" Her grandmother almost yelled as she adjusted her own laptop in some attempt to get a better picture of Paige, as if it would answer her questions faster.

Paige laughed at her grandmother's sudden change of tone and demeanor. "So, you're not worried I am spending lots of time with a 22-year-old guy that you don't know, but you are very worried I might have shot a gun?"

"Well, when you put it that way it may seem strange, but you don't know how to shoot a gun. Do you?"

"I do now. At least a little bit. Seth was super patient and walked me through it all. We went to a local range and were only there about a half an hour."

Her grandmother leaned back. "Girl, you're going to give me a heart attack."

"Let go and let God work it out, Gram. Isn't that what you always told me?"

"Yes, but I'm not quite ready to let go," she stated quietly.

"I'm doing fine, and I promise I won't let all your teaching go to waste. God's got me surrounded by some great people here, too."

"There's another answered prayer. Be safe tomorrow and send me a quick text about how it went, O.K.?"

"I will. Love you!"

"Love you too, hon. Bye." Paige waved as she hit the red button to end the call. She laughed a little at her grandmother's worries and couldn't believe she didn't get a hundred questions about Seth.

After he dropped her off earlier in the day, she got on her email and found all the information from her aunt. Paige put the address in her phone and visited the jail's website to see her mom's name on the inmate list for herself. It all seemed like a dream.

Thinking back to the last moments with Seth, she wasn't sure exactly what she was thinking in asking him take her to the jail. The more time she spent with him, the more she wanted to tell him. Yet, as soon as she was on her own and thought about it, the doubts seemed to pile up.

Let go and give it to Me.

She knew she had to trust God to work it out. She just wasn't sure she could tell the difference between God's leading and her own flesh trying to control it all.

After her research and planning earlier in the evening, she showered. Looking down at the pile of clothes in the bathroom, she realized she would need to find a way to do laundry soon. There were probably a hundred different things she hadn't thought through yet this week.

She made a sandwich for dinner and read on the couch before calling her grandmother. With all that done, it was not even ten yet. She felt depleted and ready for bed. She dozed off somewhere in between the stream of repetitive thoughts and concerns about Seth, her mom, and what would happen the following day.

Chapter 21

arah watched Paige cross the street to the café. The young girl seemed so alive; smiling and a skip in her step. What a change from the shy, uncertain girl she was last week.

Juggling her books from one arm to the other and moving her small purse farther up on her shoulder, she opened the door.

"Morning, Paige. How was your weekend?"

It didn't seem possible, but Paige's face brightened even more. "It was wonderful."

Sarah tried to suppress her assuming grin, but it didn't work. "A certain young man by the name of Seth wouldn't have anything to do with that, would it?"

Paige stopped moving and her eyes got huge, revealing more of the crystal blueness of them, while her cheeks turned a soft red. Her mouth dropped open a bit, but no words came out.

Sarah's laughter bubbled up. "No need to say anything. Your response said it all."

Paige shuffled forward and her face relaxed leaving an embarrassed yet grateful grin. "Seth and I did hang out a couple times." She placed her books on the counter. "It was really nice."

"That's wonderful," Sarah said. "He's a great guy."

"Yeah, I've never met anyone like him." Paige's look of joy increased. "He took me shooting yesterday." The girl's delight was infectious and Sarah found her somewhat dreary, morning mood fading away.

"Wow. I've never gone shooting. Was it fun?"

"Very. I was so nervous, but he was super patient and taught me a lot."

"I'll have to go sometime." Sarah thought it might be a nice change to her routine as of late. The eagerness of wanting to start a family and then being devastated every month was putting strain on her once joyful and problem-free marriage. "What can I get you?"

"I'll have a bagel with butter and cream cheese, please. Can I also get a white chocolate latté?"

"Sure. I'll bring it all out to you."

"Thanks."

Sarah saw Paige put some cash in the box. She tried not to focus on the customers when they were paying for their items. It seemed to put undue stress on them, and Sarah had found they didn't feel comfortable getting change. She wanted the experience of a donation-based café to be pleasant and not stressful. Most folks put more than she expected--often matching the high prices of the big coffee chains. Or maybe they really wanted to give more. Sarah rarely worried about it either way. The café was helped by the church each month and for that she was very grateful. Many small groups met there and the church also recommended the location to new members.

Sarah's desire to own a coffee shop had started in college. She spent many early mornings and late evenings studying for exams at a local café. The low hum of patrons coming in and out gave her just the right amount of sound to study and not get distracted. She realized how much life happened around coffee shops, and how almost all of those shops had no other purpose than providing coffee and some food.

It was the realization of a coffee shop's potential to be life changing that led her to finish her degree, ironically in business, and start working her non-profit coffee shop dream. The process had been long and difficult, but well worth the effort. Her coffee shop had now been open almost two years and more folks were coming in all the time to do more than just drink coffee.

Although the desire had been there for years, it was Tim who had made the dream come true. He had been an employee at one of the businesses Sarah had worked for right out of college. She needed to save money, so she was only there for a paycheck. Her heart wasn't into the job, but she did her best and God blessed her. She met her future husband.

Tim had embraced her passion and zeal and helped launch the shop with his savings. It had been his wedding gift to her.

Now the two of them waited and prayed to be a family of three.

~

Trudy watched her son get out of his car and look first to the apartment door and then over to the café. He was so taken with Paige and it made her heart glow. But with about four years between them, she knew that any romantic relationship they started would have its struggles.

Paige was so young and barely out of high school. Beyond the reason she was in Vegas, she didn't seem to have any plans for her future. The girl seemed lost, yet fully where she knew she needed to be at the moment.

Trudy saw great changes in her son over the years; even before coming to know Jesus as his Lord and Savior. He had matured exponentially while in the Navy, and he seemed ready to settle down. He rarely dated since moving to Vegas. His time was focused on helping her with the shop and helping his new church family. Of course, settling down would be hard if he didn't plan to spend time with any girls he met.

Trudy made it a point to try and not talk to him about such subjects. She had learned long ago that if you want your son to talk to you, then you ask very few questions and wait for him to speak. She made herself busy counting receipts and looking over reports while she waited for him to come in.

"Morning, Mom," he said before the bell stopped ringing over the door. "You remembered to lock the door. Well done."

Trudy loved the little-boy grin that was still a part of him when he praised her for doing a simple task. "Yes, dear. You're old, withering mother remembered to lock a door. Wonder of wonders." She shot him her most sarcastic face and then a smile. Seth rolled his eyes and laughed.

She came around the counter. "Sweetie, I know I've been a little scatter-brained these past few weeks, but I think I'm coming back to my senses."

"You were not that bad, Mom, and opening up a new shop is a big deal."

"Well, today is the start of our first full week. I am excited to see how it goes. I pulled the sales reports you showed me, but I need to start balancing the accounts. Can you remind me how to access the merchant account?"

"Sure. Do you want a coffee first? I can run over and get one for you?"

"Thanks, hon, but I brought coffee with me. How about you show me how to bring up that account, and I will start working on it while you go get some for yourself?"

Trudy saw the brief moment of disappointment when she declined his "coffee-run." How many glimpses of her little boy was she going to see today? His face had the same look when, in middle school, he would run into the store for her and try and buy a pack of gum with the change that was left. He always thought he was getting away with something, but they both knew the other was not fooled. Yet neither said anything, even as she had held out her hand waiting patiently for a piece of gum to drop into it before she put the car into drive. It had become a personal joke between them as the years went by.

She looked over at him and raised her eyebrows and gave a motherly smirk. He smiled. Maybe he was remembering those moments in the car all those years ago like she was right now.

"Thanks, Mom." He came over and walked her through the steps to bring up the account. He did it a little too fast for her liking, but she was not going to slow him down.

He was out the door almost instantly when it came up, but no one could tell what a rush he was in by how casually he walked across the parking lot. But she knew, and it warmed her heart.

~

Lisa went to her favorite sub shop for lunch and took her laptop with her. She almost never did work during lunch, but she couldn't get Alexandra Hanson out of her head. She rarely had such a desire to follow up with a case. She knew limited research would be done to contact the family once a prisoner was admitted to the mental health unit. However, she could update the arrest record with the best possible contact information that would likely increase the odds of the hospital contacting the family.

With Facebook, the ability to find family was extraordinarily easy. In fact, most people put too much information on the site and unknowingly put themselves in danger.

Lisa ordered her usual meatball sub and took a seat. The shop was filled with people from the courthouse. judges, clerks, and family. Yet it never failed, police officers were always looked at with dread in any restaurant when in uniform.

She glanced up to check her surroundings and saw people peeking over at her every once in a while. If she could read their thoughts, Lisa figured many wondered if they were doing something illegal as they sat there eating their subs. Some looks gave off fear that she might know what they did last night—or this morning.

It had taken a couple of years to get used to the change that overcame people when they saw her in uniform or discovered that she was law enforcement. Among her family and friends, she answered countless "what if" questions about the law, and ignored most of the requests made about the outrageous people who recently came through booking.

Thankfully, she learned to leave most of it at work and not rehash every detail of her day when at home or in social circles. In the beginning, telling stories came naturally and willingly after a long day. People had no idea what was going on in the dark alleys, remote buildings, or sidewalks outside the classy hotels. However, she felt sharing was slowly becoming her identity among people she knew, like it was satisfying some Reality TV fix in their lives.

At the end of the night, she felt drained and dirty.

Over time, Lisa learned to start directing conversations before they could focus on her life. She found ways to be interested in other people's lives to a level that never existed before just to avoid talking about her day.

In the beginning, it felt like she was deceiving people into sharing more details than they wanted to share or she wanted to hear. Surprisingly, asking questions and listening turned out to elevate her relationships to a new and unexpected level. She began to enjoy listening to the little details of her friends' and family's daily lives, jobs, and dreams.

It took three minutes on Facebook to find Alexandra's family. She was mentioned on numerous public posts, mostly by her sister, which drew awareness and support for homeless shelters--especially those in Vegas. The girl in the pictures and the girl that was now incarcerated were obviously the same person, but the streets and drugs had taken quite a toll on the young woman.

After a few more internet searches, she had her sister's name, city, state, and a phone number to add to the report. The family, many of whom had come up in the search, obviously had no idea if Alex, as they called her, was alive. Hopefully they would know soon.

Chapter 22

Seth was impressed that Paige was able to get through work all morning before they left to go downtown. She seemed to be a bundle of excitement, nervousness, and anticipation--like a kid with a firecracker!

He had no idea why she wanted to go downtown and the secrecy of it all had his stomach in knots a bit. Having her next to him and finally alone didn't help either.

She worked hard when the store opened to do anything his mother had needed done. She greeted every customer that walked in and began making fat quarter packages of amazing design and color combinations. She seemed a natural in the store, unlike him fumbling like a fool when it came to organizing fabric.

He had put together a few combinations of his own after watching Paige go at it so easily the first few times. Like a proud kindergartener, Seth brought her the combinations only to see her press her lips tight in a great effort not to laugh.

He smiled to himself as he thought about how she had tried to show encouragement in his first attempt. She had grabbed it like a mother takes a child's painting--applauding his effort while trying hard to decipher how the blob on the paper was supposed to be a majestic animal of some sort.

Patiently, she gave him some pointers on coordinating colors and patterns. He finally admitted that any quilt made with his fabrics would not be suited for a wall or a bed. He laughed at himself, and she joined in.

Those moments with her were intoxicating.

Finally, alone with her in his car, he was taking this girl he barely knew to some unknown place downtown and all he knew was that he couldn't take his gun. Were they going to a Post Office? A church? The list of places he couldn't take his gun poured forth easily. A court house? A jail? A school?

But Seth knew the gun laws. He knew that his vehicle was considered "a castle" in the concealed carry laws. Therefore; his vehicle was his home away from home and, as such, he was allowed to always have it with him. He had locked it in the glove box for this trip, just in case.

"Are you hungry? We could stop for a late lunch?" Paige looked over at him with a questioning look, as if the thought of food never occurred to her. She bit her lower lip.

"We don't have to stop now," he quickly added, as he laid his hand on her arm. "I can wait."

She had her hands on her lap and she'd wrung them endlessly since getting into the car. Her nervousness was starting to elevate his own anxiety. It took every effort to not ask what was going on. He wanted to trust her. He felt like she needed him to trust her.

"No. You're right. I need to eat something. But do you mind if we wait an hour or so? I don't think I would be great company right now."

"Sure." He hesitated before asking his next question. He had to at least know where exactly they were going. "What exit do I get off at?"

"We're going a few blocks from Fremont Street. Do you know how to get there?"

He groaned inside. Fremont Street was definitely not a place he wanted to go without his gun. Some Navy buddies told him to check out the place once he moved to Vegas. He quickly realized that he had very little in common with them if they enjoyed such places. You couldn't go 20 feet without seeing someone practically naked or someone else so drunk they couldn't stand--and that had been during the day and slow season.

"Yeah, I think I remember."

She grabbed her purse from the floor. "I'm usually on the bus, so I don't pay a ton of attention to the exits. I have maps though if we need them." She pulled out a couple, looked over a few, and put them back.

Seth picked up his phone in the console and handed it to her. "We can just use the GPS on my phone if we need to."

She let her head drop back and laughed. She looked over at him with a smile. "I have my phone, too. That's probably the better way to go." She bit her lip again, this time in amusement at herself. "Using maps is just a habit. I've had them for so many years now. They were always paper treasures to me."

Seth had another irregular piece to her puzzle. She was again lost in her own world as she looked out the window. He had no doubt that Paige believed that paper maps being little treasures was just a common thing everyone felt or said.

"I have to ask," he said, drawing her out of her thoughts. "How did old, paper Vegas maps become treasures to you?"

~

Is this the moment, God?

She felt so comfortable around Seth. Thoughts and memories she had hidden for years seemed to flow from her when near him. Or was it just the anxiety that she might see her mom for the first time in over seventeen years that left her without self-control?

Paige thought about the first map of Vegas she ever received. "When I was eleven, my Aunt Marie sent me a birthday gift. Inside was a map of Vegas. She'd visited Vegas that year and had used the map to get around."

Paige reached down and took one of the maps from her bag. She'd received multiple maps since that first one from her Aunt. Even though it was over seven years old, Paige took it with her whenever she went into the city to look for her mom.

"My Aunt Marie had been to the city a number of times before she used this map. Those trips had been for work and visiting her sister. But when she came and used this map, it was not for visiting family. It was for finding family."

Paige opened the map, and felt the sting of tears in her eyes. The emotional surge of sharing this precious part of her life with someone outside of her immediate family was mixed with relief and apprehension. *Will he think I am crazy too, Lord?*

She looked over and saw Seth glancing at her with a small smile of compassion and patient interest. Being side by side in the car helped take the pressure off of looking at him directly as she poured out the intimate details of her family and her purpose for being in the city. She was thankful she had waited for this moment.

"Each mark has a meaning. There are stars, circles, and triangles. The stars are places that my mom and Aunt visited together." She pointed to a star on the Strip. "This is Paris. They loved to go to a French restaurant there called Mon Ami Gabi. They both loved all things French, and they would practice speaking with the staff while enjoying croissants and crepes. My Grandpa was there once with them, also."

She felt a tear drop on to the map. She quickly brushed it off. She knew she was taking her story via the most indirect path and nothing was making sense yet. She had not planned how she was going to share the hope and pain. Perhaps God had a purpose in the confusing direction she was taking her explanation.

"This star is inside the Venetian hotel. My Aunt went there a lot for business. They both loved sushi and went to a place called Sushi Samba. My mom was a Navy Veteran." Paige saw Seth's head quickly turn to her. She smiled at his reaction. "She was stationed in

Okinawa for a while and had learned to love Japanese food. My aunt was also in the Navy."

"Both of them?"

She laughed at his shocked look.

"My aunt didn't go overseas though. I'm ashamed to admit that I don't know what my aunt did for a job in the service. I think her job was more administrative. My mom, however, worked on airplanes. I don't know a lot about her job either. My aunt says she has all of my mom's military paperwork, if I ever want to go through it. What I do know is that she didn't like her job."

Paige suddenly was aware that Seth may be hurt that she didn't share her family's Navy history with him since he was fresh out of the service. She knew it would have led to questions that she was not ready to answer. She pushed the fear of his hurt down, and went on.

"The triangles are the places my aunt looked for her sister after she went missing." Paige pointed to one big star near Fremont Street. "This star is the last place my mom and aunt talked, if it can be called that. My aunt said it was one of the scariest moments in her life." She looked up and out the passenger window. Breathing deeply, as if she could gather courage from the air God gave her at that moment, she said the sentence that had been longing to come out all week. "My mom is mentally ill and homeless here in Vegas somewhere." Paige let out what was left of the air in her lungs and looked over at Seth. Tears still streaming down her face, she watched his features sympathetically morph from surprise to empathy. She sucked in another breath quickly, this one of overwhelming gratitude, as she looked back down at the map.

She suddenly felt his hand take hers and the soft squeeze felt like pure bliss in the midst of uncertain chaos. "I am so sorry, Paige. I can't imagine how hard that is to live and to tell."

She squeezed his hand in thanks, unable to bring forth any other words through the knot of emotions.

"What do the circles mean?" he asked. She reluctantly let go of his hand, which he then put back on the wheel, and grabbed the map again.

"The circles are where I have looked for her."

Paige felt the car shift and looked up to find them on the exit for downtown. She grabbed her phone and copied the address she had written on the edge of map into her Maps app.

Chapter 23

Seth followed the GPS prompts and was relieved their destination was more than a few blocks from Fremont. They were in the business and government district. If they were going into a courthouse, then Paige was right that he couldn't have his gun. They were not allowed in any government buildings, even if carried by a concealed handgun permit holder.

He found a spot in a nearby lot and turned the car off. He was still processing what she had said about her mom. Never would he have guessed that she was looking for a family member in the city—a homeless one, too. He could not imagine the emotional heartache she had endured in her life.

"So, is this where you are going to look for your mom next? Can I help?" She looked over at him with so much fear. She was breathing more rapidly and looked like she didn't know what to say next.

"When we were at church, I got a phone call. Do you remember?"

"Of course. You seemed to go through a lot of emotions, but I think you ended with happy."

"It was from my Aunt. She continues to look for my mom every year. It's been many years since she saw her sister. I was less than a year old the last time I saw her myself. Most in the family believed she was dead and labeled a Jane Doe by authorities. Yet this past Saturday night, to the shock of everyone, my mom was arrested at the Strip."

Seth held back all the questions popping into his head and listened to her. She was looking down at the maps again, and the tears were rolling off the end of her nose. He reached into his glove compartment and pulled out a few napkins.

"Thank you." He noticed she wiped off the map first and then her tears. "My Aunt Marie looks at inmate lists every day here in Vegas to try and see if Mom is there. And now, after all these years, she's been arrested. And here I am in Vegas at the same time. God's amazing, isn't he?"

Seth felt his own throat close up with emotion. "He is."

"So, I am hoping to see her today. My Aunt has warned me that my mom won't recognize me and may have forgotten she has a daughter who is no longer a baby. Mom is psychotic, and I guess there was a lot of emotional trauma after I was born that has caused her to think I am still the same age as when she saw me last."

"We're going to the jail?" Seth watched her nod. "I'll be there with you, Paige." He grabbed her hand again. "God has given you this moment. I am sure He has great plans in store for you on this journey. They may not be the plans you have imagined, but He will work it all out for good. You love Him."

"I'm glad you're here, Seth." She took a deep breath and knew it was calming her. "But would you mind waiting for me outside? I'd like to go in alone. I don't want my mom to be distracted at all. Once, my aunt came to see my mom here in Vegas years ago. Mom had an apartment then, right down this street in fact." She picked up the map and pointed to a triangle. "My aunt had to do a lot of work to get into the apartment complex. Security was tight. The apartment manager told my aunt that my mom had caused a lot of trouble with the residents and would probably be evicted soon.

"When my aunt knocked on the door, my mom answered. I guess she looked horrible. Frail. Thin. Aunt Marie had a book with her which had a cross on the spine. She didn't bring it for my mom though, it was just a book my aunt was reading while on the bus." Paige looked over at him. "My mom has always hated any mention of

God or Jesus. Before my aunt could even get out a hello, my mom saw the cross and flew into a fit of rage--thinking my aunt was part of some local church. It was like my mom didn't even recognize her own sister.

"Mom slammed the door in her face. My aunt kept knocking and calling my mom's name and telling her she was there to visit, all while reminding her that it was her sister. Aunt Marie was sure her own sister was going to hit her when the door flew open again."

Seth watched Paige nervously fidget with the map as she told the story. "But my mom came out abruptly and started walking down the hallway. My aunt followed and my mom started asking the weirdest questions about what had brought her there. Questions about money for a church and if my aunt was a nun or something.

"My aunt started talking to my mom about home, their parents, and family news—anything to try and draw my mom into reality. But the more she talked, the angrier my mom got. What my aunt discovered though was that anger brought her sister closer to herself than anything else. Mom remembered the family, but didn't seem to care. She didn't care who had died. She didn't care about her own history.

"Her rage got worse as they walked down the road. My mom started yelling and telling my aunt to never come back. That is when my aunt feared her sister was going to get violent.

"My aunt cried and let her sister walk away. She followed Mom for a while. At one point, my mom did come back, but only to yell at her again. Nothing my aunt said got through. Mom walked away one more time and made sure my aunt didn't follow. My mom was super paranoid, even of her own family."

Paige put the map in her bag and looked over to him. "That was the last time my aunt saw her sister. So, any distraction could set her off."

Seth took it all in. He felt a sudden gratitude for his own family. He missed his dad terribly, but he was grateful that the times he did have with him were positive. Seth couldn't imagine not growing up with his parents.

~

As they walked toward the detention center, the nervousness of seeing her mother was periodically shattered by the comfort and understanding Seth had shown her as she poured out her family history. She was, at that moment, glad she had waited to tell him. Their relationship and respect for one another had grown exponentially over the past days, and he had not disappointed her in the most difficult and treasured moments of her past. Excitement and gratitude for the future with him now weaved endlessly within her, along with the apprehension of visiting her mother.

They paid the parking toll and made their way to the front of the building. She stopped at the last bench before the entrance. She felt her heart beating faster throughout her chest, arms, and temples. All the "what ifs" started pounding along with the acceleration of her pulse. *What if she hates me? What if she doesn't remember me at all? What if she spits on me and calls me a liar?*

What if she does?

She felt God's voice in her spirit. A still, small voice.

Won't I still be with you? My grace is sufficient, Paige.

She took another deep breath. She felt her heartbeat slow down for a few seconds and then speed back up, but not as fast as before.

"I'll be right here," Seth whispered over to her, drawing her attention to him. His small smile, filled with empathy and courage, seemed to hear and feel all the fear in her.

"Thank you." She took his hand and squeezed it as she looked back at the doors. She took a few steps, and felt her heart speed up again.

She would not let fear win.

She saw the guards inside, one sitting at a booth and one by the scanning machine. As she entered, she felt all their eyes lock on her.

"Empty your pockets, please." The guard nearest to the machine handed her a bowl to put her items in. She grabbed her phone and dropped it in. "Walk through. Info desk is there." He pointed to a lady sitting behind an encased office of plexiglass with a small hole at the center.

Paige moved, as if in a dream, to the window. The middle-aged woman, hunched over and occupied with reading a novel of some sort, seemed highly irritated with the incoming interruption as she saw Paige approach. "Can I help you?"

"Yes." Paige was too short for the small, circular window and went up on her toes. "I would like to see my mother. She was arrested recently and is on the inmate list."

The woman turned to the computer to her left. "Inmate's name?"

"Alexandra Hanson." Paige watched her input her mom's name. Paige looked down at what she was wearing to meet her mother for the first time in years: jeans and a light, plain green t-shirt. She had no cross on, but wore a simple silver chain necklace with an oval jade stone.

"Your name?"

"Paige McKinnon. I'm her daughter."

A quick look of sadness crossed the woman's face. She turned her chair toward Paige and crossed her arms. "You're not on the list of people allowed to see this inmate."

Paige felt her breath catch. "No. Probably not, but I am her daughter."

"I understand, but each inmate gives a list of people they give authorize for visitation."

"She wouldn't put me down. She is mentally ill, and hasn't seen me in over seventeen years!" Paige felt the sting of new tears, and her heart raced again.

"I'm sorry, dear, but those are the rules. I can't let you in."

Paige looked around. *Lord? What do I do?* She saw the police guards looking toward her and paying more attention than they did before. They heard the exchange from their positions. Did they think she was going to flip out? She felt like flipping out. A rush of anger and hopelessness seemed to grip her. She was paralyzed.

"There's nothing I can do. You will need to leave," the lady said, drawing Paige out of her state of shock.

"Can you tell me if there is anyone on the list?"

"The woman looked over quickly at her computer. Another sad expression momentarily passed over her face. "I can't give you that information."

"I understand. There probably isn't."

Who would her mother add? After all these years, which person was at the forefront of her mother's list of friends and relatives? Did she even remember any of them?

Dejected, and with tears streaming, Paige turned toward the exit. Leaving the building, she walked with her head down in a complete daze. She looked up, remembering Seth was there. As soon as their eyes made contact, it was like the dam of everything she felt broke. She ran to him, needing his support more than anything at that moment. He moved quickly forward; he knew exactly what she needed when she stepped into that courtyard.

She fell into his arms.

Paige was lost in the unbelievable pain of disappointment. She sobbed against his shoulder, and he stroked her hair. She didn't want to be anywhere else. His arms gave her a strength and comfort she didn't expect she would need that day.

"Shh...it's alright. What happened?"

"I...couldn't...see...not...list." She tried to get the words out, but she choked on her tears and couldn't get her breath.

He hugged her harder for a moment and then turned them toward the bench. "Here. Sit down. I don't understand what you're saying. Take a deep breath." He sat her on the bench and grabbed her hand as he took the seat next to her.

Paige hiccuped and then took a few deep breaths. She rested her head on his shoulder and took a couple more breaths. She felt herself regroup and calm down. Seth seemed to feel it, too. He wiped the tears off her face.

"You weren't even in there five minutes? Was she released?"

Paige took a deeper breath. "She's there, but they won't let me see her. Each inmate gives a list of authorized visitors, and I'm not on it."

"Oh." He reached up and stroked her hair. He held her head on his shoulder and rocked her gently." I am so sorry, Paige."

"There's no one on the list. The lady didn't tell me, but I could tell by her look. She is all alone in there and no one can visit her. After all these years..." She started crying again, and Seth held her a little tighter.

"Maybe there is a way somehow. We can look into it, Paige. We'll find a way."

She gulped and breathed in and out again until she could speak. "Maybe God doesn't want me to find her. Maybe this was all a waste of time."

"Don't give up. You've come this far."

"It feels impossible."

"I know, but God can do the impossible right?" He raised her chin and smiled at her. "I'll help you. Don't give up."

She searched his eyes and saw only compassion. She looked down at his lips. She was so close to him, and wanted so much to kiss him. He must have sensed her thoughts. He put his head down slowly and kissed her tenderly. It was the most precious first kiss Paige could ever imagine. Far too quickly, like the scent from a deep inhale of the first spring flower, it was over. He lifted his head and smiled at her.

"Come on. Let's get you home. We'll figure out the next step later." He gently took her hands and urged her up. He took one hand in his own, gave it a squeeze, and didn't let it go as he turned them toward the parking garage.

~

Lisa saw the young couple on the bench as she approached. The front of the detention center was not a usual spot for young couples to sit. After searching on Facebook and the Internet for Alex's family while at lunch, she needed fresh air and went past the officer entrance on the other side of the building.

It was the girl's blond hair that had Lisa mesmerized as she got closer. She had seen pictures of a girl with blonde hair in photos of the Hanson family less than ten minutes before. Lisa found herself hoping it was her, knowing the odds were slim.

Lisa could see the girl's shoulders' shudder and the young man wiping tears from her cheeks. She kept walking toward them, even more certain that this was the girl in the pictures. Perhaps it was the sister's daughter.

Suddenly, the two kissed and Lisa felt her feet slow down naturally. The couple was obviously having some type of moment and a cop showing up at such a time would be unnecessary and awkward for the two. She let her gaze roll over to the detention center doors and then down the street. Lisa knew the couple didn't know she was there or that she was looking at them, but it was a small way to give some privacy.

Glancing back to them, she saw them get up. "Excuse me," she said, as she approached. "Are you here to see Alexandra Hanson?" Lisa was shocked at her own boldness.

The two turned to her and then to each other. The blond, who couldn't be older than nineteen and a little shorter than Lisa's five-foot six height, had puffy, red eyes and blushing cheeks. "Yes, I'm her daughter."

Daughter. The pictures and posts Lisa had seen started to make sense. Alexandra had had dirty-blonde hair in some of the pictures. It had never occurred to her that the woman who seemed to occupy Lisa's mind non-stop lately was a mom. It seemed to energize Lisa's quest even more.

The two, now holding hands, exchanged glances again with small, hopeful smiles. "I'm Sergeant Kennedy. I handled your mother's booking when she came in the other night."

The young girl took a step toward her. "How is she? They won't let me see her since I am not on her visitor list."

Lisa knew the procedures. Even family couldn't come in without being on a list supplied by the inmate. Privacy and security rules sometimes were ironically so tight that help couldn't get in when it was needed most.

"I'm sorry. I can't do anything about that." Hope drained from the girl's face as she looked toward the ground. The young man seemed to squeeze her hand and she raised her head to look at him. Lisa went on, knowing her words would hurt more. "She did not look well when she came in." The young girl looked back at Lisa with an immense sadness. Lisa felt her own emotions starting to stir. "What's your name?"

"Paige McKinnon."

"I'm sorry, Paige. I wish I could help you see her. At booking, I did recommend she go through a mental health screening, and, if that happens, they will move her to the hospital downtown. You can see her there; they don't have the same rules as here."

"How do I find out if they move her?"

Lisa pulled out her small, spiral notebook and pen from her front shirt pocket. Give me your cell phone number, and I will call you when I get the news. I will also update you if there is any further information I can give you that will help.

"Thank you so much. That would be awesome. I can't believe it." The girl looked up to the man, who was smiling, and gave him a quick kiss on the cheek before giving Lisa her number.

"You're welcome. I'll be in touch." Lisa turned to walk back the way she came.

"Wait!" Paige said, "How did you know I was here to see her?"

Lisa looked back. "I saw your picture on Facebook when I searched for her relatives."

"Do you always help inmates find their families?" the young man asked.

"Never."

Chapter 24

S eth and Paige pulled into the parking lot of the shopping center. They had talked all the way back about the amazing turn of events following the disappointing news.

Seth saw that Paige's car was now back and a rush of sadness went through him. "Looks like John has your car fixed and ready to go."

Paige looked up, and Seth could tell she was emotionally spent. A flash of new sadness crossed her features. He was not seeing this from her perspective. She was probably scared to stay there. Seth reached over and took her hand.

"John also installed cameras and signs at each entrance, which should help deter any more problems."

Glancing toward him, he watched her bite her lower lip again. "That was so nice of him. But honestly, I wish he would have taken a couple more days." She looked toward her car again. "I've liked our time together."

Seth squeezed her hand. "Me, too. In fact, it wouldn't matter if you had three cars. I'd still like to spend time with you every day."

Her smile, despite her exhaustion, lit up her face. "That sounds good to me."

"But right now, I think you could use a nap. You've had an emotionally taxing day. I could pick you up for dinner, if you'd like."

"I think a nap sounds like a great idea, and dinner, too. I'll need to contact my aunt and gram before I lie down; both are probably freaking out that I have not texted or called them today."

Seth parked in front of her door and turned off the car. "How about 6:30? We never did stop for lunch."

Paige glanced at the time on her phone. "That works. I don't think I could've eaten anyway. Do you have any other plans this afternoon?"

"I'm going to stay here for a bit and let mom know we're back. If she ran into any problems over the last couple hours, I'll try and fix them, and maybe teach her something new about reports."

"She's blessed to have you."

Seth, now knowing the secret Paige had been protecting over the last week, nodded with even greater appreciation. "No, I'm blessed to have her." He pulled the key out of the ignition and looked over to Paige one more time. "May I tell my mom about today? Do you prefer to keep the reason you are here to yourself still? I completely understand if you don't want me to say anything."

Grabbing her maps from the side pocket of the car, she gently put them back in her bag. She leaned forward, hugging her bag as if it would give her courage in the next decision she was about to make. "You can tell her. I'm not going to keep it a secret any longer. She's sweet and everyone has been so nice to me: John, Sarah, and you, of course. I'm amazed at the people I've met here."

"They all like you."

He watched her lower lip tuck in behind her teeth again as she looked over at the quilt shop.

"I know."

~

John and Trudy sat on the terrace of the restaurant watching the evening sky multiply in colors as the sun made its way behind the Spring Mountains. Their meal finished, they drank red wine and listened to the smooth music of a jazz band, helping to put the sun to bed for the night.

The white lights, pinwheeled from the center of the deck above them, added a new layer of joy to the glowing twilight of the evening.

Trudy felt like pinching herself. She felt as if she was on the outside looking in as she sat there with John. Not in a million years did she think she would be at a fancy restaurant on a Monday evening with anyone. She took a deep breath and closed her eyes to memorize the moment and take it all in.

She knew she wasn't too old to experience such an emotional and romantic adventure, but she had assumed it would never happen after Bruce's death. She had committed herself to being on her own for the rest of her life and planned to fully enjoy it. God, it would seem, had other ideas.

"Thank you so much for taking me here, John. It is beautiful."

"You're welcome. I thought you might enjoy it, but I must admit, it is even better than I imagined it would be. I've never been here in the evening. I came for lunch once and the view was perfect; all the casinos hidden behind us and nothing but the Spring Mountains ahead. The owners do a great job of bringing it up a notch on the classy scale for the late-night dinner crowd."

"Yes, in fact I am starting to think I am underdressed for such a marvelous evening." Trudy straightened her long, ecru colored linen skirt over her folded legs. She had spent too much time thinking about what she was going to wear and ended up choosing the solid, knee length skirt, a simple white blouse, and brown sandals.

"Nonsense. If anyone is underdressed it is me. I should not have worn jeans."

"I disagree. You have a sport coat on and it looks very distinguished."

Trudy watched him blush as he straightened his dark brown jacket over his tan button-down shirt. She thought him the most handsome man on the terrace by far. Although he was fifty, just as she was, he had an air of being so much younger. Trudy was sure she had far more wrinkles than he did. She guessed they most likely had similar amounts of gray hair, but his looked distinguished and hers were covered with dye every couple of months.

Trudy picked up her wine and carefully took a sip. Ordering red wine with her white shirt was probably not the best idea. She was so nervous her clumsy, nervous hands would get the best of her. Setting it down, she leaned back and clasped her hands on her lap.

"What did you do when you got out of the Air Force?"

"Surprisingly...nothing. I had no plans at all. I just knew it was time for me to get out. I had some offers for civilian jobs, but I turned them down. I saved enough over the years to take a few years off."

"How did you end up in Vegas?"

"My last duty station was right down the road at Nellis Air Force Base. I spent my last three years of service here in Vegas. I had a nice, simple house I was renting, and I loved the temperature and surrounding area. A couple of years ago the shopping center came up for sale and I saw potential in the area, so I started a little realty company and bought it. I also bought the little house I was renting from the previous owners."

"Did you have experience being a landlord before that?"

John laughed softly. "Not at all. I'd rented from others all my life when I lived off base. What I did know is how the good landlords I'd had handled issues when they came up. I wanted to break the stereotype of horrible landlords and be an asset to the community until I figured out where the next step in my life journey would take me."

He picked up his glass and took a sip of his wine. He smiled over at her. Trudy reciprocated, but felt a flash of concern.

"Are you planning to leave Vegas soon then?" She tried to hide the surge of disappointment in her voice.

He leaned forward and quickly put his glass on the table. "No, no. That was how I felt then. Actually, it is how I felt all my life until recently. I've been waiting to move to the next duty station every few years since I was eighteen. It's hard to settle down. I didn't know how to do it."

He moved his wine glass and brought his hands to the middle of the table. "Give me your hands, Trudy."

His soft voice seemed to pull her body towards the table and her hands to his of their own accord.

"Knowing you has given me feelings I've not had in many years. I have new hope and a greater determination to make Vegas my permanent home more than at any other time over the past six years I've lived here. In the back of my mind, I always assumed I would sell the properties and go to a new location to do it all over again. It seems so silly to say and hear out loud. Why keep moving when the military is not forcing you to do it? I never let myself think about it— but I think it is fear. I don't know how to make a place my permanent home. What if I choose wrongly?"

"That doesn't sound silly at all. It is quite understandable."

"Maybe." He grew quiet and watched his thumbs softly stroke the back of her hands. "I don't have that fear now. If I do, it has been eclipsed by you being in my life."

She smiled. "You're a poet, John."

He laughed. "I imagine one surprisingly good line does not make one a poet."

Trudy was mesmerized by him. He was still looking at their hands. She wondered if he was feeling the same rush of emotion that started running through her when he first took her hands. He finally looked up and they squeezed each other's hands. She loved his honesty.

"I have some fears, too. You're not alone."

"I can imagine you do, Trudy. It is hard to lose a loving spouse. You are always welcome to share those fears. I believe that God can help us with them."

She took a deep breath of unexpected possibilities.

"Yes, He can."

~

Seth pulled out his phone from his back pocket. "Hello, Patrick."

"Hey, Seth, is this too late to talk?"

"Nope. I'm just heading into my apartment. Anything up?"

"Not really. I was leaving work tonight and saw a guy who looked a lot like you kissing a blonde on the boardwalk of the shopping center." Seth could almost hear Patrick's smile. "You wouldn't know anything about that, would you?"

Seth sat down on the steps of his townhouse and laid his arms across his knees, feeling like a kid who got caught stealing a cookie from his grandma's kitchen.

"Hmm...that's interesting."

"Seems like things have escalated a bit since we saw each other on Friday night."

"It has, but I'm not sure that is a good thing."

"Want to talk about it?"

Seth wondered what his biggest concern was when it came to "unofficially" dating Paige. He had been pressing down his trepidations as soon as they popped up throughout the week, but he was ready to be honest about it now—out loud.

"It's been an amazing week with her, Patrick. She opened up to why she's here in Vegas and she's the type of girl I am looking for in a relationship. She's level-headed, funny, smart..."

"Being beautiful is just icing on the cake, right?" Patrick joked.

"She *is* gorgeous."

"What's the problem then?"

"She's only eighteen and just out of high school."

"Does she like you?"

Seth leaned his back onto the upper steps and stretched out. "Yes, she definitely likes me, too."

"Well, then you probably can't fault her for being the age she is right now. That's not within her control."

Seth laughed. "I know that."

"Is it illegal to date her?"

"No, of course not."

"Is she a Christ-follower?"

"Very much."

"Then you don't need to worry about it anymore on your end. You need to ask her if the age difference is a problem. Why does it really bother you?"

Seth took a deep breath. "I think I'm more fearful of what other people might think. Yet, I know three and a half years between us is not that big of a deal. I think I might also be concerned that I would somehow hold her back in life."

"That's ridiculous, Seth. I'm sure you would be supportive of her desires, and since you know she is a Christian, you can be confident that she would be doing what God has led her to do—whatever that may be. You can still be together through all that. It will be hard work that will require patience, but there is a lot of potential for God to do amazing things through you guys. I think you are focusing too much on this."

"I know you're right," Seth said sitting up and running his fingers through his hair in frustration.

"I'm surprised you didn't mention that she isn't old enough to drink."

Seth smiled. "Besides it being a given, it would be pretty shallow of me to let a great girl go because she can't have a beer."

"Finally, something we agree on." Patrick laughed and Seth couldn't help but join in.

"Thanks, Patrick."

"No problem. Keep in touch, alright? I'll talk to you again on Thursday."

"Sounds good. Night."

"Night."

Seth stayed on the steps a few more minutes soaking up Patrick's advice. It was foolish to hold Paige's age against her if she didn't care either.

After a wonderful dinner with her, and seeing her refreshed and excited about the potential of Sergeant Kennedy's help, he knew it would be a good time to ask how she felt about their age difference. He just hoped she wouldn't hold his age against him either.

Chapter 25

P aige was ready the next morning at 8:30 to help Trudy prepare to open the shop. Seth had not arrived yet and Paige was pleased to have some time with Trudy alone.

"How is it going with John?"

Paige watched Trudy smile as she arranged a new shipment of patterns onto the carousel.

"Better than I ever expected it would, that is for sure. We had dinner at a wonderful place last night. Oh, Paige, it was so romantic. It didn't feel real most of the night."

"That's wonderful, Trudy, I'm so happy for you."

"Thanks, sweetie. I have to admit that I think our relationship went to a new level. We connected, and he held my hand so tenderly. I feel like a teenager again."

Although Paige knew she should feel awkward talking to Seth's mother about dating, it also felt very right. "I know what you mean."

Trudy, now kneeling on the other side of the rack, peeked around to catch Paige's eye. "I am very excited for you and Seth. I am also happy he is helping you during this difficult time. He told me about your mom and what happened yesterday. I am so sorry, hon."

Paige was putting fabrics together at the cutting table. She expected one of them to bring up what happened at the jail and why she was in Vegas at some point in the day. Paige had decided not to be the one to do it.

"Thank you, Trudy. I'm not sure how it would've gone had he not been with me. I also don't think we would have run into Sgt Kennedy." Paige kept it to herself that the delay of crying, and then kissing her son, allowed the encounter to happen at the perfect time.

The other kisses that evening, enjoyed only twenty feet from where Trudy was working at the moment, were also left unsaid. The memory of them; however, made her want to tell someone. Paige smiled at the thought of two women, ages apart, wanting to jump up and down like little schoolgirls. It was hilarious.

"When he told me about the officer, I just couldn't believe it. We forget how much God is working behind the scenes of everything. We are truly powerless without Him."

"It is definitely something I will never forget, even if it doesn't result in seeing my mom."

"I'm very glad we met that night outside the shop, Paige. Please let me know if there is anything I can do to help you find or see your mom. I can't imagine what you are going through. You're very brave to come down here and look for her all alone. Don't forget that although you came here alone, you've now got a handful of people who are with you on this journey and will help in any way they can."

"Thank you, Trudy. I definitely don't feel alone here."

"Good." Trudy glanced at her watch. "We have five minutes until we open. Let's pray, alright?"

"Sure." Paige put down the fabrics and came over to Trudy. She stood up and grabbed Paige's hands.

"Father, help us to have a great day here at the shop and please move in a mighty way to help Paige see her mom. In Jesus' name, Amen."

Trudy let go of her hands and pulled Paige into a big hug. Paige felt her tears come closer to the surface. She didn't want to lose it so early in the morning and before customers—and Seth— came in. She squeezed Trudy back and let go. "Thanks."

"You're welcome, dear. Let's turn on the sign and unlock the doors."

~

Seth had not run for months. He was slowly getting out of shape with no one forcing him to do mandatory Command runs. He didn't miss it, and hadn't thought about running until that morning. He woke with so much energy—energy he had to burn off before going to the shop. He had texted his mom and Paige to let them know he wouldn't be in until lunch.

He was grateful he was not scheduled to play at this Wednesday's worship service. He knew he was too distracted to learn the new songs.

Patrick's phone call had given him the push he needed to have the serious conversation Paige and him needed to have about their ages. Yet, with all that was going on in her life, he felt selfish to even consider bringing it up.

After a three-mile run, in an embarrassingly slow time, he showered and then made his way to the shop. He prayed non-stop for wisdom and clarity. He didn't want to screw up this opportunity with Paige, but he also didn't want to assume God's plans. Ironically, despite desperately needing God's discernment on the situation, he had skipped his usual Bible study at the coffee shop. He didn't need any caffeine and he couldn't sit still.

When he opened the shop door, he saw Paige off to the side of the room on her phone. The news was obviously good and she motioned for him to come over.

"Wonderful. Thank you so much. We will be down later today." She paused, listening and whispering to him that it was Sgt Kennedy.

"Sounds good. Bye."

She hit END and threw herself into his arms, surprising him. He hugged her back and laughed. "Well, that is a nice hello, but I am guessing you have good news you are celebrating."

She pulled herself back but kept her arms wrapped around his neck.

239

"That was Sgt. Kennedy. Mom was evaluated earlier this morning by a psychiatrist that works for the police department. He, or she, agreed that my mom is a good fit for the Legal 2000 program. It's a program that guidelines who can be committed and how it is done when someone who seems mentally unstable is arrested. They did a physical exam at the jail and declared her healthy, physically anyway, to go to a treatment center. It's a 72 hour hold and then there is another evaluation. Sgt. Kennedy gave me the number and website address. She says I could probably see her this evening."

"That's great, Paige." Seth pulled her in and hugged her again, lifting her feet off the floor.

Once they were back on the floor, Seth saw his mom coming over. "That is wonderful news, Paige. I am so happy for you."

"Thanks, Trudy. It all feels so unreal." Paige put her hand to her head. "I can't believe that after more than 16 years, I am going to meet my mother."

"You are going to have one amazing testimony when all this is done," Trudy said. Seth smiled. His mother always could see the positive in almost any situation.

Seth looked around the shop. "We don't have any customers right now. Why don't you use the computer, Paige, to get all the details on the hospital, and we'll go straight over whenever you want to leave. Mom, can you call in some backup?"

"Sure. Judy is always free now that she is retired from teaching and she loves hanging out in the shop."

"Great." Seth looked over to Paige. "Does that sound good?" She had a strange, quirky grin on her face. "What's that face for?"

"I love that you knew I would want you to come."

"Oh." Seth inwardly cringed. "I should have asked you first though. I'm sorry."

"Don't be." She walked over, planted a kiss on his cheek, and made her way to the computer.

Seth caught his mom's knowing, joyful eyes, and Seth rolled his own while trying to suppress his smile.

~

Marie, having received the text from Paige that Alex was committed, was still in a state of shock.

This new wave of good news was already making its way through the family and all were hopeful. She contemplated getting on the next airplane to Vegas, but she wasn't sure if a trip to see Alex would cause more harm than good. If she did go out to see her, Marie knew that it would have to be toward the end of the 72-hour hold—when the medicine for Alex's psychosis was in her system. That would be the time, if at all, that Alex would mostly likely be approachable.

Deciding that she couldn't wait for a status update from Paige, Marie dialed the number to the hospital. Paige had sent all the details she had, including Sgt Kennedy's name. She needed to find a way to thank the woman.

She dialed the number and prayed she would get some more information. "Mental Health Unit. May I help you?"

"Yes. I believe my sister has been admitted to your department, and I was hoping to get an update on how she is doing."

After being redirected two more times, Marie hoped she would eventually get someone who could help.

"This is Linda. I understand you are looking for information on a family member?"

Marie took a deep breath to calm her voice. "Yes, on my sister, Alexandra Hanson."

"Ms. Hanson was brought in this morning. I am the head nurse for the department she is staying in right now. We handle those who have been arrested and then brought in. Are you Marie?"

"Yes!" Marie couldn't believe the nurse knew her name. "How did you know that? Has Alex talked about me?"

"No, I'm sorry, I don't think she has while being here. I got your name from the next of kin information sheet. Looks like your name was either on her when she was arrested, or added later by an officer or physician during the evaluation. She may have mentioned you then."

Marie realized that must have been some of the information Sgt Kennedy had discovered when searching online.

"How is she?"

"First, I need to verify some information for security purposes." After relaying details on Alex's form, Marie heard the nurse take a deep breath herself.

"Ma'am, your sister has been on the streets for a long time, correct?"

"Yes."

"Although she is not in any obvious physical pain, she has not seen a doctor or even taken a shower in weeks, maybe more. She was quite dirty, and even basic feminine needs were not being taken care of while on the streets. I doubt she has gone to a shelter for more than a meal in over a month."

Marie felt her stomach clench with sadness.

"Is she a Veteran, Ma'am?"

"She is."

"They may transfer her to the VA hospital, but at this time I am not recommending any transfer until she is cleaned up and has a chance to see a doctor for further evaluation."

"Thank you so much. She has been admitted before, many years ago, and had a good response to medicine within days—she just never wanted to stay on it."

"I understand. We will take care of her the best we can."

"Her daughter is in Vegas now and will be coming to see her soon. Is it possible to put her name on a list or something so that she will be allowed to visit?"

"We don't have approved visitor lists, but I can add her information as a local contact."

Marie gave the nurse Paige's information and hung up.

It was clear, despite Alex's hate for Him, God was still looking out for her. How many opportunities would she get? Will she ever respond to them? Only God knew. He wouldn't give up on her and Marie knew she couldn't either.

Chapter 26

Paige and Seth entered the mental health wing of the hospital and asked to see Alexandra Hanson.

Paige's legs bounced up and down while she sat straight up and at the edge of her seat in the waiting area. "I am so nervous."

Seth placed his hand on her leg and gave it a soft squeeze.

"I know. You're doing great though, considering all that is going on and how big this moment is for you."

She was so thankful he was there with her. She had rehearsed this moment over and over again in her mind since she was little. She had pictured their meeting in hundreds of ways: on the street, in a coffee shop, at the book store, at a shelter, in a jail, at a hospital, or in a morgue.

Her heart was racing, her hands sweating, and her stomach growling. She couldn't eat anything all day, despite Seth and Trudy's urging.

"I am so glad Marie sent me a text to remind me that Mom's medication won't kick in for days. It has given me a little reality check, but I still have this fantasy meeting in my head."

"I would imagine that is normal for anyone who has never talked to their parent."

"Paige McKinnon?"

"That's me." Paige stood and took a few steps. She looked back at Seth. "You're coming, right?"

"You sure you want me too? You told me she can flip out very easily, and I didn't want to be the cause of any issues."

"Honestly, I don't care if she does. I need the support."

Seth got up and grabbed her hand, following the nurse to a small room down the hall.

Paige entered the room behind the nurse. It was a double occupancy room and the nurse went to the center and pushed the curtain separating the patients to the side.

"Alexandra? You have some visitors."

The nurse stood aside and let Paige by.

In a chair, next to a barred window, was a skinny woman with dark circles under her eyes and a scarred face from apparent skin problems. She had on a blue hospital nightshirt with a pair of blue, loose pants. Her hair, uneven and shoulder length, was still wet from a shower. She was slouched back in the chair and had her arms crossed. She stared at the TV in the corner.

"Hi Alex, I'm Paige."

Her mom didn't even look at her. Paige looked over at Seth, who gave her hand another squeeze. Paige prayed she would say the right thing.

"We came to see how you were doing and if you needed anything?"

"You can get us out of here."

Paige's heart raced uncontrollably.

"Where would you like to go?"

Her mother looked over at her for the first time. Paige held her breath, waiting to see if her mom recognized herself in Paige's own blond hair and blue eyes.

"Wherever we want. Why do you want to know? Who are you?"

"Your family sent me. I am a friend of theirs."

"Really? Did you bring our stuff?"

"What stuff?"

"All the stuff they took from us. Our computer, furniture, and clothes."

"I didn't bring anything, but I could ask them."

"You'd probably just take it yourself. Get out."

"Would you like me to give your sister or your daughter a message?"

Alex stood up so fast that Paige took a step back and Seth took one in front of her. He put his hand up to stop Alex from going any closer.

"What do you know about our daughter? Who are you?" She knocked Seth's hand down and Paige saw her mother's own hands clenched in fists.

"I'm your daughter. I'm Paige."

The wait for her mother's response to the words she dreamed of saying her whole life felt endless. Then her response came.

Her mom laughed.

Paige's heart broke.

~

"Remember what your aunt said, the medicine hasn't had time to kick in yet. Let's come back tomorrow and try again."

As the tears continued to stream down her face, Paige nodded her head.

Seth put his arm around her shoulders and squeezed as they headed to the parking lot. Her mother just laughed, loud and obnoxiously, at Paige's declaration. Neither one of them expected what happened next either. As if a flip had been switched, she started yelling. She called Paige a liar and a spy. The whole interaction had been the most bizarre thing he had ever seen.

Paige texted her family and let each of them know how her mom had looked and acted. She had just finished when they arrived back at the plaza.

"I'm going to go lie down. Thanks for taking me, Seth."

"You're welcome. I'll walk you up."

Seth waited for Paige to unlock the doors and followed her into the apartment. She mindlessly threw her keys on the table. She was depressed and emotionally spent.

Seth led her into the bedroom. He laid her down, removed her shoes, and covered her up.

"I'll be downstairs for a while. Come down or call me when you are up and around. We'll figure something out for dinner, if you want."

"Sounds good. Thanks again."

He bent down and kissed her forehead. He wanted to hold her until she fell asleep, but he knew that wasn't a good idea. He made his way back to the store.

His mother was waiting for him at the register. "By the looks of her when she got out of the car, I'm guessing it did not go well."

"She got to see her mom, at least. But, no, it did not go well. Her mother laughed at her and then screamed and accused Paige of all kinds of weird things. It was awful."

"Poor girl. Is she resting?"

"Yeah."

"What will she do now?"

"She'll go back tomorrow and try again. Apparently, when her mom had been committed years and years ago, she responded well to medication and was lucid within the few days she was there. It was just enough sanity to convince the panel that she was fine, and so they let her go. She didn't stay on the medication though and just relapsed back into her paranoia."

"See if she wants to come over for dinner tonight at the house. She shouldn't be alone."

"Will do."

Seth went to computer and checked the sales. He tried to concentrate on cost of goods sold, but his mind couldn't get the crazy laughing out of his head. He had suppressed the urge to shake the woman and tell her to listen. He probably would have broken something; she was beyond frail. Seventeen years on the streets had taken their toll. Seth was glad Paige had seen her after she had been cleaned up. He couldn't imagine how she looked, or even smelled, prior to getting to the hospital. He didn't understand why she wasn't cleaned up after being arrested.

Seth found himself hoping that whatever panel decided the fate of those in the mental ward, they would not be fooled after a couple days of treatment.

~

Paige looked around at the stones and shrubs in Trudy's back yard as the sun went down over the mountains. The stars were starting to come out as they rocked on the free-standing swing in the middle of the rock garden. It was a narrow but long backyard with a surrounding wood fence.

"Your mom has a cute house and nice backyard."

"She does. Judy helped her find this place. Mom bought it without even seeing it first."

Paige couldn't imagine having such a close friend that you would trust them to find a home for you. Her friends from high school were great, but Paige always had trouble connecting with people her own age. She spent most of her time alone, with family, or with her small group at church.

"Did she also sign the lease for the store before she moved here?"

"No. She found the plaza when driving around and learning the area."

Paige glanced over at him. He had his head leaning back on the swing, a beer in his left hand perched on the arm rest, and his other hand clasped with one of her own. He seemed so calm and content, despite the whirlwind of crazy she had brought into his life.

"Has this stuff with my mom freaked you out at all?" The question seemed to blurt out before she even thought about it.

He rolled his head over toward her. "Not at all. Did you expect it to?"

"Yeah, of course. That's why I waited to tell you."

"I doubt it would have changed anything even if you told me that morning when I met you in the café."

"I don't know about that."

"I do." He winked and rolled his head back to watch the red glow of the evening sky.

"You do look pretty relaxed with it all."

They heard Trudy cleaning up the dinner dishes and singing though the kitchen screen door.

"What is she singing?" Paige glanced back, trying to look through the mesh of the swing, if Trudy was dancing too.

"She loves Abba songs. She's listening to the 'Mama Mia' soundtrack."

"I've never heard of Abba, but I do remember a 'Mama Mia' movie years ago. My gram watched it."

"Abba is pretty good. I grew up listening to all kinds of musicals. She's always been a Broadway fan."

Paige turned back around and leaned her head back as well.

"I do have something on my mind, Paige."

She swallowed and felt fear rise up in her. "Really? What is it?"

He lifted his head and looked down at their entwined hands. "We probably should talk about us and what we are thinking about each other."

She hadn't expected him to bring up their time together, but she knew it had to be talked about sooner or later.

"Sure." She waited to see if he was going to start first.

"Paige, I did the dating and bar scene when I was in the Navy, and I never want to do it again. I'm waiting for the person that I'm meant to spend the rest of my life with. I have felt like this for months, but you are just out of high school. I'm sure you are not interested in a serious relationship at eighteen. I should have thought of all this before I let myself..." He hesitated. Paige had a feeling he was going to tell her he was in love with her. He took a deep breath and started again. "I am willing to back off and leave you alone, if you want.

Besides the obvious difference in our ages, we probably have different goals, too."

"Besides looking for a wife, what other goals do you have?" She had a hundred things she wanted to say, but he had never mentioned any goals before that she could remember.

"Right now, my goal is to do whatever it is God asks of me. So far, the only things He has led me to do are get out of the Navy, move to Vegas, and be here for my mom."

She brought her leg up onto the swing so she could turn toward him. "Of course, I didn't expect to meet someone while I was here looking for my mother. It's been amazing to get to know you and share this difficult time with someone." Letting go of his hand, she grabbed her ankle and pulled it close to her body so she could lean in closer to him.

"You're a great guy, Seth. It's sweet of you to worry that I might be missing an important part of my youth if I don't venture out into the dating world. That world, I hear, can be really dangerous."

"That's definitely true."

"What's funny is that I've never even thought about going out and meeting a bunch of guys and trying them on like they were gloves. I am far more interested in the people God brings into my life."

"What about our ages? College?"

"There are less than four years between us and there is no money to send me to college. I think you need to ask yourself what *you* think about our ages."

"We can't help being the ages we are, right? I guess it would be silly to punish ourselves for something out of our control."

"Plus, God knew what ages we would be when we met."

"Very true." He reached for her hand on her ankle and brought it toward his chest. "You're pretty smart, you know that?"

Laughing, she leaned forward. "Of course, I do."

They kissed softly and cuddled up side by side to enjoy the view.

Chapter 27

Two Months Later

eth couldn't believe how late he was getting to the church. Forgetting the rings, he'd headed back to his apartment when he should have been getting ready in the back room of the church.

He opened the back door next to the band's practice room and made his way to the pre-service lounge where the groom was required to hide himself while waiting for the marriage coordinator to give the signal that the bride was ready.

Kelly, the chosen coordinator for the big event, rushed in.

"Oh, thank God, you're back. She's ready and everyone is seated."

"Kelly, I was only gone ten minutes."

"We were all worried you would drive too fast and get into some tragic accident, creating horrible memories for the bride-to-be."

"Glad to hear no one is freaking out in the bride's lounge," he said dryly.

"Very funny." Kelly walked over and straightened the green button mum pinned to his tuxedo. "Alright men, you're up!"

Seth watched her exit the door she had come in while he opened and exited through the door to the sanctuary.

John, in his full-dress Air Force uniform, and Patrick, in a sleek tuxedo, was with him.

They took their places at the front.

"Ready?" Patrick asked the husband-to-be.

"Definitely."

The three men lifted their eyes as the music changed. Down the aisle came Sarah in a floor length, emerald green grown. She winked at her husband in the chair to her right as she walked the aisle holding a white and yellow bouquet of flowers.

The planning of the wedding had gone so fast with all of the help from friends and family. Many joked, tongue in cheek, that it had to be a shotgun wedding.

When Sarah took her place, Seth saw Paige begin her walk down the aisle. She was so beautiful with her blond hair pinned back and white roses in her hands. Her dress, elegant and simple, was also floor length. It was Paige's turn to give a smile and Seth matched it wholeheartedly. As she neared the front, the music changed once more and everyone stood.

Seth forced himself to take his eyes off Paige and watch his mother, the gorgeous bride, make her way to the altar. Seth elbowed John, and he gave Seth a knowing and shy smile.

Trudy tried to smile at everyone, but always turned her eyes back to John before acknowledging more of her family and friends along the aisle.

Paige and Seth's eyes met and they couldn't help but grin. Paige had helped Trudy so much over the past two months to prepare for this day. John had proposed only a few weeks after they started dating, and Trudy accepted upon hearing that Seth was alright with the decision.

Days before the proposal, John had caught him at the coffee shop and had asked for his mother's hand in marriage. After the initial shock, Seth quickly gave his blessing. He had come to respect and admire the older gentleman.

Trudy wore a simple white V-neck dress with sleeves that went just passed her elbows. The fabric, a matte white silk, swept over to her left hip where it bunched into fabric-roses before trailing down to the floor.

She carried a beautiful bouquet of yellow roses, green mums, and white lilies. Her shoulder length brown hair was curled and pulled up with a clasp holding a small spray of baby's breath.

John took his bride-to-be's hand as she approached and they faced the pastor. Each beamed at the other and the guests took their seats.

John had accepted Christ as his Lord and Savior just two weeks after his first date with Trudy. She had been the one to teach him how to take that step of faith, and the man truly was a new creation.

Seth had been honored when John came to him and asked him if he would be his spiritual mentor. However, Seth felt the Lord's prompting and told him that Patrick would be a better fit. In hindsight, Seth understood why God had put that on his heart; mentoring your step-father would probably be a very awkward situation for them both.

~

Paige held Seth's hand as they made their way out of the sanctuary toward the reception hall.

She watched Trudy and John walking in front of them, arms linked, and whispering about something. They were an absolutely adorable couple.

Paige was over the shock of Trudy asking her to stand up with her, but only barely. Paige knew it was probably more for Seth's benefit than any deep personal connection, yet the two of them had developed a wonderful relationship. Trudy treated her like a daughter and Paige loved the woman's motherly tenderness.

She had hugged Paige and whispered words of encouragement after the second day Paige visited her mother at the hospital. The reaction had been the same; no change in her mental state.

After the third visit, Paige fell into despair and cried all evening in her apartment. Her mother had been calmer and more approachable.

It was amazing to see how just three days of medication could help someone so much. The food and care also left its evidence—her cheeks had color and the skin around her eyes didn't seem so dark.

Despite the mental and physical improvement, the paranoia and fear hovered below the surface of the calm.

"Hi, Mom. How do you feel today?" It was the first time Paige chose to call her mom and not Alex, hoping it would stimulate a memory.

Her mother turned from looking out the window in the patient lounge. She was sitting in a chair wearing the dark blue pajama set that all the patients wore. She picked at her finger nails, chipped but now clean, when there was nothing else to do. She still was not able to relax.

"My name's Alex. Get it right." Paige cringed at her response, not even letting the change in her third person point of view bring a little hope.

The hearing for her 72-hour hold would be in an hour, and Paige was authorized to attend. Her mother was improving, but there was so much brain damage. Aunt Marie had warned Paige that the court would only be concerned if she was a threat to herself or others. Sergeant Kennedy had kept Paige up to date on the legal side of things. Her mother would not go back to jail, essentially serving her time at the hospital. She would be released and required to return for her court hearing for the arrest taking place the next month. Paige knew her mother would not be well enough to go, and her mom's absence would put another arrest warrant out for her, essentially starting the entire process over again.

"Your court hearing is in an hour. Would you like to talk about it?"

Clearly not remembering Paige's visit yesterday, Alex turned to her with a look of confusion. "Who sent you? What do you want?"

"I'm your daughter, Paige, remember? Your sister, Marie, helped me find you."

Alex's fury rose. *"My sister is always interfering. I don't need her."*

The anger with her family seemed to block out any of the words Paige said about being her daughter. she pushed down her own anger and took a deep breath.

"Mom, I met this really nice guy. He's not with me today, but he came yesterday. His name is Seth. Do you remember me bringing him?"

Her mother rolled her eyes and looked away. Paige took a seat and looked out the window too. She prayed and occasionally glanced over at her mom who was talking to herself softly.

Paige waited and waited for her mom to say something. She never did. Paige asked a few more questions and had some one-sided conversations before a nurse came to take them to the court hearing.

It went exactly like Aunt Marie predicted. Mom answered their questions calmly.

"Are you ready to leave, Ms. Hanson? Do you feel well?" asked the older man at the large desk. The court room was a simple office for the hospital.

"I feel great."

Paige couldn't believe the simple changes in her demeanor. It was almost like her mother knew she had to trick the man. Paige thought the judge would get a more honest reaction if he came to the lounge and took off his white coat.

"You have been on medication for three days now, do you feel it is helping?"

"Sure, but I don't need it."

"It may seem that way, but you have greatly improved since being here. You need to stay on the medication if you want to try and get off the street and continue to get well."

"Doctor, how would she get the medication?" Paige interjected.

"I will give her a prescription. She is a Veteran, so I am referring her over to the VA Hospital for follow up and for the refills. She will get some to take with her today when she leaves."

"You're letting her leave?" Paige couldn't help but raise her voice.

"I can no longer keep her here, Ms. McKinnon. She is well enough to leave."

"But she doesn't remember me. I am her daughter and she doesn't believe me. She is sick."

"It is out of my hands. I can only keep her if there is no evidence of improvement since admittance. The VA will take care of her."

"She won't go unless someone makes her go!" The sting of tears bit at her eyes as Paige looked pleadingly at the judge.

"I understand your frustration. I'm sorry." He turned to Alex. "You will be released today at five. Will you be taking her, Ms. McKinnon?"

Paige nodded.

"Your daughter has offered to take you where you need to go—I recommend the women's shelter."

Paige knew her mother would not go with her, and Seth highly recommended Paige not give her a ride without him. He felt it would be too dangerous, and she knew he was right. She regretted having said yes to taking her, but how could she say no? Her mom had no one. Paige knew she would need to follow through with the plan Trudy and Seth had helped her create once the hearing was over, if her mother allowed it.

"Do either of you have any more to say at this hearing?"

"No." Alex immediately said. She picked at her nails as if the meeting was of least importance.

Paige stared at her and was amazed at the stupidity of the entire situation. She looked at the judge. "You're making a big mistake."

He sighed. "You may be right, but there is no other decision I can make at this time."

"She won't go to the VA. She won't refill her medication. She never has in the past."

"I know. Again, I'm sorry. Don't give up hope."

An hour later, Paige and her mother walked out of the mental hospital. Alex, back in her clothes which were now washed, put the strap of her black purse over her head and onto her shoulder. It was evident that the bag had not been cleaned. Once out the door of the hospital, she began rummaging through it, oblivious of her daughter standing next to her.

"Would you like me to take you to the shelter?"

Alex gave her an irritated look and continued looking in her bag. "I've got to get back to the casino."

Paige opened her purse and pulled out the map and ticket Seth had purchased for her that morning.

"Here is a three-day bus pass."

Looking up, Alex grabbed the pass instantly. "Why do you have my bus pass?" Paige took a deep breath and prayed for patience.

"Here is a map, Mom. It has all the places you have been with Aunt Marie marked plus other areas of the city you like to go. There are a lot of symbols on it, but this one here," Paige pointed to the star, "is where I live. You can come and see me if you want. And my phone number is on the back." She forced her tears back down. "I've had this map a long time. I hope it helps you."

Her mom looked her in the eye for a few seconds. The longest she had done in the last three days. A flutter of hope joined Paige's racing heartbeat.

"I don't need a map. I know this city by heart." Alex grabbed the map. "I do like to write on things. I will take it for paper." She stuffed it in her bag and walked away.

Paige watched her mother leave and sadness consumed her. She wanted to yell and scream at her, but she knew it would do no good.

"Thinking about your mom?" Seth pulled her out of her thoughts with a soft squeeze of his arm around her waist.

"Yeah. I just keep replaying it over and over again, wondering what I could have done differently."

"I know. Don't forget about all the opportunities you'll have to try and help her again, now that you've decided to stay here."

"You're right and this is a celebration, so I won't dwell on it anymore today."

"You can think about it and talk about it as much as you want. It doesn't bother me, and I know it won't bother my mom." He kissed Paige's forehead. "She's way too occupied anyway to notice." They both looked at the older couple still whispering and laughing ahead of them.

Paige decided to concentrate on the newlyweds for the rest of the day. "They are so cute."

"They make a good couple. It's strange to think I have a step-father now."

"He's going to be a very good one."

"I think he will make a good father-in-law, too."

"Was that a proposal, Mr. Seth Redding?"

"Nope. It's just a reminder of the good things to come. We agreed we would wait four months before making any future plans to give God time to guide us in the right direction, and I intend to live up to that agreement." He leaned over and put his lips near her ear. "I just didn't realize it would be this hard when we agreed to it." He kissed her on the cheek and held her a little closer.

"We have two months to go. I'm sure it will fly by." Paige tried to strengthen her own resolve with her words, but she too felt like the four months were going to take forever—especially when Seth's kisses accentuated his words of kindness and understanding.

"It will be an adventure for sure. I doubt; however, it will fly by. And have I told you lately what a horrible liar you are?"

They laughed and entered the reception hall. Seth took her hand as they lined up past the newlyweds to greet the guests making their way to the celebration.

Epilogue

Paige continued to work part time for Trudy and live, rent free, in the upstairs apartment. Trudy refused to accept any money and encouraged her to volunteer at the local women's shelter to help her lookout for her mother.

Sergeant Kennedy connected Paige to the Clark County Family Court Self-Help Center where she was able to petition for her mother's commitment to the inpatient mental health facility when she was picked up on the street again.

She never gave up hope that her mother would get better, even after multiple involuntary commitments over the next few years. The times in the hospital would clean her up for a few days, and then the entire cycle would start again. The nurses at the mental unit would call her when Alex arrived and Paige would visit, always praying her mother would remember her.

Occasionally, Alex would mention her baby daughter and how she was taken away from her, but she always spoke as if it was just months earlier. Time stood still for Alex—another reminder of the heartbreaking reality of what drugs can do to the mind. At times, she would look at Paige as if she was seeing her baby girl. Paige embraced those moments as blessings.

She continued to trust in God's love and sovereignty, even after she was called to the coroner's office to identify her mother's body.

Alex was found dead in the underground tunnels approximately four years after Paige arrived in Vegas. A small memorial service with military honors was held for Alexandra Hanson and her ashes were buried at the Southern Nevada Veterans Memorial Cemetery.

Seth opened up his own gun shop, thanks to the help and guidance of his friend in Virginia and the super-low rent for the empty suite in the plaza offered by his step-father. Paige helped him with paperwork and the two became a great business team.

Almost five months after meeting, Seth and Paige announced their engagement. They were married exactly one year after that first awkward, and most memorable, conversation in the café. On June 21st, 2017, all the family came together to celebrate their union. Aunt Marie became good friends with Trudy and stayed with her and John when she visited a couple times a year. Sergeant Kennedy also came and Marie was able to personally thank her for all the help years earlier.

John's faith grew and he embraced Seth and Paige as a son and daughter. He paid for Paige to attend night school, and the tradition of Sunday dinners every other week continued for years.

Paige formed a ministry for the homeless at Creek Community Church in honor of her mother. The church provided lunch three days a week and developed a program to help families looking for their homeless relatives in the Las Vegas area.

God fulfilled Paige's dream of meeting her mother and provided her a complete family in His own amazing way. He gave her a new father and mother in Trudy and John, a best-friend to be her husband, and a network of sisters and brothers in Christ at her new church home.

When Seth moved into the upstairs apartment after the wedding to save money for their own future home, Paige started a new box of treasures. She filled it with small, meaningful items that created the collage of a new and beautiful season in her life—a season when Paige saw the ordinary of everyday living as the extraordinary threads of God's purposeful tapestry.

Threads of Pain

Tangled in threads of pain.
Confused and torn by unseen ropes of hurt and hate.
With one voice ill and access removed,
And one gone, never heard again.

Loved much and purpose still alive.
The ending unknown, the past seems compromised.
Stories filled with half-truths and delusions.
Ultimate peace comes from the Son.

The present seems lost in questions of why,
But even Jesus arrived in dirt and grime.
The future is seen only by Him who knows
Why the present must be for His plans to unfold.

Loved much and purpose still alive.
The ending unknown, the past seems compromised.
Stories filled with half-truths and delusions.
Ultimate peace comes from the Son.

So, hold on, let His work be done.
Don't lose hope, He is still the One
Who covers, Who seals,
Who heals His little one.

Tangled in threads of pain.
Confused and torn by unseen ropes of hurt and hate.

--Artist: Timberlake Dawn, Album: *All of Me*

Other Books by Lilly Horigan

Dear Anxious Christian: You're not Less if you Need Something More

Lilly shares her anxiety journey, what she has learned over the past twenty years as a Christian with an anxiety disorder, and practical steps for dealing with it.

Chapters Include:
- Is My Anxiety a Disorder
- Circumstantial Anxiety
- God Knows and Cares
- Self-Reflection
- Daily Living
- Have a Talk with Yourself
- Accepting the Less Than Perfect Days
- Relationships

Your Mommy Was Little Too

Children can rarely imagine their parents as kids. "Your Mommy Was Little Too" is a Christian children's book that shares how Mommy played and dreamed, and how God made her dreams come true with her precious little one. Lilly has filled this book with her own thread art and reminds the reader that God is the great Creator. Everyone is a part of God's great work of art. Also included in the book: learning activities, Bible verses, and encouragement for parents.

Does Everything Happen for a Reason, God?: A Study on Suffering from God's Word and Seasoned Believers in Christ

Are you looking for direction when it comes to understanding suffering? Maybe you wonder why bad things happen to good people. Or perhaps you want to understand why you have personally suffered.

The good news is God wants us to understand suffering. He welcomes us to ask the question, *Does Everything Happen for a Reason, God?*

In this book, Lilly shares:
- Why there is suffering
- The benefits of suffering
- How to profit from suffering

Journey through God's Word and the insight of seasoned believers in Christ to discover the truth about suffering.

Shimmering One: A Short Story

Background for the writing of this short story: Many years ago, I went to Richmond to pick up my wandering, lost, and mentally-ill sister. My short story, *Shimmering One*, is a fictional recount of how we miraculously found her. Or maybe it isn't fictional at all…

When eleven year old Emily walks down her street, she passes by a woman who is always sitting on her porch--day after day. The summer passes, yet the porch lady remains. Until, one day, she doesn't. The missing woman is a mystery that will only be solved with time and the help of one of God's wondrous creations.

If you enjoyed watching *Touched by an Angel* and *Highway to Heaven*, but always wanted Jesus' name mentioned, you will enjoy this story.

Acknowledgements

I would like to thank God for the idea, ability, and time to put this story, which is non-fiction for many hurting families, into a tangible product that will help others in whatever way He desires.

I am thankful to my earthly father for encouraging me to write and to never give up—even if an idea takes years to complete.

I am grateful for my dear friends at my local Celebrate Recovery group (www.CelebrateRecovery.com) for reading my book and giving me their feedback.

I appreciate my husband and boys being patient with me throughout all my projects.

In Christ,

Lilly Horigan

Connect

Email: info@LillyHorigan.com

Website: LillyHorigan.com

Facebook: fb.me/LillyHorigan

Twitter: twitter.com/LillyHorigan

Mail: Lilly Books
           PO Box 223
           Bolivar, OH 44612

About the Author

Lilly lives with her husband and teenage boys in Bolivar, Ohio.
She is originally from Horseheads, NY.

Made in the USA
Middletown, DE
22 April 2024